Hateful Promise

B. B. Hamel

Get your free book!

Chapter 1

Hellie

I t's raining outside and Dad's been missing for three weeks. I finish putting away the last of the paints, wipe down spilled wine, and toss the easels left behind by guests who didn't really care about what they were making right into the trash. This paint and sip place specializes in bland landscapes and holiday themes, and tonight's waterfall is basically burned into my skull from making some version of it every night for the last year. Most folks don't come to Picasso's Drinking Problem to make a masterpiece, and that's fine by me.

As I continue the clean-up phase of closing, I remember the last thing Dad said to me before he went on the run. *Heloise, don't you ever give it up, girl. You've got a gift. And hey, lend me a few bucks, I need to grab some smokes.* That was my old man, the only person in the world that used my real name, quick with a compliment and never shy about asking for a loan. He took my ten bucks and never looked back.

Now he's gone after pulling off the biggest job of his life. If he ever comes back, someone will put a bullet between his eyes.

Good old Dad. I throw the last of the used paint in the big trash can in the back and stare down at my hands, covered in blue and purple and shaking. Good old Dad, gone now, and left behind a big target on my back. Good old Dad.

"Hey, Hellie, you okay?" Nicky sticks her head in the back room, squinting at me. I jump at her voice, look back over my shoulder, and stifle a yelp.

"All good, just finishing up."

"You've been standing there looking at the floor for, like, a minute. You sure you're fine?"

"I'm totally good, just tired is all." I turn up the dial on my fake smile and that makes Nicky pat the doorframe, her lips pushed together.

"Alright, well, we're all set out here. Is it cool if I head home? I gotta get changed before Molls comes and picks me up."

"Sure, get out of here, I'll close up."

"You positive you don't want to come meet us out at the Palm? Her cousin's bartending and we're getting free drinks."

"Nah, I'm not in the mood for a casino tonight." *And I'm pretty sure my dad robbed one, which means I need to lie low,* but I don't add that part. "I'll see you tomorrow."

"Text me if you change your mind." She waves and leaves. I pause for a minute, gathering myself together, before I get everything locked up.

It's not like this is the first time Dad's fucked up. I should be used to it by now.

The Great and Wonderful Daniel Accardi's been running around Las Vegas for the last fifty years causing mayhem, conning locals and tourists alike, and generally being an all-around sleazeball. Most people know him as Danny, but I call him Dad, and he's been an intermittent light in my life since I was a little girl. I remember following him down the Strip as he pointed out all the different schemes going on, from pickpockets to fake beggars, and he grabbed me by the shoulders outside of a huge casino, and he made me look up at the top floor, and he told me something I haven't been able to get out of my head since: *sweetie, they don't let people like me and you up at the top, but they also can't lock all the doors even if they wanted to.*

My grandmother raised me. I never knew my mom—Dad told me half a dozen stories about her, most of them conflicting, probably none of them true—and I barely have any family.

Which is why Dad always mattered so much.

Now he's gone, and I don't think he's ever coming back.

At least if he's smart.

I finish closing up Picasso's Drinking Problem while ruminating on my con-man father's latest fuck-up and how it's going to ripple into my life. The night's dark and quiet, dry as the desert, the parking lot slow and still. I hurry toward my car, cutting across a couple rows of SUVs and minivans, until I slow and nearly stop when I spot a man leaning up against my ancient Ford Focus's rear bumper.

I nearly scream.

He's tall. Broad, muscular. Scruffy beard. Dark brown hair, light tan skin bordering on olive colored. His eyes are dark, his form-fitting suit is pure black, and he's one of the most gorgeous men I've ever seen in my life.

I also know exactly who he is, and this is very, very bad.

"Hello, Heloise," he says, not smiling. His voice is low and soft-spoken. I move closer to him without thinking about it before I force myself to stop again. We're completely alone.

My heart's racing into my throat.

"Hello," I say. "Can I help you?"

"I hope so. My name is Erick Costa and we need to talk about the money your father stole from my casino."

I take one step backwards. "I don't know what you're talking about."

"Yes, you do. It's been all over the news." He pushes off my bumper. Erick's enormous, athletic, muscular. Tattoos peek out from his collar and at his wrists. His shoes are probably worth more than the contents of my apartment. Everything about him screams danger. A sleek, beautiful, deadly terror rolls down my spine.

"If my dad was involved, I don't know anything about it. I haven't seen him in three weeks, and I've barely spoken to him over the last year."

"Doesn't surprise me. Your old man's been very busy and very patient. It would be impressive if it also didn't make me look bad."

"Like I said, I can't help you."

"Maybe, maybe not, but unfortunately you don't have much of a choice. Come with me, Heloise, and we can figure this out together."

"My name's Hellie," I blurt out since it's weird hearing him call me that. "And I need to go home. Maybe we can talk tomorrow, or—"

"You misunderstand," he says. "This isn't a request. I'm being polite right now, but that can change. Last warning —Hellie." He tilts his head and I swear the ghost of a smile brushes over his lips as if he's almost forgotten how to. "I like that, *Hellie*, like you're a little devil."

"Please," I say, choking out the word. I look around for help but there's nobody around, only rows of empty cars.

"I don't know anything about what my father did. I just want to go home."

"Last time I'll offer. Let's make this easy."

I take one step away from him and suck in a deep breath.

Dad didn't teach me much. He didn't show me how to braid hair or throw a ball. He didn't teach me math or reading, never talked about history or philosophy.

But he did show me other stuff, and one of his most important lessons was this:

Never let the bastards catch you, Hellie. Run!

I turn and take off. I'm in decent shape—I like taking long jogs around my neighborhood after I get home from work —and I'm quick enough to dodge between a pair of trucks, heading for the open street. If I can make it to the far end of the strip mall where Picasso's Drinking Problem's tucked in the back corner, I'll be able to yell for help from the people waiting for the bus or the people heading into the fancy new Mexican place they opened up last week.

I run hard, sucking in air, adrenaline and terror ringing through me like a gunshot. Erick's not following, or I don't think he is, and I turn to reach the open space, and if I can just make it—

Something hits me like a truck. The breath gets slammed from my lungs and I land on my ass hard, barely keeping my head from smashing back onto the pavement. I skin my palms and hurt my ankle, and I sit there, dazed and blinking tears from my eyes, as an enormous body looms over me.

"Should've been polite," he says. It's another massive guy, muscular, almost square, with a small nose and curly hair combed back. "Now we gotta do this."

He kneels on me. It's like an anvil dropped on my chest. I gasp for air, try to speak, but I make only a pathetic wheezing noise. I'm choking or getting crushed to death, I don't know, but my legs start to kick when Erick appears. The guy on my chest grabs my right arm and pins it to the ground so hard I can't move, even though I'm fighting as hard as I can.

Erick unrolls a leather satchel and takes out a needle.

"Don't worry," he says. "We're careful. Ren will keep you nice and still. I figured out your height and weight. I checked your medical history to make sure you don't have any allergies. Propofol's relatively safe, anyway, but the doctor's waiting just to make sure. You'll be okay, Hellie. My devil girl."

"Wait," I gasp, trying harder to fight as the needle lowers to my arm. "No, no no no, *please*."

"Sorry," he says, and genuinely looks like he means it, as he sinks the needle into my vein. It's a sharp pinch, and I release a terrified groan. "It'll be quick. Faster than you think. I bet you won't even—"

Blackness hits, and I'm gone.

Chapter 2

Erick

I place the unconscious Heloise—*Hellie*—into the back seat of the SUV idling nearby. "Check her, Doc."

Roger Okara leans over and starts fussing with her vitals. I make sure she's comfortable, her seatbelt tight, her limp body propped against the door with a small pillow under her head. This isn't my first kidnapping and it won't do to give the girl a concussion.

"Did you give her the full dose?" he asks, clipping a heart rate monitor to her finger.

"Just like you said."

"We have approximately one hour before she wakes. If something goes wrong—"

"That's what you're here for."

Roger's bushy eyebrows pull together. He's in his mid-fifties and he's been loyally serving my family for decades.

I can tell he hates this. "I can't do much if she starts to choke on her own vomit or if she goes into cardiac arrest."

"She won't. You'll make sure of it." I stare at the doctor before I decide to climb into the back too. Ren sits up front with the driver, a young guy named Wolfram that everyone calls Wolfie.

We head out. The doc keeps a close eye on Hellie while I do my best not to stare at the unconscious girl. I've known her tangentially for a while now—her father's infamous in this town—but I haven't seen her in person since she was a kid.

Hellie's beautiful. Gorgeous, actually, with this thick, curly raven-black hair that falls in waves around an angular face. Full lips, fierce eyes—when she's conscious, anyway—and a body that's clearly used to exercise, but still full and soft in all the right places.

I had no clue my new toy would be so shiny and pretty.

The doc keeps her comfortable, constantly checking to make sure she's doing okay, and Wolfie gets us out to the desert compound as quickly as he can. He knows this drive better than almost anyone else in the world, and he's one of the few people I'd trust to make it at night. The desert house is hidden out among the mesas and the cliffs at the end of a long, dangerous stretch of gravel road and a barely marked pathway.

Once there, I carry Hellie into her room and place her softly onto the bed. "I'll stay and monitor her," Roger says. "But this is going to cost you."

"It always does, Doc." I pat him on the shoulder and leave him to tend to the girl. But I pause in the door, glancing back at her sleeping body.

What's that I feel in my chest? An elevated heart rate, but something else, like my nerves are jangling and on fire. The moment I saw her, I felt it, a raw blast of pure emotion, something like desire, something like hunger. But I don't even know her, and I can't imagine why I'd feel much of anything at all.

I head back to my office. Ren's off making his own calls, updating everyone on a successful mission, while I sit behind my desk, pour a whiskey, and phone my older brother.

"How'd it go?" Adler asks.

"Better than expected. She tried to run."

He grunts. "You have her though?"

"Nobody saw. I was thorough."

"Good. I'll let Frost and Gallo hear the good news."

"Don't bother, Ren's already spreading the word." My jaw works as I take a long sip of the whiskey. "Not that you give a shit, but I don't like this."

"I know. You told me already."

"She's not involved."

"True, but she's her old man's only link back to Vegas these days, especially ever since the old lady passed a little while back."

I grunt. The old lady is Hellie's grandmother, the only guardian she's ever known. "He won't come to help her. You know that."

"I can't say for sure. I'm a father now, and I've got to admit, parenthood fucks you up in very specific ways."

"Not him." No, the great and wonderful Danny Accardi, one of the most successful Vegas con men to ever work the Strip, does not care enough about anyone to get himself killed trying to help them.

"There's no other option. Would you rather give the girl over to those animals?"

"That's the only reason I agreed to your plan."

"Then be thankful it happened at all. My people told me Frost was about to make his own move, and you know what that psychopath would do to her if he got the chance."

"Hm," I say, leaning back with a sigh.

"Make the girl understand. Be reasonable about it. Yes, her father knew what he was doing when he knocked over that fucking truck, but she's got to know something. She's not dumb enough to protect the old bastard."

"We'll see."

"I hope we will. Get this shit cleared up, Erick. It's embarrassing for the family."

"Wouldn't want to embarrass the family."

Adler sighs, frustration obvious in his voice. "Just figure it out."

He hangs up. I stare at the phone for a moment before sipping my whiskey, thinking about Hellie back in that room, her thick, black hair spread out around her like a demon's halo. Why did she have to run like that? She had to have known I was going to catch her. She knew me the second she saw me, which means the girl isn't stupid.

But then again, she ran.

Ren comes into my office not long later and sits in one of the chairs. He stretches, cracks his knuckles and tilts his head from side to side. "It's done," he says.

"They know?"

"They know," he confirms. "And they're pissed."

"Good." I look over at the window.

"They're gonna want her, you know. Frost especially. He's not gonna make this easy. That old asshole stole their money, too."

I close my eyes and sigh. It would've been so much easier if Danny the Con had taken just my money—but instead, he stole an entire armored truck full of cash from three of the largest casinos on the Strip worth over eight million dollars, the score of a lifetime.

"They can wait their turn. I have a plan for her."

Ren's eyebrows raise. "You gonna put it to her?"

"No," I say. "She's innocent."

"She's Danny the Con's daughter. She's not innocent."

"I'm going to have her work off the debt."

Ren doesn't move. His eyebrows raise. Then he laughs. "There were nineteen million dollars in that truck. There's no way in fuck she can earn that kind of money, even if you whored her out to every tourist in town."

"She won't be a whore."

"Then what good is she?" Ren scratches his chin. "I bet Danny taught her some stuff, but—"

"She can paint."

Ren takes that in. I let it linger in the room. I've found that saying less is always more. Let other people fill in the gaps with their own ideas and misconceptions; the way they respond can say a lot about who they are as a person and what they value most.

"Like that ugly crap at the store?"

"Better than that. She can really paint."

"I don't see how that can earn money."

"You will." I check my watch. "She'll be up soon. Go check on the doc and tell him I want to be there when she comes to."

"You sure?"

"Positive."

"Your call." Ren gets to his feet. He frowns at me, shaking his head. "Fucking painting? You lost me there, man."

My best friend is a simple man. He cares about money, about sex, about loyalty. He's strong, aggressive, ruthless, clever in some ways, but he thinks too small.

When Hellie wakes up, I'll show my little devil girl how big I can think, and how she's going to save her own life.

Chapter 3

Hellie

I wake up in a bed.

It's a big, comfortable bed, with soft sheets and luxurious pillows, and I'm pretty delirious as I try to make sense of my surroundings. An older man's sitting near me, checking my eyes, talking to me through the haze. I try talking back, but it's like clearing cotton from my brain.

"You were given propofol, it's a common drug in surgeries. Recovery is quick and it should leave your system soon. Please, don't try to get out of bed for a while."

"Who are you?"

But the older man's already getting up. He snaps closed a doctor's bag and walks to the door, glancing back at me with a sympathetic smile. "Good luck, Heloise."

He leaves, shutting the door behind him with a click.

I groan, try to sit up, but my head swims. It takes all my willpower just to stay still and stare at the ceiling as I try to recount how I ended up in this place.

The room's beautiful. Like something from a modernist painting. Clean lines, expensive furniture, thick rugs, and an actual fireplace. Windows overlook something, I can't tell, I only see black sky. It's still night, which means I haven't been out too long.

I remember Erick. I remember running, getting pinned to the ground, the needle—

Then nothing.

I have no idea where I am.

Fear swims into my mind. It's muted and distant, held at bay by the drugs still swirling in my brain, but with each passing moment, more of my strength comes back.

Along with my determination to get out of here.

Just like Dad said, don't make it easy. Just keep running.

He's been running from trouble his whole life; he should know how to keep one step ahead.

I push myself up, swing my legs over, and stumble to my feet. My eyesight swims and I nearly lose my balance, but I steady myself, wait until the dizziness passes, then I stumble to the door. I'm trying to remember how a knob works when it turns on its own and I'm forced backwards as Erick steps into the room.

He stares down at me. I'm struck again by his sheer sexual masculinity. The man's a specimen, oozing strength and intensity, doing nothing but looking at me like he wants to pick me to pieces for his own pleasure. His rugged beard, his tattooed hands, the small scar on his right jaw under his ear all suggest a hard life, one filled with pain and violence.

But it's his eyes that hold me. Those dark pools, liquid and expressive. He says nothing, but he still speaks to me by the way his body angles in my direction, by the way his gaze drags from my lips to my chest to my legs and back up again. He seems happy with what he finds.

"The doctor said you should stay in bed." He breaks the silence. I take a step back.

"Where am I?"

"My house. Please, lie back down before you hurt yourself."

"You drugged me. You stuck a needle in my arm."

"Yes, I did."

"That's crazy. This is crazy. I can't—" I stagger forward and try to get past him, but he grabs me, lifts me off my feet, and carries me to the bed. I try to struggle, but I have no strength as he drops me back on the mattress. I stare at him, my breath hitching in my throat, aware that he can do whatever he wants with me and curious about how it might feel for this brute, this massive monstrosity to peel my clothes off and brush his rough lips along the soft skin of my inner thigh.

Which is an objectively insane thing to think under the circumstances.

"If you leave my house, you will die." He stares down at me and I squirm under his attention.

"You mean, you'll kill me?"

"No. You will either die in the attempt, or you will be killed back in town. Either way, you're stuck here for now."

I want to ask him what he means by that, but I shut my mouth. I'm trembling with fear. I'm at his mercy, completely vulnerable and intensely aware of it. He remains standing at the foot of the bed, his enormous shoulders and sculpted chest flexing with some inner emotion. Frustration? Desire? Rage? I can't tell—his face is a mask.

"What do you want from me?"

He nods once. "That's a better question."

"Are you going to answer it?"

"In time." He paces away, hands behind his back. "Your father stole a lot of money from me, but he also stole from two other men. Clifton Frost and Alberto Gallo." He glances over. "Do you know who they are?"

"Vaguely," I admit. "Frost is a big-time investor. Gallo owns the Lucky Seven."

"That's correct. Frost currently controls three resort hotels in the area, most notably the Villa Fortuna. Your father owes all three of us a lot of money."

"I told you. I don't know where he is." My heart's beginning to race. My head's clearing as adrenaline begins to burn away the lingering drugs. "Who was that before? What did you give me?"

"The doctor was making sure you weren't experiencing any side effects. You were given a common drug called propofol." Erick tilts his head, considering. "I'm here to offer you a job."

A laugh rips from my throat. A job? This man can't be serious. How in the hell could I ever work for someone like him? Except I suspect this *job* isn't really an offer, but more of a prison sentence.

I want to scream. I'm not a part of my dad's scheme. If he stole money from these big-time casino owners, that's on him, but I'm totally innocent.

I've kept my head down. I did okay in high school, got a scholarship to an arts college out in California, I earned my degree and moved back to Vegas. I've been painting ever since, trying to sell stuff on Etsy and Instagram, while earning enough to survive by picking up hours at Picasso's Drinking Problem. I've done my best to stay away from my father's long, storied criminal career.

Now it's returned to eat at me. Threatening to tear me to pieces.

B. B. Hamel

"I don't want to work for you," I tell him, raising my chin and trying to find some little piece of defiance left.

Mostly all I fear is terror.

"That's not a smart answer. Let me try again. I'm here to offer you a job in exchange for not killing you."

I shuffle back as I suck in a few quick breaths. "You wouldn't. You can't just murder me."

But of course he can. This is Erick Costa, casino magnate, mafia lord. Everyone knows what he is and what he does, and nobody can touch him, not even the Vegas police. Especially not them. How else can they afford their pensions, if not from Costa bribe money?

"I don't want to," Erick says. "That's why I'm offering you a job instead. However, my compatriots Gallo and Frost see value in sending a message to any other would-be thieves roaming around town."

"What's the message?"

"Fuck with us and we will murder your family." He delivers that line without a hint of emotion.

"Oh." I'm on the verge of panic. "Right. Okay."

"You're here because I think you can be valuable in other ways." He walks over and sits on the edge of the bed.

I shiver and close my eyes. Disgust floods my mouth. I want to spit, scream, throw up. He wants to use me, make me *work* for my father's debt. I'm being trafficked, turned into a whore, used for my flesh and skin.

20

It's horrible. It's worse than death, and if I weren't such a coward, I'd beg him to end me instead.

I hate this man. I despise everything he represents. His unchecked power, his obscene privilege. He's big and gorgeous, and I feel an erotic thrill whenever he comes close, but that's only a physical response. That's only my body making a very stupid decision.

My heart wants to stab Erick Costa in the neck until he dies.

"Please. I don't have anything to do with my father." Pathetic. I'm so pathetic. Begging won't do anything, not with a guy like this. But maybe if I play quiet, act submissive, make him think I'm weak—he'll turn his back and get complacent.

That's when I make my move and get out of here.

"You have a talent I want. You have something—" He reaches out as if to touch me and I flinch back, both afraid and strangely excited by the prospect of his fingers on my skin. He stops and lowers his hand.

"I'm bad at sex," I blurt out before I can think better of it. His eyebrows raise. Well, crap, I might as well commit. "I'm boring. I've never had an orgasm before. I don't know anything. I can't give head or whatever. You won't make any money trying to sell me like that, nobody's going to want me."

Amusement crinkles his face. "Is that what you think?"

"What else could you want from me? I'm worthless otherwise. My dad never taught me anything real and all I have is some stupid art degree. If you think I'm going to pay off millions of dollars with sex—"

He laughs. He actually laughs. If I weren't terrified for my life and convinced I'm about to be forced into sexual slavery, I'd be really insulted right now.

But Erick shakes his head. "No, my little devil girl, that's not what I want at all, although I think you're under-selling yourself. You'd make an extremely attractive fuck doll."

My mouth falls open. *Fuck doll?* This man's mouth sends a tingling shiver down between my legs. "I don't understand."

"I'm not going to whore you out, Hellie. Although now that you say it, I wouldn't mind tasting you for myself."

I let out a whimper. "No. Please."

"Don't worry." He leans closer. "I prefer my women willing. Very willing, and begging."

I blink rapidly, head going blank from his sudden pure sexual heat. This man's masculine energy is sex personified, and the way he's licking his lips while staring at my mouth makes me want to either throw myself out a window or directly into his lap.

"What do you want then?" I manage to ask, surprised that I'm still able to form words. I need to get it together. I hate this man and I hate his world. Just because he's hot doesn't mean I can let it get to my head.

"You are going to paint for me." He stands up. I wish he'd stay on the bed, close to me, but this is probably better. I can think clearer once he's a few feet away.

"Paint?" The word doesn't make sense. "How? Paint?"

"I told you, you have a talent that I want." He turns away. "Can you walk?"

"I, uh, think so?"

What the hell is going on right now? The fact that Erick's talking about my painting is too absurd to process.

"Come with me." He walks to the door and waits for me to follow.

I get out of bed again. This time, I'm much steadier on my feet. I manage to stagger after him, trailing into a hallway. He turns right and walks to the end of the corridor, and I'm frantically trying to memorize the layout of this place —doors, steps, all that stuff, but it's a blur.

He opens the last door on the left and gestures for me to go ahead.

I give him a look. "Is this some kind of trap?" I ask.

"No trap. No joke. Go ahead and look. I made this for you."

I open my mouth to tell him off—

But instead, I peer into the room.

Chapter 4

Hellie

The space is large, bigger than the room we just left. In the center are several driftwood tables with designer chairs around them. Stacked against the walls are dozens of blank canvases of all different shapes and sizes. On shelves are paintbrushes, all of them brand new, and rows and rows of paints. There's an easel, another desk with paper, charcoal, pens and pencils, big sketch pads, and past that are more cabinets and storage vessels filled with more materials.

"It's an art studio," I say, barely believing the words.

A brand-new art studio.

Hardwood floors, beautiful, sleek design, and lots of windows overlooking—something, I can't tell, it's too dark outside.

"Do you like it?" he asks.

I step inside and start to look around. Everything is expensive, top of the line, no expense spared. It's the sort of stuff I've always dreamed about but could never afford. Colors, so many colors, and lovely soft brushes of different cuts, types, sizes, thicknesses, and angles. There's a utility sink in the back corner and what looks like a small en-suite bathroom. Books line another shelf—they're references, beautiful art references, all packed with the most famous paintings in the world, thousands of them.

"This is hard to process," I admit, practically salivating at the idea of spending time in here. What I could make—the things I could paint—

But I have to get it together.

It's a beautiful space. A dream space, really, but it's also a cage, and there are dozens of invisible strings that I can't quite see yet, but I know Erick will make clear very soon.

I can't let him seduce me.

No, not when he drugged me, dragged me here against my will, and talked about making me work to pay off my father's debt.

And also laughed at the idea of sleeping with me.

My cheeks turn red and I ball my hands into fists to keep myself from feeling embarrassed.

"This is your job." He drifts into the studio, looking around at everything. "It took a lot of effort to put this together, but I believe you will have what you need."

"I don't understand. You own one of the biggest casinos in Vegas. What the heck do you need with some nobody painter like me? You can buy whatever art you need."

"No," he says, holding up a finger. "You're wrong."

I open my mouth to argue, but I'm missing something. I close it again, thinking.

What could I paint for him that would hold value? My work is good—I've had a few gallery shows, most of them small and local, and I've sold some decent stuff online—but I'm nowhere *near* popular enough to be worth kidnapping.

None of this makes sense.

Until he walks over to the row of books, selects one, and pulls it out. He flips it open until he lands on a particular image: a red brick building, tall on the right, sky on the left, a woman bending over something in an alley, another woman sitting in a doorway, cobbled streets, the hint of a tree.

"Vermeer," I say, mystified.

"*The Little Street*," he says, pointing at the title. "You'll paint this."

I narrow my eyes, staring at him. "I'll do what now?"

"You will paint this. You will make it perfect in every way, indistinguishable from the original. I don't care what it takes, but you will make it happen. That's how you'll pay off your debt."

I take two steps away from him as his plan clicks into place. "You want me to forge art."

"I want you to paint masterpieces." His gaze burns into mine. "I've seen your own, Hellie. You're talented. Extremely talented. I want you to paint for me."

I shake my head. I want to laugh, but he's not kidding. This is a joke, a travesty, a nightmare all wrapped into one.

He wants me to paint for him?

No, he wants me to commit fraud, to cross the line I swore I'd never cross.

"I can't," I say, shaking my head.

"You have the technique. I know you do. It might take some time to perfect it, but we have everything you'll need, and anything else can be found. Material is no problem."

"That's not the issue."

"If you think it's skill, then don't worry. Like I said, I've seen your work, and you're talented. You can do this."

I rub my face. This is crazy. Even if he's right and I'm good enough to make a proper copy of the old masters, there's no way in hell I can do it.

"You don't understand," I say, desperation oozing from my pores, because some part of me wants to accept this challenge. Some part of me wants to stay in this beautiful room for the rest of my life and paint forever. "I won't break the law."

He leans back, lips pressed into a line. "You won't what?"

"My dad's the con man, not me. I swore to myself a long, long time ago that I'd never be like him, and now you're forcing me to commit fraud. You're dragging me down where I never wanted to go. I can't do it."

"You refuse to paint for me out of some moral pride?" He seems genuinely confused. "You realize the alternative is death?"

"I can't do it."

He stands silent, studying me. A chill runs down my spine at the way he seems to eat up all the light and attention in the room like a charming black hole. A very muscular, very scary black hole. I slam closed the reference book, hands trembling, trying not to look at him, because the more I stare at Erick's mouth, at his eyes, the more tempted I am to find out what it would feel like to be his *fuck doll*.

"You have to understand what I'm offering you here." He taps a finger on one of the easels. "If Frost catches you, he won't only end your life. No, he'll do it slowly in some suitably horrific manner. Something painful and terrible. You won't like that." He runs a hand over a blank canvas, not looking at me. "Gallo will give you to his men as a prize." He shrugs and glances over. "That's simply how it's done among men like him."

I bite my cheek to keep from making a sound. "I can't," I whisper. "There has to be another way."

"I'm offering you that other way. Paint me masterpieces. I'll sell them on the underground art market. We'll earn back what you owe, pay the others, prove that you're useful enough to keep alive. That's my offer. Paint for me and live. Refuse and die. There's not much more I can do." He walks to the door, opens it, and is about to leave.

"Wait," I say, panicking. "What about me? I mean, what am I supposed to do?"

"You have freedom in this house. Do not go outside. Beyond that, take tonight and tomorrow to think about what I said. But remember, I'm not exaggerating what will happen to you, and it *will* happen if you don't accept this opportunity."

He leaves. The door clicks shut. I'm alone in the studio, in the pristine place, this dream of a room. It's everything I've always wanted, but it's my prison cell and my personal hell.

This isn't the person I want to be. Painting forgeries, becoming my father. I've avoided that for so long.

Now Erick Costa's forcing that life on me, and I don't know what I'm going to do.

Except keep my head down, play the role he expects, and take my chance when it appears.

Chapter 5

Erick

I walk through the crowded halls of the Shadespring Hotel with Ren by my side. The place is all motion, color, light, and distraction. "You know that rumor about casinos pumping pure oxygen into the place?" I ask as we follow the carpeted path around a slot machine forest. People sit in front of the huge, bright edifices, staring at the screens, jabbing at buttons, essentially playing nothing more than a random number generator. I still don't understand the appeal.

"I've heard that once or twice," Ren says, giving me a look like he's wondering why I'd even mention something so stupid.

I choose to ignore the attitude and continue. "We obviously don't do that. It'd cost way too much money, and besides, people are amped up enough already."

"I'm aware. I've been working in casinos as long as you."

"But, we do pump this place full of something else. Can you guess?"

He holds up a finger. "Desperation."

"Well, yeah, but I'm thinking more along the lines of surveillance. Every inch of this place is covered by a camera. Every face is run through an AI algorithm searching for bandits, thieves, and con men. Everything from the sub-basement to the top penthouse is covered. So how the hell did Hellie's father manage to fuck everything up so bad?"

Ren grunts in response. "That's why we're having this meeting."

I stop outside of a conference room. We're in one of the back halls, away from the action. "No, we're having this meeting because I don't want to see that girl get her throat cut. I need you to solve the theft issue."

"I have people working on it already."

"You work on it personally." I squeeze his shoulder. "You're the only guy I trust on this."

He nods once. "I'll figure it out."

I turn to the door, take a deep breath, and shove my way inside.

It's a gorgeous space. Sleek, modern, updated. A big table dominates the middle with a presentation screen at the far end. Two men sit across from each other at the center, while their associates are spread out covering them from all angles. I pause, taking in the scene, before walking to the head of the table.

On my left is Clifton Frost. Late forties, graying hair, blue eyes, thin face. He looks like he could coach a German soccer team. On my left is Alberto Gallo, in his seventies, wearing a cheap pinstripe suit, big nose, dyed black hair. Looks like he's an extra from a gangster movie.

Gallo speaks first. "Alright, Costa, we're fucking here. You got my ass to the far end of the Strip. Now why the hell did you need this little meeting?"

I nod a greeting to him. "Nice to see you as well, Alberto."

The old man waves me off. "I'm tired. I'm in a shit mood. My fucking arthritis is acting up. Don't be a prick and get to the point."

"Hello, Erick." Frost gives me a respectful nod. "Thanks for setting up this meeting."

"Oh, suck a dick, Frost," Gallo barks at him and laughs. Frost's smile is strained.

These two men hate each other. They represent completely different versions of Las Vegas. One is the new-school developer, coming in with his big money and his dreams of making the Strip a family-friendly destination, while the other is an old-school gangster who would love nothing more than to see Vegas never change.

I hold out my hands. "Gentlemen, please, we have a mutual problem and I want to discuss a solution."

"I heard you made a move last night." Frost's eyes hold mine. "Is it true?"

"You know it's true," Gallo says. "This wily little shit snatched the girl out from under our noses. Isn't that right, Costa?"

"Yes," I confirm. "I have Heloise Accardi in my possession, although she likes to be called Hellie."

"Hellie," Frost repeats, head tilted. "I like that."

"Fuck what she wants. That girl's head needs to be mounted on a spike outside my goddamn casino doors." Gallo sits forward, glaring at me. "When are you going to give her up?"

"I'm not."

"Bullshit." Gallo looks at Frost. "Tell him we need to kill the girl."

"For once, I agree with the old man. We need to kill the girl." Frost keeps staring at me. "But if that's all you planned on doing, you wouldn't have called us all here in person."

Gallo groans as he sits back. "That's a good point. Ah, shit, Costa, what do you have planned?"

"The girl is too useful to kill. That would be a waste."

"It would be fucking revenge." Gallo practically spits the words.

"She didn't steal from us," I point out. "The actual thief is hiding out somewhere on a Caribbean beach enjoying his millions. If we kill his daughter, he'll be sad and maybe some other would-be con men might think twice if only to preserve their own precious spawn, but it won't bring Danny out of hiding."

"Perhaps getting at Danny isn't the point anymore," Frost says. "Hurting the girl, and doing it in a very brutal and public manner, might be all the revenge we need."

I glance at the woman sitting in a chair behind him. Her face shows nothing: his personal assistant must be used to this brutality by now. Across the table, Alberto looks pleased, and the two thugs behind him are grinning like idiots.

"Torture sounds great to me," Gallo says. "Cut the girl's toes off. Make her eat them."

"Brutish, but that would be effective." Frost strokes his chin. "We could film it. Release the footage online or trot it out whenever someone gets too fresh. That would be a very good deterrent."

"I like it." Gallo's beaming. "You're not so bad, Frost, for a fucking stuffed suit."

"We aren't killing the girl, let alone torturing her." I speak loudly to draw their attention back to me. "No, we're going to use her. Did either of you do any research?"

"What's there to research? She's some bitch spawn of a shithead thief. She's got to die." Alberto's not smiling anymore.

"She's a painter," I say, looking over at Frost. "A good painter."

He frowns at me. "I don't see how that matters."

"Instead of murder, I propose we make her work off the debt. I've provided her with a list of important paintings that have been stolen over the years, some completely lost, some thought to be destroyed. She'll make forgeries, damn good forgeries, and the three of us will sell them on the black market. We split the proceeds three ways until we're all made whole."

My plan sits in the air between the men. Gallo barks a laugh after only a few seconds, shaking his head like I'm the most insane person in the world, but I never expected him to go along with it.

Frost, however, seems thoughtful.

"Can she do it?" he asks. "It wouldn't be easy, making a passable fake."

"She can do it," I confirm, and I genuinely believe that's true. I've seen her work; there's a wide range of styles and technical abilities on clear display. "Making the forgeries isn't the problem. Selling them is, which is where you two come in."

Gallo sighs. "We should just kill her and be done with it."

"We can kill her later," Frost says. "I'm interested."

With that, I have them. Gallo will make more noise, he'll complain and delay, but eventually he'll play along. Which is good, because his family makes their real fortune selling stolen goods, from art to electronics. Meanwhile, Frost's got a huge network of filthy rich collector friends who wouldn't mind breaking a few laws to get their hands on something truly rare and historical.

And all of this will be fake.

Orchestrated from my house in the desert.

Masterminded by myself.

Created by Hellie.

There are a dozen ways this can go wrong, but I was raised to go after profit no matter the stakes. Risk is acceptable, so long as the risk can be managed.

And I believe I can manage Hellie Accardi, whether she wants it or not.

Chapter 6

Hellie

I get a fitful night of sleep before waking up early. I stay in bed, still unwilling to accept my current reality, but eventually I have to use the bathroom, take a shower, and put on my old, dirty clothes. That's something I'll have to figure out.

But for now, I check the door, and it's unlocked.

Erick said I'd have freedom in the house, and I can't help but test those boundaries. I sneak out into the hall, but instead of going down toward the art studio, I take the stairs to the first floor.

The place is enormous. At least two wings, furnished with modern, expensive paintings and decorations, and entirely empty. There's nobody else, not a guard, not a maid, nobody. I poke my head into a sitting room, a pool room, a media room, a smoking room, a drinking room; so many rooms I start to lose track. Finally, I find the kitchen in the back of the house, and nearly let out a shriek.

An older woman's in there, kneading dough. "Oh, hello," she says. "You must be Heloise."

I stare at her, my heart racing. She's shorter than me, stout, round, gray hair, wrinkled face, wearing a white shirt and simple jeans, her sleeves rolled to her elbows. She slaps the dough, turns it, kneads it, and eventually shapes it into a bread pan.

"Um, hi," I say. "Hellie."

"Hellie," she repeats. "Very pretty. I'm Marina, Erick's housekeeper and cook. There's also a cleaning staff but they only come once per week, though maybe they'll come more now that you're here." She laughs to herself, a pleasant sound, and pops the loaf into the oven. "Are you hungry? I can make you whatever you like."

"No, sorry, I didn't realize there was anyone else here." I laugh awkwardly, shuffling from foot to foot. Can I ask this woman for help? Does she know who I am and what I'm doing here? "Do you know how I can get out of here?"

She gives me a sympathetic shake of her head. "Sorry, dear, you know that's not possible. Erick gave me strict rules to follow regarding you. Now, how about some coffee? Maybe eggs? I can make an omelet if you like."

"No, thank you." I turn away, my stomach feeling sick. This woman is aware that I'm a prisoner here, and yet she seems completely okay with it. She seems kind, like a gentle grandmother, but anyone who works for a guy like

Erick must be cold-blooded. "I think I'll keep looking around."

"Feel free, dear," she says. "I'll be here. Come find me if you need anything."

I leave the kitchen as the smell of baking bread starts to fill the room. I'm shaking, my stomach a knotted mess, my heart racing. What sort of bizarre upside-down world am I in right now? Can it really be completely fine that I'm being held against my will? Anger fills me all over again, anger at Erick for stealing me away, anger at my father, anger at my situation. I want to scream, but what will that get me?

Instead, I find a back door.

It leads to a patio. A beautiful stone patio overlooking a gorgeous swimming pool. There are a few plants, mostly low desert shrubs, immaculately landscaped. I crunch down on gravel and stare out past the fence. There's desert straight back, rolling hills, red rocks, and nothing else.

An insane idea occurs to me.

There has to be a way in and out of this place. If I run now, find the road, and keep going—

I hurry to the fence, find a gate, and step through.

Nobody stops me.

I'm feeling sick. My hands tremble. Is this still from the drugs he gave me? No, these are just nerves. I hurry forward, over the rocky, dry terrain, and toward the hills. I stomp over scrubby brush, skirt around small cacti, and begin my ascent toward high ground.

It takes a couple hours. I'm drenched in sweat as I keep going and the house gets smaller behind me. I have to stop and catch my breath a few times, but eventually I reach the top, cresting out onto a flat peak.

More desert spreads all around me, desert for miles and miles in all directions.

I stare in shock. Awe overtakes me. There's a path that leads down to the house, now toy-sized in the distance, but even that snakes away for miles and miles, before disappearing around a bend.

We're secluded. Completely and utterly secluded. It must be an hour or more by car just to reach the next road.

If I tried to escape, I'd die.

My god, no wonder there are no guards.

Finally, I let that scream break from my chest.

I scream and scream, tears in my eyes.

The house isn't my jail cell. The house is keeping me alive.

The desert's my real prison.

It takes a little while before I can calm down. I wipe away my fear, staring out into the distance, willing myself to find some landmark.

There's nothing. Only more rocks.

Eventually, I head back to the house. I'm exhausted to my core when I stumble into the kitchen and collapse at the table. The bread's sitting on the counter, cooling off. It smells incredible.

"Coffee?" Marina offers. She places a large glass of water by my elbow. I drink it down greedily. "How about something to eat?"

"Pancakes," I say, shoulders slumped. "Please. And I'll take some coffee too."

"Coming right up." The old woman gives me a sympathetic pat and doesn't ask where I've been. She knows all too well.

She whistles as she cooks, and outside beyond the windows, I can see the bars of my cell glowing red in the sunlight, beautiful and breathtaking, but horrible just the same.

There's no escaping this place.

Even if I can get out, I won't survive the hike back. I'd need water, supplies, probably a vehicle. It would take a full day to reach a road, and even longer to reach civilization.

Erick knew what he was doing when he brought me here.

"We're fully self-sustaining," Marina says when she places the food in front of me. "Solar panels on the roof, batteries in the basement, a well for water, regular shipments of food. Erick should be back shortly if you want to discuss things further with him."

"No, thank you."

"Don't worry, dear. You'll be okay. Do your job and he won't hurt you. Erick's fair."

"How do you do this?" I stare as she pours coffee. "How do you work for a man like him?"

She tuts as she brings over the mug. "There's much worse in this world than him. Besides, the pay is fantastic. There you go, eat up, you need it."

Marina begins to wash the dishes and I stare down at my food. I take a tentative bite and it's so good I can't stop myself from devouring it all like an animal, desperate and unable to control myself, wondering when I'll have my last meal, and if it's happening right now.

Chapter 7

Hellie

I'm curled up on the couch in my room watching TV when Erick comes back. I hear him downstairs talking to someone. There are several voices; I don't recognize them at all. Soon, someone knocks at my door, and enters before I can call out.

Erick lugs two heavy bags over to my bed and dumps them down. I stand, staring, as he pours one out. Clothes tumble all over: shirts, pants, underwear, all of it with tags.

"What's that?" I ask, unable to help myself.

"I assume you don't want to be in that for the foreseeable future." He gestures at me. I'm in my dirty, sweaty work outfit still from last night. "This stuff is yours now. Everything should be your size."

I drift to the pile, my mouth falling open. It's all designer: Dolce, Prada, Yves St. Laurent, a few names I don't recognize, but the price tags are all obscene. "You could've just gone to Target," I murmur.

"My casino doesn't have a Target. This will have to do for now."

"Right. Sure." I clear my throat, lifting up a tiny black dress. "What's this for?"

"That's for when we have dinner together."

His face remains straight, but he's got to be kidding. "We're not sharing meals, and I'm definitely not wearing this." I toss it back onto the bed.

"You can wear whatever you like, but you might change your mind."

"I doubt it."

"This doesn't have to be difficult. You understand why you're here and what your role is. We can work together."

"You kidnapped me." I stare at him like he's gone insane. I'm reminded all over again of his pure sexual magnetism: the man's a sculpted, gorgeous machine of raw masculine energy. I'm taken aback by the stare he pins me with in return. It's unguarded, the desire in his gaze unmistakable. He doesn't try to hide as he looks me from top to bottom, licking his lips as he does it. This fucking guy is absurd.

"Yes, I did, but I kidnapped you for a good reason."

"To make art forgeries."

"Because your father stole from me and two other men."

"Right, and now I'm stuck paying off his debt, even though I had nothing to do with that."

Erick gestures back toward the door. "Feel free to leave again. Marina told me you went for a hike."

I grind my jaw. I guess I'm not surprised, but I liked her. "How far does it go?"

"Far," he says. "You can try to make the main road if you like, but it's too hot during the day and too dangerous at night. You'll die of heat stroke or get bitten by a rattlesnake."

I shiver. "But you make the drive."

"It's not bad by truck." He runs a hand through his thick hair. I stare at it, unable to help myself, thinking about what those fingers have done. How many lives they've taken. How many bodies they've touched.

"That's why you don't have guards."

"I don't need them out here. Nobody knows about this place except for my inner circle. You're safe."

"I wasn't really thinking about my safety, more about how the hell I'm going to get out of here."

"You're not, and don't try. I'd rather not scrape your cooked body from the dirt. Corpses swell in the heat. It's unpleasant."

I glare at him. "Why are you doing this to me? You have to know I can't pull off a real forgery."

"I think that you can." He moves away, heading over towards my windows. "I looked at your portfolio, and not only the one you have online. I checked your work from school, too."

"You did?" I ask, surprised. "How?"

"Money opens doors." He stares out at the desert. "Your work is good, Hellie. Very, very good. I like art, love it actually, and I know what I'm talking about. You're talented. Your technique is phenomenal."

I want to be pissed that he spied on me, but I'm kind of flattered. "Thanks. I guess. Also, screw you."

A ghostly smile crosses his handsome mouth. "Paint for me. Otherwise, my protection will run out, and Frost and Gallo will torture you for their own amusement and as a way to send a message to this town. I'm your only shot at getting through this alive."

"Says my kidnapper. Is this the part where you Stockholm Syndrome me into feeling grateful you stole me?"

He shrugs, turning back. "That would be nice."

"No, thanks. I'm not painting for you. I'm not digging myself into a hole like my father did. And I'm sure as hell not grateful for this fucking beautiful prison you've got me in."

"I hope you change your mind. I was just meeting with my associates, and I told them you were on board. Right after Gallo gave a very vivid description of how he wants to hurt you."

I flinch, looking down at the floor. "I don't believe you."

"I have no reason to lie. I'll give you another day to reconsider." He walks towards me, coming over like a panther. Oozing confidence and sexual energy. His muscles are bulging, his lips slightly pursed, and I want to dig my fingers into his back. Fuck, what is wrong with me? Get a grip!

"I won't change my mind."

"You will, or I'll have to get creative." He stops inches away and reaches forward. I shy back, scared of his touch but also craving it like a skydiver begging for the ground. Instead, he continues past me and picks up that black dress. "Maybe I'll take away everything but this. I wouldn't mind you parading around in only this outfit, though it would be very distracting."

"I'd rather be naked than let you dress me up."

His eyes flash to mine. Hunger lurks behind that gaze and it scares me, because I feel that same need reflected in my core.

"Don't tempt me, little devil girl."

"Stop calling me that."

"Why? You're my devil girl, causing me so much trouble while I'm trying to keep you alive. Paint for me, Hellie."

"Or you'll strip me down and make me be naked? What happened to not treating me like a whore?"

His lips curl. "*My* whore. Nobody else will ever touch you."

"But you will?" My spine shivers with terror and a strange undertone of desire. Curious need.

"I don't need to fuck an unwilling woman. If you're going to be my whore, you'll do it because you want to." His hand comes up and he touches my chin. I suck in a breath, heat racing into my guts. This guy's got the kind of confidence that pisses me off, but he's also got the good looks and charm to back it up, the bastard.

"That'll never be me. And I won't paint for you. Just let me go."

"I can't." He leans closer. I think he's going to kiss me, or press his mouth to my neck, or rip out my throat with his teeth. He could break me, crack my spine, snap my neck. He's a beast, and I'm attracted to the monster in ways I never dreamed possible. "It would be such a waste of a beautiful woman to let my associates have their way. Paint for me, Hellie." His hand wraps around my throat, but he doesn't squeeze. I release a terrified whimper as my body pumps adrenaline into my veins. Unadulterated lust slams into my core, mingled with fear. "Paint for me, and I will make it worth your while. It just might save your life."

He releases my throat and turns. I gasp, even though he hadn't been choking me. He walks to the door, pauses only for a moment to look back at me, his expression unreadable. The mask is back on, his emotions gone.

But for a moment, when his hand was on my neck and his mouth was inches from mine, I saw something in his eyes.

A man beneath the creature. A man filled with lust, just like me.

What the fuck am I doing?

Erick leaves, and I collapse back onto the bed surrounded by expensive designer clothes, all of it worth more money than I'll ever make in my entire life, but all of it worthless.

Chapter 8

Erick

I dream of chasing her through the desert. Hellie runs and runs, gasping for breath, until she stumbles. My teeth are fangs, my hands are claws. I hold her down and spread her legs, and she's screaming as I tear off her clothes, and she's begging me to keep going as I fuck her.

I wake, drenched in sweat, and have to stroke my cock in the shower to get the dream out of my head.

I'm not forcing myself on the fucking girl.

God damn, Hellie. The sun hasn't risen yet, so I take the opportunity to go for a run around the property. When I get back, the sky's pink and purple, and I'm drenched with sweat.

"Coffee and the usual?" Marina asks me as I chug down water and towel off my bare chest.

"Please, but I should shower first. Has our guest been down yet?"

"Not yet. I think she's still getting used to the place." Marina gives me a look. "You could be nicer to her, you know."

"That's your job. I'm the bad cop. You're the good one."

She smiles and shakes her head. "I'd rather not be a cop at all."

I go over and kiss her cheek. "Judge then. You can tell me when I'm out of line."

"Would you listen?"

"I never do."

She pats my cheek before I head upstairs. Marina will make me toast with jam and some yogurt with granola. I prefer a light breakfast to get the day started.

Before I can disappear into my room to shower off, a light at the end of the hall catches my attention. I drift closer, moving silently, past Hellie's room and down to the studio.

I peer inside, barely daring to breathe.

She's alone in the room. Around her, the sunrise throws beautiful slants of light over books, paint cans, brushes, the tools of her trade. She's in only a cotton t-shirt and a pair of tiny shorts with a big DG on her ass.

My mouth opens. I want to find words, but I can't speak, terrified that I'll break the spell.

She's incredible. Beautiful in a way I've never experienced before. Her raven-black hair falls in tresses, the curve of her spine leads to her small, sloped shoulders, and her upturned nose gives her an almost regal look. Her ass is lovely, heart-shaped and firm; her breasts are small, but palm-sized, in the perfect proportion to her athletic frame. I lick my lips, my mouth watering as the dream from the night before drifts back.

I'm about to speak when she moves over to the canvases. I bite my tongue and watch as she picks one up, studies it, carries it to the easel, and puts it down. She doesn't get paint, doesn't get brushes, only looks at the blank canvas, at the white. She touches it, strokes it almost lovingly. Like she's coaxing something from its depth.

I wish I could see what she's seeing.

I've always wanted to be an artist. Not in the sense of wearing a beret and saying insipid bullshit. But I want to make something beautiful, something meaningful to people. Instead, I am what I am—a man that runs a casino as a member of a crime organization that spans back decades.

That can't change. I won't ever be something I'm not.

But she can create. She can do things I worship.

In the same way I worship the long lines of her legs, her beautiful thighs, those lips.

"You can stop staring at me now." She looks back over her shoulder. "I know you're there. I saw you in the mirror."

I glance to her left. I spot myself in the reflection in the mirror propped against the floor.

"What do you see when you look at that blank canvas?" I ask, unable to help myself.

She looks away. "Nothing. Just white."

"I don't believe you."

"It doesn't just come to me. My paintings, I have to—" She stops, shaking her head. "It doesn't matter, because I won't do it."

"But you're here. You're in here." I step into the room.

She looks at me again and her eyes widen.

Yes, I like that look. I like it a lot. She stares at my bare chest, still damp from sweat, glistening in the light. Her mouth opens and her eyes take in my tattoos, my scars. My body is like a canvas of my life. A hard and ugly life, but also privileged in so many ways. A contradictory life, one I never asked for.

"You could wear a shirt, you know."

"I just got back from a run. Tell me what you want to paint."

She chews her lip and tears her eyes from me. "Nothing. I don't want to paint anything."

"Then why are you in here?"

"Because it's comfortable," she blurts out and looks annoyed with herself. "Look, I know why you did all this. You want me to make you forgeries. You made me this room because you'll profit from it. But I've always dreamed of having a studio like this. It's like... it's perfect. Like you knew I'd love it."

Which I did. I studied her before creating this space. I looked at her Pinterest, her Instagram, read her thesis at college, and carefully curated this studio in such a way as to maximize her creative output. It was a labor of devotion, and maybe she can feel that.

I walk over to the reference books and pull one down. She watches, curious, saying nothing as I flip through the paintings until I end up on another Vermeer. "The Gardner Museum."

"The what now?" she asks.

"It's an art museum that got robbed in the nineties. Some important pieces were taken, in particular this Vermeer." I jab a finger at it.

She comes over, like she can't help herself, and leans over my shoulder, her warm body pressed to my shoulder.

The image is simple. A dark room, the light coming in from a window on the left. A girl sits at a piano in a yellow dress with yellow ribbons in her hair, maybe a teenager, maybe older. On her right is a man in a red chair. To his right is an older woman, maybe the girl's mother, gesturing at the man. On the wall are two paintings, lost to shadow, and in the foreground is a piece of

cloth draped over a table. I can almost hear the girl playing, the noise echoing off the checkerboard tile floor, her
parents having a soft discussion by her elbow.

Hellie makes a soft noise in the back of her throat, half of
excitement, half erotic.

"It's incredible," she says.

"You can make this." I run my finger down the page.
"This and the others taken from the Gardner. We'll start
here, take it slow, make sure we have plausible stories for
how they surfaced again, and you'll do your thing in this
room."

"I can't." But she's staring at the image, her voice a whisper, her body pressed to mine. "I won't."

"Paint for me, Hellie."

"Would you stop saying that?"

I shift myself, turning to face her. She stares up into my
face. "Paint for me, because if you don't, I can't guarantee
you'll be safe."

A low hum escapes her throat. It's a purr, or maybe it's a
growl.

"That's how you'll manipulate me, isn't it? You'll pretend
like you're the only person standing between me and
certain death, and if I do what you say, you'll keep me
alive. But I don't believe you."

She walks away. I feel the space between us like that
blank canvas.

Haunted by potential.

"I'm not lying."

"Again, I still don't believe you." She stands by the window. "Just leave me alone, okay? If you're going to kill me, then kill me. I can't live like this, playing some stupid game."

I try not to smile. She thinks she's calling my bluff, but she has no clue what she's doing to herself.

I turn away. "Start work today. Start with *The Concert*, if you want. I'll check up on you soon."

"I'm not going to do it," she calls as I head to my room for a shower.

But I think she will. I saw the way she looked at the book, the way she gazed at the canvas. She wants this. She's tempted.

And I'm just as tempted, but for something so much worse.

Chapter 9

Hellie

"Asshole."

I pace around the studio, glaring at all the art supplies.

"Asshole."

I keep thinking about Erick, his self-satisfied smirk, his muscular chest glistening with sweat, covered in tattoos and scars.

"Asshole."

Each time I pass it, my eye strays to the Vermeer paintings. *The Concert.* How does a man like Erick know about something like this? I'm into the art world and I'd never heard of the Gardner.

He probably likes the crime aspect.

"Asshole."

I run my finger down the glossy page. It's strange, the woman on the right side, her hand's up in the air as if mid-gesture, and her face is glowing from the light slanting in from the window. There's the vague, blurry image of the sky and some trees on the inside lid of the piano, and I can't tell if that's a reflection or if it's a decoration. In the foreground, under the table draped by cloth, is a little basket. Almost lost in shadow.

It's beautiful.

"Asshole."

"You don't have to keep saying it, he knows."

I yelp and jump, flinging myself around. The other man from that night's standing in the doorway, grinning at me. He's in a dark suit fitted to his muscular frame. Around Erick's height, but wider, like a damn refrigerator.

"You scared me."

"Sorry. My name's Ren." He doesn't move to enter the room. "I heard you were hanging out in here and I had to see it for myself."

I get myself together, straightening my clothes. "Here I am, his little circus show."

"Aw, don't be so down on yourself. Erick really thinks you can pull this off." Ren stared around, a skeptical frown on his face. "But based on the way you keep muttering *asshole* to yourself, it seems like this job is off to a bad start."

"I'm not doing it." I turn away from him, arms crossed. I slam the art reference book closed. "He can just kill me if that's what he wants."

"You're right. He could."

The way Ren casually says it makes a chill run down my spine. "I don't know where my dad is, if that's why you're here. I don't know anything about the theft at all."

"Oh, I believe you. So does Erick, which is why you're not in the basement right now getting your skin peeled off your body."

My jaw drops open. Ren's smiling at me like he's discussing the menu for Sunday brunch, but there's a sharpness in his eyes. A willingness to do anything that needs doing. Which includes torturing me, if needed.

"He's serious about this." I gesture around me.

"He's very serious. Brought it up to the other two just yesterday, and I gotta say, both of them were pretty keen on making your demise very slow and very painful."

"Did he send you to convince me or something?"

Ren snorts, shaking his head. "Hell, no. He strictly forbade me from entering this room." He gestures at himself, still standing on the threshold. "I'm obeying the word but ignoring the spirit."

"It's really true then?" I drift to the windows, hugging myself. "Those guys really want me dead?"

"Nothing personal, but hey, that's the way it goes in this town when you steal from the casinos. They'll gladly murder a girl if it means scaring the rest of the would-be thieves away."

I take deep breaths to steady myself. Ren's talking about my death like it's no big deal—like he almost wants it to happen. His tone, more than anything, scares the hell out of me.

"I really don't have much choice, do I?"

"The way I see it, you either paint like your life depends on it, because it does, or you take your chances in the desert." He follows my gaze to the brown-and-dark-green landscape. Beautiful and arid and deadly. "Who knows, if you're smart and lucky and you follow the road, you might make it."

I stare back at him, eyebrows knitted. "Are you serious?"

"Not at all. You'd die, but hey, that'd make my job a lot easier." He sighs, turning away. "I'm in charge of liaising with Frost and Gallo, and trust me, that's a real fucking pain in the ass. It'd be a huge weight off my shoulders if you just killed yourself."

I stare at him, my mouth hanging open, trying to understand how someone could talk about something horrific like it's putting on a pair of comfortable jeans.

"You could always let me go. Give me some water and good shoes, and maybe I'll make it."

He snorts. "Not on your life. Get smart and listen to Erick. Prove you're useful or he can't keep you safe much longer. Or not, whatever." Ren waves as he walks off.

I stare after him, heart racing, head spinning. I have to sink down into a stool, my hands on my knees, taking deep breaths.

Finally, for the first time since coming here, my situation feels real.

It's not some joke. It's not some game. Erick isn't manipulating me for his own amusement.

Two of the most powerful men in Vegas want me dead, and my kidnapper is the only thing keeping me from a very gruesome and painful death.

Oh, fuck. Oh, fucking fuck.

How the hell did my dad think this was going to end? He steals all that money, disappears, and what? He figured the casino lords would just leave me alone?

Fuck. Fuck. FUCK. He left me for dead, knowing damn well they'd come for me.

All for one more score.

My dad isn't a drinker. He's not a smoker, he doesn't take drugs, but he's an addict all the same.

Addicted to the score. To the thrill of pulling off a job.

To the point that he'd even get his own daughter murdered for the win of a lifetime.

My hands clench and tremble. I'm so mad I could scream. I stand up and pace again, but this time, it's like I'm a wild animal.

Ren's right. I won't survive out in the desert. Maybe for a little while, but even with water, there's a good chance I'd get lost. One wrong turn and I'm finished. One misstep, one turned ankle, one snake bite, and it's a slow, agonizing, and lonely end.

I turn back to the reference book. I whip it open, flipping through the pages, heart racing, until I find the Vermeer.

The Concert.

Can I really do this?

Turn into my father to save my own life? Leave behind all my personal morals, my beliefs, my ethics, just to keep breathing one more day?

It's a horrendous, impossible choice, and Erick made it clear that I don't have long to figure it out.

Chapter 10

Erick

"I get why you want to keep her around." Ren crosses his legs in the chair across from my desk and swirls a glass of whiskey. "Honestly, Erick, she's nice to look at."

I give him a flat stare. "I told you to stay away from her."

"No, you said her studio was off-limits. You never said anything about talking to her."

I grind my jaw. "Let me be clear then. You are not to speak to Hellie. You are not to look at her. Pretend like she doesn't exist."

Ren's expression sharpens. His smile turns savage. "This one's special then, is that it? You're not going to share the spoils with the boys?"

I lean forward, my body tense with anger. The thought of giving Hellie over to my men, to be fucked and used and torn through, sends a hot spike of rage through my guts. I could stand and murder Ren right now, except I understand what he's trying to do. The man likes to rile me up, and for once, it's working.

"No more jokes." I stare at my best friend. My second-in-command. The man I trust with my life. "Hellie is off limits."

He sighs. "Fine, whatever you say." He takes a long drink. "Gallo's been on my ass since our meeting. He wants proof that your girl can pull this off. The guy's chomping at the bit to end this."

"Delay him. She needs at least a week or two."

"I doubt he'll wait that long. Get him something in a few days."

"Gallo can come out here if he wants her that badly."

Ren snorts. "Come on, don't be obtuse. He'll make our lives harder in other ways. Well, my fucking life, since you won't have to be on the ground dealing with it."

"Stall him. I'll see what I can do."

"Fine." He stands and stretches. "I'd keep an eye on your girl, by the way. She keeps looking outside like that's a viable escape plan. I tried to make it clear that's not going to happen."

"Marina told me she already took a walk."

"Then hopefully she understands." Ren shakes his head, looking at his glass as he swirls it. "What a fucking crazy plan. You really think anyone will buy these fake paintings?"

"She's good," I say, sitting back. "It'll work."

"Yeah, I hope so. It'll be one hell of a story if we pull it off." He salutes me with the glass, throws it back, and heads out.

I look at the ceiling. Somewhere up there, Hellie's prowling around and raging at her situation. I can't blame her for being angry, but I wish she understood the risk I was taking for her.

Which begs the question—why am I doing all of this?

The profit is real. Her talent is real. I see something in her that the others don't, and maybe it's because I love art, I love paintings, and I know the art world better than they do, even if they have better direct contacts with collectors.

But it's something else. There are plenty of talented painters out there, many of whom would gladly accept my little scheme.

It's Hellie herself.

After her dad pulled off the job, I was fucking livid. I wanted to burn down the Strip to find him—and nearly did. But once it was clear he'd skipped town and disappeared, it was time to go for the next best thing.

Which is how I found her.

I stand and wander to the doorway, thinking about that first night I followed Hellie home from her job. How I stared at the way she moved, her dark hair, those fucking hips. I felt something, even then.

She's the opposite of what I should want in a woman. Messy, artistic, in her own little world. Her father stole from me, for fuck's sake.

Everything about her is wrong.

And yet everything about her makes my skin burn with pure lust.

It's fucked. Beyond fucked. It's going to get everyone killed.

I linger near her studio door. I should turn back—there's other work to be done. Hellie's not the most important thing in my world, not even the top ten.

But I can't help myself.

I peek inside, breathing softly so she doesn't notice.

The girl's sitting at a drafting table, hunched over a large sketchpad. She's got charcoal in her hand, and she's making these quick slashes with the tip, then longer lines with the side, filling in shades of light and dark. On an easel to her right is the reference book, open to *The Concert*.

She's sketching it.

A practice run. Getting the feel for the composition. I stare at the way her arms move, her shoulders, her back, the muscles in her hands. The concentration on her face is magnetic, the intensity of her stare, the way her tongue pokes out from between her lips ever so slightly. She's whispering to herself, muttering something I can't hear.

It's incredible, watching her work. I've never been this attracted to a woman before—it's her focus, her determination. And, yes, it helps that she's sexy as fuck, the sort of woman that draws looks wherever she goes, only she's so used to dressing in nothing but sweats and big sweaters it's easy to forget that she has an incredible body.

Lean and toned. Light brown skin. And that raven dark hair. I want to wrap my fist in that hair and taste her lips.

But most of all, I want to stay here and watch her work.

Instead, I move away. If she catches me, it might ruin the moment, and right now things are delicate. Whatever Ren said to her, she's finally breaking down and making the right choice.

I want her to work.

Hell, I want her to survive this.

But that can only happen if she obeys me.

"Asshole."

I stop in the hall. It was her voice, clear as day.

I turn halfway back, and I hear it again, louder this time.

"I know you were watching, asshole."

I smile to myself, my heart racing in my chest.

My little devil girl.

Chapter 11

Hellie

I find Erick down in the kitchen. Whatever he's eating smells incredible. He takes small bites from a large bowl while reading the paper on a large tablet. Marina's at the stove, whistling to herself. Outside, the sun's setting.

"Here, asshole." I toss the drawing down onto the table in front of him and flop into the chair opposite. "Take a look."

He stares at me for a long moment. I should really try to be less abrasive, but I'm exhausted from working all day and I haven't really eaten anything. Besides, he's my freaking kidnapper, and I don't really owe him anything.

Marina comes over with a bowl and a glass of wine. "Enjoy," she says, smiling warmly as she pats my shoulder. I'm too starved to wait—I start shoveling forkfuls with rice, beans, shredded pork, guacamole, and fresh vegetables.

"Holy crap," I say as the flavor hits me in the skull and my stomach growls. I gulp down some wine and keep eating. "Marina, this is so good!"

"Glad you like it," she says and sounds like she means it.

Erick's staring at my sketch.

"It's rough," I say with my mouth full. "Just blocking it out. Getting the forms. If you think it sucks, I don't really care."

He says nothing. Only keeps staring, which makes me unreasonably mad. The least the guy could do is say something. I mean, I get it, he's got a lot riding on whether I can convincingly fake an old master's painting style, but to hell with him. I worked hard on that stupid charcoal piece, and even though it's pretty basic, it's got all the right elements in place.

"This is good," he says finally, looking up. "This is very good."

"Oh." I lower my fork. "Really?"

"Yes." He sets the drawing aside carefully. It's the way he makes sure that the paper doesn't touch anything, not the food, not his glass of water, that's how I know he really means it. He treats the sketch like it's an actual prize.

Which lights up a strange feeling in my chest.

I'm proud of the way he's looking at me.

"Thanks," I say, cheeks flushing red. I go back to eating to cover my embarrassment. "It's just a start. I mean, doing the whole painting, making it as realistic as possible, it's going to take a lot of work. I need first-hand accounts of what the painting looks like, you know what I mean? Close-ups of the brush strokes if possible. We'll also have to figure out what colors he used and what those colors were made from so we can make it as historically accurate as possible. If we're smart, we can make it such that nobody can ever tell the difference, even the experts."

He's staring at me again with that look, like he's glowing on the inside. Like he's freaking into the way I talk, which I hate. I hate to keep remembering that no matter how handsome this man is, he's my kidnapper. He drugged me. He stuck a needle in my arm in a goddamn parking lot.

"We can do that," he says at last. "I'll get you whatever you need."

"Start with the pigments. Hire someone to do the research, or get me books and I'll do the research myself."

"No, you paint. I'll hire someone."

"Fine." I clear my throat and take a slower sip of wine. "Okay. Great."

"I am very happy that you decided to take me up on my offer."

I shake my head slowly. "I haven't done that yet."

"No?" His eyebrows raise. "Then what's this?" He gestures at the drawing. "Why talk about pigments?

71

You're excited. You're planning. And I'll be honest, it looks good on you."

I hold up a hand. "First of all, quit complimenting me. You're so full of shit."

"I mean every word. Your excitement is intoxicating. I love the way you light up when you talk about your work."

I grind my jaw, annoyed that he's making me feel good. "I haven't accepted yet because we haven't discussed terms."

He stiffens. His face drops into that mask again. Erick is so good at shutting down, it's terrifying.

Marina comes over and refills my wine glass. "Can I get you anything else?"

"No, this is so good, thank you."

She winks at me and shoots Erick a look like she wants him to behave.

He takes a long breath. The man's gorgeous face remains impassive. "You want to discuss terms."

"I figure I have something you want, so I might as well get something in return." I stare at him.

Inwardly, I'm freaking out. This is stupid. I'm aware that it's stupid. I'm basically dangling myself into the tiger's den with a hotdog necklace around my throat trying to ask them questions about quantum physics or something. I'm *begging* him to cut my throat.

But something Ren said put the idea in me. Erick's keeping me alive. The others, they want to make an example of me, but Erick doesn't want that. Which means I'm valuable to him for some inexplicable reason.

Maybe he's the only serious art-collecting mafia psychopath in the world and he really does think I'm talented.

Or maybe this job has some serious potential, and I can't see it yet.

Either way, I'm in a negotiable position.

"What do you want in return? Aside from my promise not to kill you, which is itself already a lot."

"Money." I put my fork down and raise my wine glass. "Let's say, ten percent of your cut of the profit."

He shakes his head. "No."

"Five percent then."

"You are in debt to me, little devil. You're not getting any money."

"I won't be in debt forever, right? Eventually, I'll break even. But here's the thing, I won't know that until you tell me. I'm at your mercy."

He leans forward, his eyes glinting. Handsome and dangerous.

"You're right, you *are* at my mercy."

A sharp clench stabs into my core.

What the fuck is wrong with me?

Some part of me actually *likes* that idea.

"Fine, okay, forget the percentage. I want five million. I'll do ten paintings for you in total, and when I'm done, you let me go with five million in my bank account."

"Ten paintings might not cover your debt."

"We both know they will, assuming you can sell them for what they're worth."

"And are you sure they'll pass inspection? How positive are you that you're good enough?"

It's a question I've been asking myself ever since I started work earlier today.

Can I really pull this off?

I keep coming back to the same answer, no matter how I look at it.

I have no other choice, so I will.

"I'm sure."

"Then let's say this. Ten paintings. If your debt is covered before all ten are sold, I'll give you five million, regardless of what's left."

"Five million and you let me go."

He nods once. "And I let you go."

"And you guarantee the other guys won't try to hurt me."

"That'll be harder, but I think once everyone's got their money and then some, we'll be in a good position to make that happen."

I lean back in my chair, studying him. Can I really trust this guy? Erick Costa, mafia boss, casino owner, fucking psycho monster? He's handsome, and he likes my world, and he's weirdly complimentary, but I still can't get over the whole parking lot drugging thing.

Still, if what he's saying is true, this is my only shot at staying alive.

I hate myself for this. I hate him for it too. All my life, I worked hard to never become my father, and now I'm diving in. I'm not just trying to save my life—I'm profiting too.

I guess being a shitty con-man asshole runs in my blood.

"You have a deal then." I shove my hand out.

He takes it. His palm is huge, and he rubs my knuckles gently, sending my head spinning into space. My god, even the slightest touch from this beast sends my heart rate skyrocketing. He licks his lips, looking at me, and that stare is utterly erotic. He drips with masculine intensity, and I could scream with desire, if I also didn't want to stab him with my fork.

I release him first, pulling away.

"Glad we could get to this point," he says, pushing his chair back. "Although there's a problem."

I groan. "What now?"

"You need to produce something in the next three days."

"The fuck?"

"I know, it isn't much time." He tucks his tablet under his arm. "But Frost and Gallo want proof that you can pull this off. Ren's running interference, and I'm guessing that's the best we can do before they get impatient. Three days."

"I can't do something like *The Concert* in three days. I need the right supplies, pigments, whatever!"

"Use what we have. Make it eighty-percent there. That'll be enough for me to explain that it's only a prototype."

"Even eighty percent there is like—" I close my eyes, trying to imagine the amount of work. "I won't be able to sleep."

"Then you'd better get started, devil girl." He walks over to Marina, kisses her cheek, thanks her for dinner, and leaves.

I sit staring at my floor, my appetite gone. I lift the wine-glass to my lips, hand trembling.

This is insanity.

Three days? I can't make an entire master-quality oil painting in three days. Not something even passably good. I need multiple attempts to make sure I get it right. Three days isn't enough for multiple attempts.

Three days is enough for one fucking moonshot.

"Here you go, dear," Marina says, refilling my wine.

I shake my head. "I better not. Can't paint while drunk."

"Nonsense." She beams at me. "Picasso did it all the time."

"You saw the stuff he made, right?"

"Looks can be deceiving, dear. Go on, loosen up a bit. Erick seems scary, but he's doing what's best for you."

"I hope so," I mumble, but I take the glass, and I head back to the studio, already planning out the next three days of pure hell.

Chapter 12

Hellie

My shoulders ache. My hand cramps. My back feels like a bunch of toddlers have been headbutting me in the spine.

I crack my neck and make the smallest paint mark and curse. It looks like shit. It all looks like shit.

The sun's rising outside. My eyes are goo. My face is jelly, my brain mush.

On the canvas is not much more than an outline. The shape of the composition is sketched out in pencil. Just rough blocking—I'll get the details right later—but it's enough for now.

And in the center is the mother.

That's how I think of her, the mother.

She's the focus. Her strange, pale face glowing with light, the pearls around her neck, her hair up in looping curls. There's a piece of paper in her hand—how did I not see that before? I think she might be reading it, reciting it, or maybe she's singing along to her daughter's music. I can't really tell. I like to imagine it's both. The father, meanwhile, is nothing more than a head, some hair, shoulders, a sash across his back, and a chair. He's a lump, a nothing, while the women shine, especially the mother.

I've been working on her for hours. She's coming into focus, the rightness, the shadows, and she looks good. Very good, actually, as close to the original as I can manage given my constraints. Eighty percent there, maybe even better. She has to be perfect, or else the whole thing falls apart. The mother is the painting. The mother is the heart.

I have two-and-a-half days, and I'm barely making any progress.

My mouth is dry. My tongue swollen.

I could scream.

I make another mark on the canvas.

"Hellie."

I jump. Grunt in surprise. Nearly knock over the whole set-up, which would be freaking terrible. I turn, glaring.

Erick's standing in the doorway, watching me.

"How long have you been there?"

"A half hour."

"You've been standing there watching me for a half hour?" I look around, bleary-eyed and only half-conscious. "What time is it?"

"Six fifteen in the morning."

"Oh. Right." I rub my face and carefully put down my brush. "Are you here to gloat?"

"No. I'm here to make sure you take a shower and get some sleep."

I laugh once. "Sorry, but no. I don't have time for any of that."

"Hellie, if you push yourself like this, you'll never finish."

I gesture at my work. "If I don't push myself past my limits, you're absolutely right, I won't finish. I spent all freaking night on this."

"You're getting faster."

"What? No, I'm not."

"You will after you've slept." He comes into the room wearing a pair of tight joggers and a t-shirt that clings to his biceps. Freaking guy's gorgeous. Absolutely drop-dead gorgeous. I could cook a pancake on his abs and eat it off his tight ass.

Wow, I really am sleep-deprived.

"Maybe that's a good idea." I let him help me up. He's gentle as he steers me into the hallway. I'm shuffling along, zombie-ish, feeling like my brains are going to seep out of my ears. My head's a buzzing mess of painting techniques. The mother's face is seared onto my eyelids.

And there's Erick. The smell of him, warm and spicy, musky and nice. I like the way he touches me. I like how big he is, how muscular and strong. I like how he only smiles when he really means it, even though he's always hiding behind that face. His mask and his armor.

He takes me back into my room. I kick off my sandals and lift my shirt over my head, tossing it aside. I reach back and unhook my bra without thinking, staggering to the bed. It only occurs to me after the bra drops to the floor that maybe I shouldn't start undressing yet, since Erick's still very much in the room.

I turn to look at him. Which is stupid, since now my tits are on full display. My god, I'm out of my mind and I need to sleep.

His eyes stare at my chest. His mouth is open, his gaze sharp, needy. He licks his lips and lets out this incredibly erotic grunt like I've punched him in the guts.

I cover my breasts with my arms.

"Shit. Sorry. I'm a mess. I'm on autopilot. Sorry."

"Don't apologize." He doesn't look away from my body, totally unashamed that he's checking me out. "You're beautiful."

"Okay, big guy, go easy."

He comes toward me. I stay rooted in place, shivering. Suddenly cold, despite the desert heat seeping in.

"I told myself I'd stay under control. I'm not sure I can hold myself to such a high standard."

"That's creepy and I don't know what it means."

He stops inches from me. Big, so big. Wow, what a big, beautiful man.

"You know what I'm saying, devil girl. I swore I wouldn't touch you. I told myself I'd keep this professional."

"If you're about to cross some line, reconsider."

"Would you like that? Really, would you want me to keep my hands to myself, Hellie? The way you're looking at me now, I don't think you do."

He's right. The asshole. I'm aching for him, deep into my core, my pussy pulsing wet with the thought of him peeling my arms back and licking my nipples. God, I have such sensitive nipples. They're hard with excitement right now, and I have to keep them covered, or else he'll know he's right.

"I can't control my actions. Sleep-deprived, remember?"

"Being tired isn't the same as being impaired. You need a shower. Let me finish undressing you."

"Erick," I whisper as he steps closer, his hands on my hips.

Slowly, he tugs down the hem of my pants. They slide over my hips. I could reach out to stop him, but that would mean uncovering my breasts and showing off my hard-as-iron nipples, and that's an absolute no-go.

I shimmy slightly, helping him as the pants come down, leaving me in only a pair of black panties.

He lets out a low purr. "Beautiful girl." One hand reaches around and grabs my ass tightly, the other on my hip. "I'll wash you with my tongue."

"That won't get me clean." I want him to do it. Freaking hell, yes, lick me all over, every effing inch of me. Suck my nipples and fuck my pussy with your fingers. Make me come. "I should shower and sleep."

He releases my ass. I whimper a little as his hand moves around my front. He backs me up until I bump into the wall beside the bathroom. "You should," he agrees. "But you won't."

"Erick," I gasp as his hand cups my pussy.

My warm, wet pussy.

"Oh, devil girl, I knew you liked this," he says, his eyes burning. "You're fucking soaked. My god, you're *dripping* wet."

"I'm not," I groan as his hand slips down the front of my panties.

And fuck, that feels good. Oh my god, the slightest touch sends fire into my spine.

"Soaked," he repeats, his big fingers gliding up and down my slit, teasing my lips, rolling around my clit.

Asshole's completely right about that.

I'm so wet, I must be dripping into his palm.

"Physical response. I can't help it." I moan as his fingers sink in and back out.

"You want this. You want me to get you off, don't you?"

"Fuck you. Asshole." Also, fuck yes, please, please, please. "I don't want anything but freedom."

"Not even this?" His fingers drive inside me and I'm done, freaking done. I lean back, gasping with pleasure as he curls his fingers inside of me, slides back out, rolls around my clit, fucks me again. "Come on, Hellie. Tell me you want it or tell me to stop, but quit lying."

"You'd like that, wouldn't you? I bet you get off when girls struggle."

"Go ahead and fight. You're right, I'd only get harder."

"Then fuck you." I stare into his eyes. "You bastard. You piece of shit. I hate you."

"Yeah? Tell me more." His fingers slide inside again, fucking me.

I'm panting. Drooling. Barely mentally capable of forming a sentence as pure bliss rips into my body. "You're a self-centered piece of shit. You don't know —fuck—a thing about art. And you sure as—oh my god, damn it—you sure don't know anything about *me.*"

"I know this," he whispers, moving closer. "You're about to come on my fingers. The second I kiss you, that's all you'll need. Think I'm wrong?"

"Fuck off."

And he slams his lips into mine. That kiss, that goddamn kiss, his mouth is like honey and heaven, his tongue invades past my teeth the way his fingers fuck deep into my soaking, dripping pussy, and he's right, the asshole, the bastard, he's right. I come like thunder on his fingers, moaning into his mouth as we kiss, as I lick his tongue and suck his lips, I moan and come and when I can't take it anymore, I push myself back, gasping for air.

He's slow about finishing. Gentle even. His fingers come out and I'm left panting hard—still covering my tits as if it matters at this point. He steps back, staring. The outline of his cock strains against his joggers. Thick, long, and so hard I'm surprised he hasn't torn through yet.

"You are incredible," he says and licks his fingers clean. "Every drop, incredible."

"Yeah, totally," I say, catching my breath, my knees shaky. "I'm the best. I just let my kidnapper get me off. I totally rule."

He laughs, shaking his head, and moves past me into the bathroom. The shower turns on. "I'll get you pajamas," he says. "Get in and get washed."

"Can you just go? I mean, I get we just did something extremely weird and intimate, but I need some alone time to process just how mentally insane I am at the moment."

"Whatever you want, devil girl." He lays out cotton shorts and a tiny t-shirt on the bed. "I have an alarm set for four hours. I'll wake you when it's time to get back to work."

"Right. Work." My reality reasserts itself. I'm a prisoner. He's forcing me to paint forgeries for him, which is a big-time crime and could land me in serious trouble if we somehow got caught. None of this is normal or remotely okay. "Four hours should be fine, I guess."

"It'll have to be." He turns away. "And, Hellie?"

"Yes?"

"I like the way you kiss. And I love the way you taste. But next time, don't cover yourself."

With that line, he gets the fuck out of there, leaving me alone.

I lean my head up against the wall.

"Asshole," I say, staring at the ceiling. "God, what an asshole."

Chapter 13

Erick

I wake her exactly four hours later.

Her taste is still on my tongue. Her moans are still in my mouth. For the last four hours, I've been sitting alone in my office, trying to get work done, failing miserably, thinking about nothing more than Hellie. My devil girl. My gorgeous artist. Every inch of her is a masterpiece.

"Time to paint," I whisper, gently shaking her awake.

She tries to hit me with a pillow. "Fuck you."

"Hellie. Come on."

"Let me sleep."

I want nothing more in the world than to crawl under the sheets and cuddle up against her. I want that warmth, her softness. I want to plunge myself between her legs, feel her beautiful wet pussy wrapped around my cock.

I am fucked up with desire at this very moment.

"Hellie," I say, shaking her again. This time, I catch the pillow and toss it across the room. "Back to work."

"Fine." She stretches, groaning like a cat. "But I hate you so much right now."

"You loved me four hours ago."

"I was sleep-deprived." She glares. "I'm still sleep-deprived. I need rest if I'm going to do my best work."

"You're not doing your best work, only your good enough work. Get up."

She slithers like an eel, wriggling away from me as she kicks the sheets away, and climbs off the bed. Her hair's piled on the top of her head, messy from sleep, and she looks gorgeous in the shorts and t-shirt I gave her the night before.

"I just want to say that I'm out of bed, but I am very unhappy about it."

"I hear you."

"Good." She stands, sighing. "I don't feel like painting. Can't I just say the muse isn't speaking today?"

"Fuck the muse. I shot her in the skull. The muse is bleeding out. You'd better get used to working without her."

She rolls her eyes as she stumbles into the bathroom. Once she's ready, I walk her down to the studio. Each step seems to wake her up slightly more until she's inside, facing her work again, the late afternoon light slanting in sideways through the window, the desert reaching out in all directions, red-brown-green.

"Fuck, I really like this room," she says, ambling over to the canvas. She stalks around it, making little thoughtful noises, fingers on her lips.

"Well?" I stay back near the door, not wanting to invade her space. I worry that if I go fully inside, if I let myself become a part of her studio, then it'll lose some of its magic.

And I *really* need that magic. She does too, even if she doesn't understand why yet.

"It's good," she says at last, slumping down on her stool. "Did I really do this?"

"In a state of mindless delirium, yes."

"Great. Get me more of that." She picks up a brush and chews on the end, getting a little paint in her mouth. I grimace, disgusted, but she doesn't seem to notice. "I did most of the hard stuff already. The mother's the focus."

"The mother?"

"Her." She points at the woman standing up beside the sketched piano. Everything's a ghost, except for her. "I'll do the daughter next, then fill in the rest. The hard part is getting the light and the shadows right." She keeps chewing on the brush end. What I would give to replace that with my—no, keep my head in the game, don't get distracted.

"That sounds like a plan. You should get to it."

But she's already ignoring me, busy mixing paints, getting herself set up. I stay and watch for a little while. The world disappears when she gets in this state, and it's incredible to witness, like a world-class athlete performing a motion they've done a million times to the point where the neural pathways are etched like ravines in their brains. Painting, for Hellie, looks like walking for other people. Natural, automatic, done with ease.

The girl's in ratty clothes with drool stains next to her mouth, her eyes red and bleary, her hair a messy nest, and I've never seen someone so beautiful in my life.

It's her talent. It's her ability to switch on, just like that, filter out everything but the work.

I'm jealous and in awe.

But soon it's clear I should leave her alone, even if I could stay there and observe every little motion, every grunt, every annoyed noise, every squeal of delight. She paints like a performance, even if it's a performance only for her. I could watch her hands, her arms, her lips pressed together, her shoulders slumped as she leans over the canvas, sniffing the paints, almost licking them.

Instead, I tear myself away and go back to work.

"You have to eat something." I knock on her door until she finally looks over. She looks like shit now. Ragged, burning out. Big bags sit under her eyes. She's been painting for another six hours, and the daughter's nearly done, the father's outline coming into view, the piano taking shape. "And I brought you something to drink."

"No alcohol," she says, waving a brush at me. Gray paint splatters all over, not that she cares. I spot little marks all over, like she's been waving her arms around. "I need to focus."

"Tea," I say. "Can I come in?"

Her head cocks as she chews on the brush again. "Why are you asking?"

"Because I want to respect your space."

She snorts, rolling her eyes. So much for respect. "You own all this crap. Do what you want." She turns back to the canvas, makes a mark, grunts in approval.

I carry in a tray with chicken noodle soup and fresh bread, both made from scratch by the lovely Marina. "It's still warm," I say, placing it down on the work table behind her. "Come eat."

"Not yet. I'm almost done. Did you ever notice this guy's hair? It's lank, greasy. He doesn't wash it nearly often enough, while the women have lovely hair, done up in ribbons and curls. He's like an ogre, ugly, round shoulders, barely a shadow. The women glow. Why do you think that is?"

"Vermeer understood who runs the house."

Hellie's clearly not impressed. She makes a mark, seems fine with it, makes another. Dab, line, dab. "No, I think Vermeer wanted to say something about the passivity of masculine dominance in a patriarchal society and the strong submission of the women that keep society running."

"I doubt that very much."

She pauses and turns to glare at me. "What do you think then?"

"I think he found these women attractive and needed an excuse to paint them. The father's just a prop."

"Typical dude. Women are always either hot or not, right?"

"Look at them. The focus of the daughter is her dress, look how much time Vermeer spent on the folds. And the mother? Her face? Come on, his dick was hard for these chicks."

"You're gross." But she puts down her paintbrush and comes over. "How come you like this stuff, anyway?"

"Oh, because I'm a mafia criminal, I can't like art."

"Yep. Basically." She eats some soup, drinks some tea, and seems to realize that she has a body with needs, and starts shoveling it down. "How'd you get into it?"

I look away. She's eating like choking sounds fun. "My father had a collection. He didn't really care about the stuff, only saw it as like status symbols and investments, but I used to run around the Sunrise, checking it all out."

"Sunrise?"

"It's the casino my family runs back in Atlantic City. It's where I grew up."

"You grew up in a casino? Really? You guys didn't have, like, some big mafia family house in the suburbs?"

"Nope, just the casino. My brothers and I raised hell in that place when we were kids, getting into trouble all the time, at least until he started sending us to boarding school for half the year. But when I was back home, I used to spend hours walking around the halls, hunting down my favorite works of art, and staring at them. He had a pretty good collection, too. Renoir, Klimt, O'Keefe, Pollock, Monet."

"Where are they now? The paintings, I mean."

"Still hanging, mostly. He sold some of them a while back. I made Adler swear he'd keep the rest."

"Are you close? You and your brothers, I mean."

I grunt, considering how to answer. "It's complicated. Yes, we're close, we're loyal to each other above anyone else, but we don't see each other often."

"I can see how that might seem difficult, but I'm kind of jealous, I wish I had siblings."

"You were an only child."

"That we know about." She smiles to herself and cradles the tea in both hands. The soup is gone, devoured. "My father wasn't shy about, you know, spreading himself around."

"You were raised by your grandmother."

"Yep, she was amazing. Grams got me, but she passed a couple years ago, right after I graduated from art school. I never knew my mom. Grams said I got dropped off on her front step one day, and that was that."

"What about your father?"

"He came around sometimes." She smiles at me. "I loved him. I still do, even though he got me in this fucking mess. He taught me all sorts of things, and he was the first person to encourage me to paint. I'm not sure he ever really believed I was serious about it, but here I am."

"You wouldn't be who you are without your father. I can empathize."

"Family's never easy, huh?"

"Not for us."

That lingers. She goes quiet, sipping her tea, already looking at the canvas again where the painting's taking shape. She's making good progress—if she keeps pushing, she'll finish in time.

But I'm worried. I don't want to burn her out. I don't want to make her suffer for this. I had envisioned a more relaxed environment in which she could work, not this bullshit time clock.

"I should get back to it." She puts the tea down and moves back to her stool. "You know, even though you kidnapped me, you're not terrible to talk to sometimes."

"Did you just compliment me?"

She rubs her palms into her face. "God, I must be sleep-deprived. Seriously messed up. I can't believe I said that out loud."

"I enjoy talking with you too. When you're not insulting me."

"You like the insulting too though. Admit it, you're into that."

"You want to start talking about our kinks? I'll share mine if you share yours."

She chokes a laugh. "I have none. I'm vanilla as they come."

I stand and gather the tray. "I doubt that very much. I look forward to learning about all your twisted little fantasies."

"My fantasies are anything but twisted. They're very straight. Very narrow and boring!"

"If I wasn't sure you're a freak before, now I am absolutely positive." I carry the dishes away, grinning to myself. "You can paint for a few more hours, but you're getting more sleep tonight."

"Are you keeping me on a schedule?"

"I'm making sure you don't kill yourself making this happen."

"It's almost like you care."

"You're an investment. Don't forget it."

She grunts, shaking her head, and turns to work again.

I stop before I leave, watching, unable to get enough of her. I can pretend all I want that this is about business and business only, that her painting is nothing more than a means to an end, but that's not true.

I don't need to bring her food. I could send Marina to do it. I don't need to keep her schedule. Marina's capable of that.

I want to be near her. I want to take care of her.

Which is an extremely new sensation, one I'm still trying to understand.

Chapter 14

Hellie

For the next couple days, I paint the absolute shit out of that canvas.

I fall into the zone. I've hit this point before, where I'm so completely locked into a task that it's all I can think about. It's an obsession, and also a super power, and it scares the shit out of me while at the same time I absolutely love it.

There's nothing but the painting. The mother, the father, the daughter. Their piano, the walls, the light—the freaking *light*—and the cello on the floor. I thought it was a basket, but no, a cello, and I spent legitimately three *hours* on that freaking instrument, painting and repainting until it looks absolutely freaking perfect.

I'm on a high I've never experienced before. I love this copying, love the challenge it presents, but mostly I'm forcing myself into this state of hyperfocus because my life literally depends on it. I can play coy around Erick all I want, but deep down, I understand what's going on.

I paint or I die.

So I paint every fucking waking hour, hands aching, fingers cramping. I go through pints of tea, so much tea that Marina's bringing it up constantly. At one point, I consider peeing into a bucket in the corner, but the mere thought snaps me back into reality, and I take the two minutes to walk to an actual toilet. Then I consume more tea.

The canvas comes to life. Vermeer's room focuses. The back of the father's chair, a reddish-brown. The tiles, checkerboard black and white. Another instrument on top of the cloth, barely in view, probably a lute of some sort. I paint it all, obsess over the details, chewing on my brushes until the ends are worn nubs.

Erick comes and goes. He brings me what I need. Food, fuel, whatever. We don't talk much—there isn't time. A day passes, I get another four hours of sleep, and I'm so deep into the process that I forget to take any breaks until I look up and realize it's mid-afternoon and I've been working for six hours straight.

When I stand, I go all dizzy from hunger as the blood rushes into my feet and legs, and suddenly I stagger, grab onto the desk, and knock over a few cans of paint.

"Are you okay?" Erick appears in the doorway. I look over, blinking rapidly. "Hellie. Are you okay?"

He comes over. I smile at him. "Fine," I say. "I'm fine. Just forgot to eat." Which is when I notice that he brought me breakfast at some point earlier, and I just never bothered to have any.

"Come with me."

"Wait. The mess."

"Marina will clean it up, don't worry about it." He pulls me away from the studio. "You need rest."

"But the painting." That's all I can think about: the painting. The light, the dark. The minute strokes. I want to get everything perfect, so perfect nobody could ever tell the difference, so perfect there *is* no difference.

Erick leads me into my room and pushes me onto the bed. "Stay."

"Hey," I protest, glaring at him, but fuck, these sheets are soft. "You can't just throw me around."

"I definitely can. Don't move, I'm getting you something to eat."

"Fine. Whatever." I mutter curses at him, not really feeling any of it. Just saying noises to say noises, as a way to keep my dignity intact. Because if I'm not struggling then what am I? Just some total pushover, giving in to her alpha captor like it's no big deal, and I can't have that.

He returns a little while later and I jerk awake. "Eat. Drink." He sits next to me, gets me upright, and places a

B. B. Hamel

tray in my lap. There's a simple peanut butter and jelly sandwich and a big glass of water.

I devour it. I gulp it down. When it's all gone, I shove the tray away, feeling more myself. "You don't have to take care of me, you know."

"I definitely do." He puts the tray down on top of my dresser and faces me, arms crossed over his chest. His gorgeous face is etched with worry. Does he care about me or about the painting? I genuinely don't know, and it doesn't matter. I am the painting right now. "You're skipping meals."

"You're the one forcing me to do ten days' worth of work in three. Remember that?"

"You don't have to kill yourself to do it."

"Actually, I kind of do, dude."

His lips scrunch up. "Don't call me that."

"What? Dude? You don't like it, dude?" I say it again, sing-song. "Dude, dude, dude."

"Get in the bathroom. You reek."

"Excuse me?" I glare at him. "Now you're just being rude."

"I'm serious. Smell yourself."

I'm about to bite off a killer insult, but instead I do a quick, very feminine sniff, and he's right. I am beyond ripe.

"Get it started," I grumble, annoyed that we're doing this again.

The shower turns on. I stand, very aware of what happened the last time, and I'm smart enough to stay clothed until there's a door between us. I clean myself off, taking my time, relaxing in the warm water. When I'm done, I towel off, and step into my room to get dressed.

He's still fucking here, sitting at the end of my bed, and he stares at me with a deep, soul-sucking intensity.

No, scratch that. It's not intensity.

It's hunger. Like some sort of galactic hell-demon searching for a planet to chew on.

I'm his latest snack.

"Drop the towel, lie on the bed."

"What the fuck?" I grip the edge tighter, holding it against my body. "Erick, absolutely not."

"You need to relax. You're a mess. Drop the towel, get on the bed."

"Stop it. You're going too far." I shake my head as he stands. Did I mention that he's big and beautiful? Because the guy unfolds himself, standing up to his full height, his muscles flexed and lovely through his tight button-down shirt, the sleeves rolled up to show vein-roped forearms. "Look, I get it, I'm tired and strung out. Let me have another four hours of sleep. I'm in good shape."

"You're right, the painting's coming along. I actually think you'll finish in time. But you need to relax. You're a mess."

"Seriously, stop insulting me, please."

"Take off the towel and lie on the bed."

"Or else what?"

"Or else I am going to force you down and that won't be fun for either of us. No towel. Face down."

I stare at him, frowning. "Face down? You're not—"

His smirk makes me want to jab a brush down my own throat. "I'm going to give you a massage before you get some sleep."

"Oh." I blink a few times. "Oh." I had other things in mind. "Oh."

"Did your brain just break?"

"No! I'm fine. I just—I'm fine."

"I'm good at this, okay? I knew this girl—"

"I don't need details." I walk to the bed, still in the towel, but climb on face-down. I wriggle free, but leave the towel draped over my ass. "Best you'll get."

"Good enough." He climbs up beside me, kneeling, looming.

"You better not be fucking around. You better—" But he shuts me up as soon as he touches my body.

Holy shit. *Holy shit.*

If this man weren't too much already, he really wasn't kidding about the massage. No, he's not a professional, but he's so damn good with his hands that it's absurd. I really want to hate it, really want to resist it, but after maybe thirty seconds I'm making these really embarrassing whale-like moans. Low, animalistic, satisfying. He doesn't seem to mind as his hands drift lower and lower, down to the edge of the towel, and then there's no towel at all, and he's kneading my ass, and fuck him, I'd scream and make him stop if it didn't feel so damn good.

Arousal fills me. I'm groaning as I turn my head. He's staring at me, eyes like fire.

"You're too low," I whisper, biting my lip, salivating at the thought of him going even lower.

"You need this."

"How do you know what I need?"

"Your body's telling me. That's what I've learned over the years. Listen to the body."

"My body's saying I need to finish that painting."

"No, little devil, it's saying you want my hand between your legs. You're wound up too tightly for a little massage to help."

"Okay, see, I knew this was where you were going." I think about escaping, but I'm very naked, and if I move at

103

all, he'll see everything. As if there's much to hide at this point.

His hands don't stop. He works my lower back. My shoulders. Down to my ass again. And this time, he doesn't stop, one hand dropping down between my legs.

"That's my Hellie," he says as his fingers find my arousal. "Oh, I knew it."

"Shut up," I say, groaning. It feels so fucking good. I arch my back, just a little, lifting my hips to give him a better angle.

He teases my clit, rubs my lips, slides his fingers deep inside. His other hand grabs my hair and I gasp in surprise.

"I want to take care of you, Hellie, in every way you need. If I don't do it, nobody else will."

"Take care of yourself. Seriously, go over in the corner, whip out your cock, and take care of yourself. Leave me out of it."

"You want to watch while I stroke myself?" His fingers slide deeper. His grip on my hair tightens. My hips raise up—magically, all by themselves, I swear I'm not doing anything at all—and he's fucking me with that lovely hand of his. "You want to finish yourself off at the same time as I come? I'll lick your fingers clean and you can lick mine."

"Uh," I say, sucking in air. "Fuck, that's hot and I hate you a little bit for putting it in my head."

"We can do that. Or I can keep going until you come. Do you want to come for me, Hellie?"

"Yes," I gasp, and he's going faster now. "Yes, I want to come, I want to come, *yes*." My hips are moving, bucking against his fingers, bliss ripping into my body. "Fuck yes, fuck yes, don't stop."

I come against his hand, his other fist gripping my hair tight, pulling back as the orgasm slams into my core, ripping into my brain. I come hard, gasping, moaning, my pussy a soaking wet bomb of desire against his palm.

He pulls his hand away and I collapse onto my belly, still twitching from the after-effects.

"That's my girl," he says, pulling the blankets back and covering me. He stands near the bed, licking his fingers clear, as I cuddle against a pillow, feeling like my body's made of clay. "Go to sleep, get some rest. I'll wake you up soon."

"Then I paint for you some more?"

"Yes, devil girl, you paint for us both. Go to sleep."

He disappears. The lights turn out.

Asshole doesn't have to tell me twice—I go to sleep.

Chapter 15

Hellie

I finish around four in the afternoon on the third day.

I'm fried. My head hurts. My eyes are like swollen balloons. My hands are cramping, and there's paint everywhere, staining my clothes, my skin. I sit cross-legged on top of the work table in the center of the room looking from the reference book to my finished piece, back and forth, back and forth, for almost an hour.

"It's not perfect," I tell him. Erick's standing nearby and hasn't said a word since he found me like this. I didn't want to engage him, not yet, but at this point there's not much more I can do. "If I had more time, I could get it there. Another week, and I think I could make the details perfect, assuming you could get me a better picture to go off. But it's finished."

He steps forward, coming into view. I watch him, heart beating hard, surprised by how much I want him to approve of this.

I don't need him to like it, or at least I shouldn't. I think of my father, during one of our little excursions together, this one much more recently, only three years ago. *Don't care what other people say about you, Heloise. You have a gift. And you're an Accardi. We don't give a shit what anyone thinks.* I thought he was being stupid at the time, because obviously we care, but I've held on to that piece of advice. It's a strange thing, not caring—it's armor against the world, a strange kind of confidence.

"I love it," he says.

I let out a long breath. "Really?"

"I'm serious." He steps closer, squinting. "I can't tell the difference between yours and the book. God, even the back wall, all the little dark and light patches, it's identical."

"You have no idea how long that took me."

"You did this in three days." He shakes his head, looking truly mystified, and a satisfied smile crosses my lips. I try to hide it, but shit. I'm proud of this. That's okay.

"Will it be enough for your partners?"

He turns to me, expression smoldering. Uh-oh, I know that look, it's the same look he gave me before he massaged my back then fucked my pussy with his fingers.

"You are incredible."

"Alright, easy now." I unfold myself and hop off the work table, putting it between us. "Your partners. Will they be happy with this?"

"Yes," he says. "Absolutely."

"Are you sure? Because there's a lot riding on whether this is good enough. Don't think with your dick."

He barks a laugh. "I'm not."

"You are. Hey, don't look at me like that. I know what you want from me, let's just set aside the bullshit for one second, okay? You want to sleep with me."

"Okay, Hellie, you're right. I want to fuck you."

Hearing it so plainly sends a sharp thrill of desire between my legs. My nipples are instantly hard. This was a mistake, but I power through.

"Put that aside. Forget about that. Is the painting good enough?"

He nods slowly. "Absolutely, yes."

"Alright." I let out a long, relieved sigh. "Great. I guess I'm not getting murdered. Yet."

I watch, exhausted, as he circles the canvas, studying it up close. I wonder if he can see the flaws, all of them so glaringly obvious to me, but he doesn't linger on any of them. Instead, he shakes his head. "Incredible," he whispers.

"It's done. I'm finished. Now I'm going to bed." I turn away and go to leave.

But he calls me back. "There's a problem."

I groan. I should've seen this coming. "What now? You need another painting done in the next twenty minutes?"

"They want you there when we present this to them."

My eyebrows raise. "Your partners do?"

"Gallo and Frost. They want proof that you're alive and that you're the one doing this work."

"We can take a video right now. Take out your phone."

"I understand this is stressful. Believe me, I pushed back hard, but Frost in particular was firm. If they're going to invest this much time and reputational risk into you paying them back, they want proof. They want to speak with you."

I slump back against the doorframe and release a frustrated whimper. "All I want to do is sleep for the next decade."

"I know. I'm sorry. We're leaving tomorrow morning, very early, and I guarantee you'll be safe."

It hadn't occurred to me that I wouldn't be, but it should've. Frost and Gallo want me dead. They want to send a message.

Erick's the one that's running this art scheme. He's the one keeping me alive.

"Can I at least get some sleep first? I mean, it's not until the morning."

"Yes, Hellie, go ahead, get rest. Sleep as much as you can." He moves toward me, his body tensed like a wild cat. "But don't think you're going to escape. Don't get some horrible idea in your head about running away, because I promise, if you do something stupid, I won't be able to protect you. Frost and Gallo are practically begging you to fuck this up. Do you hear me?"

I nod once. Sharp. Annoyed. "I get it."

"Good."

"Am I dismissed?"

He turns back to the painting, arms crossed, studying it. "You're dismissed."

Chapter 16

Erick

I keep Hellie close as the car rolls through the Strip toward our neutral location. Wolfie sits behind the wheel with Ren in the passenger seat. The painting is stowed in the trunk wrapped in layers of padding. Nobody speaks, and I can tell Hellie's nervous. She fidgets with her hair, shifts in her seat, stares anywhere but at me.

"This must be strange for you," I say softly, leaning down so only she can hear. "Being out here again."

"You mean since you kidnapped me?"

"You're probably thinking to yourself, this is your best chance of getting rescued. Make enough noise and someone might come to help, right?"

Her jaw works. "Leave me alone."

"I need you to understand that you're wrong. If you make a scene, you'll only make your own life harder. That beautiful art studio I built for you? You don't *need* that to paint for me."

"Are you trying to piss me off right now?" She meets my gaze. We're inches apart. "I'm aware that my life is on the line right now."

"Then make sure you behave."

Her lip twitches. I can tell she's pissed and barely holding it back. "You know, Erick, one of these days, you're going to fuck up, and then I'll be gone. I can't wait to get away from you."

I sit back, keeping my face neutral, but that hurt me more than it should have.

I'm not surprised she lashed out—I pushed her into it and practically begged her to come at me—only I didn't expect that to hit me so hard. *I can't wait to get away from you.*

It's irrational, this feeling. She's a prisoner, my captive, of course she wants to get away. But some part of me, some broken, needy, stupid part of me, hoped that she was beginning to understand.

There's no escape from me.

Because she's not trapped with me—I'm keeping *them* from her.

That's why I need to make sure, really damn sure, that she doesn't do something stupid and give Frost and Gallo the opportunity they want.

They'll snatch her away without hesitating and torture her until she begs for mercy, but none will come.

That's why I'm pissing her off. That's why I'm getting in her face and making sure she knows there's no running.

Because she's right—her life really does depend on it.

We reach the casino. Wolfie stays with the car while Ren, Hellie and I get out. Ren goes first, clearing a path, and I slip my hand into Hellie's. She tried to yank away, but I hold on tight, pulling her closer. She's wearing tight jeans and a creme blouse, her hair up in a messy bun, only a little bit of makeup around the eyes.

"What are you doing?" she hisses.

"Making sure you don't escape." I hold her hand tighter. "Don't let go. If you do, I'll tell Ren to carry you in."

"You wouldn't."

"I absolutely would. I don't give a fuck what the crowds think. This is Vegas, remember? Hold my hand, devil girl, and don't get any ideas."

She glares. For a second, I think she's about to defy me. But instead, she moves stiffly by my side as Ren holds the main doors and we make our way toward the conference room.

I know this isn't real. I understand that I'm dragging her along against her will.

But there's still some sick voice in the back of my mind that enjoys being this close to her, that likes having her by my side, like we're actually together. I like being seen with her in the casino. I like the way her hand feels in mine.

I like so much about this girl.

Which is a goddamn problem, because every time I get close to something I like, it always ends up corrupted and ruined.

I won't let that happen to Hellie, I just have to figure out how to protect her first.

Including from myself.

Frost and Gallo are already waiting when we arrive, their people sitting near the walls again. Frost stands, shakes my hand, and stares at Hellie for a long, uncomfortable moment.

"This is our artist," he says. "It's nice to meet you, Heloise Accardi."

"Hellie," she says. "Nice to meet you too."

I don't release her hand, and this time, she doesn't act like she wants to pull away.

Gallo's next. He doesn't introduce himself to Hellie at all, only grunts in her direction like she's a dog from the street. "You really brought the bitch, huh?" He shakes his head. "Pretty bitch. It's a shame what we have to do to her."

"Easy there," Frost says, patting Gallo on the shoulder. "Based on the way Erick's looking at you, I'm not sure you'll get away with insulting that girl anymore."

I realize I'm on the verge of snarling and quickly school my face. "Gentlemen, my driver will be up with the painting shortly. Why don't we have a seat and discuss business?"

I put Hellie in a chair next to mine. Ren remains standing, vigilant for any trouble. Gallo starts the meeting by complaining about Hellie like she isn't around, talking about how she should be dead and buried already, and how it's an embarrassment that she's still breathing. Frost cuts in, claims it's for the best, and besides, she can always be killed later on.

As the two casino bosses discuss public and horrifying ways to brutalize Hellie, she shifts closer to me and slips her hand into mine again.

I go very still. We hold hands under the table, and even though her face is locked into a neutral, pale mask, I can feel her trembling.

This is what I've been hiding her from. These men don't care about her, not at all—they'd gladly rip out her intestines if it meant showing Vegas that they're still strong.

Wolfie arrives before it gets too bad. He carries the painting to the front of the room and sets it up on an easel the casino supplied for this occasion. With a flourish, Wolfie removes the covering, and reveals the work to everyone in the room.

There's total silence. The two bosses stare. Gallo's face twists with confusion, while Frost strokes his chin.

"What the fuck is this?" Gallo asks.

"This is a Vermeer." I gesture and Ren walks to the computer at the front of the room. He types, clicks, and pulls up an image of the painting, projected onto the wall beside our fake.

The men stare. I sit back, smiling to myself, astonished all over again at the quality.

"I have to admit, that's incredible," Frost says, his voice very soft.

"So what, it's a good fucking copy." Gallo sounds pissed, which is no surprise. He didn't want this from the beginning. "Who gives a damn?"

"It's an incredible copy." Frost walks to Hellie's forgery and studies it closely. "The brushstrokes look fantastic." He looks at her, shaking his head. "You really did this in a few days?"

Nobody speaks. Everyone stares at Hellie. I nudge her and she clears her throat.

"Yes," she says. "I can do better if you give me more time."

"Better?" Frost seems delighted. "This is perfect already."

"No." Hellie's voice is small but strong. I'm amazed she's speaking out of turn, but also pleased. "There are issues. The materials are all wrong. Some of the details aren't

116

right. I had to rush some things to get finished in time. If you give me more time and the proper paints, I can make it pass for the real thing."

"Even if an expert studied it?" Frost's eyes narrow. He steps toward her, head tilted.

"Yes," she says, but she doesn't sound convinced.

"This is foolish." Gallo bangs his hands on the table. "The painting is good. Fine, so what? It'll always go like this. She'll demand more and more, a never-ending supply of excuses. We can't trust her. We might as well end her right now."

"No, I'm interested." Frost returns to his seat, leaning back. "I spoke with some friends recently. I may have a few contacts."

Gallo groans. "You have got to be kidding me."

"Can you paint us a final version in five days?"

Hellie goes stiff. She grabs my hand tightly like she wants to dig her fingers into my flesh. I know what she's thinking, and I speak up for her.

"Making this painting in three days nearly killed her," I tell them. "She barely slept, barely ate—"

"Oh, how awful," Gallo says, deadpan.

"Five days will wreck her. She needs more time. Two weeks, at least."

Frost's lips push together. "No, we don't have that long, and I worry that Gallo's right and she'll keep on dragging this out. If she can do *that* in three days, she can do better in five."

"Fine, give the girl five," Gallo snaps. "Pain in my ass. I'll even broker this travesty."

I grind my jaw, trying to stay calm. "You want to burn her out on a single deal. I want to keep her around and make us all some real money. Think long-term."

"If she pulls this off, there will be a long-term," Frost says, his tone hard. "But if she fucks it up or tries to ruin our plans, we'll hand her to Gallo and let him have his way."

"I like the sound of that." The old bastard shows teeth.

I want to cut their throats. I want to murder them here, in cold blood. But instead, I nod sharply. "Fine. Five days."

Hellie lets out a little whimper, but I put a hand on her knee to silence her.

"Then we're done here." Frost smiles as he walks to the forged painting. "Mind if I keep this? I'll hang it in my house. What beautiful work."

"Be my guest," I say, stand, and drag Hellie out of the room. Ren and Wolfie follow at a distance, both looking grim.

"I can't," Hellie says on the walk to the car. "I can't do it again."

"You can and you will."

"Erick, please. You know I can't."

I stop and face her, pulling her close and staring into her face. She looks back, her expression vacant, haunted, and afraid.

"You *can* do this. I'll give you whatever you need to make it happen. I've already gotten most of the historically accurate materials, and now it's just a matter of getting through the next five days."

"I almost lost my mind the last time."

"I know you did. But you can do this, and I swear, if you pull it off, things will be easier."

"That's what you said last time."

She's right. I know she's right. And a little piece of me loathes myself for that. "I'll fight for you."

"Like you did today?"

That hurts. A punch to my throat. But I take it and grab her hands, holding them both between mine.

"Hellie, I promise, you can do this. Five days. Okay?"

She whimpers again, a pathetic noise, but sucks in a deep breath through her nose.

"Fine," she says. "But when I'm a wreck, you can blame yourself for it."

Chapter 17

Hellie

It's strange, both dreading something and feeling completely immersed in it anyway.

The second we get back to the house, I head straight up into the studio. Marina follows with some tea and soup; she pats me on the knee and promises to check in on me soon. I don't see Erick anywhere, and that's fine.

He's only a distraction right now.

I pull out the correct kind of canvas, something Erick had sourced for me a few days ago. There are historically accurate brushes and paints in most of the colors I'll need. I sit down on my stool, get my work space ready, and close my eyes, trying to picture every detail of *The Concert* all over again.

Except I see that conference room instead.

The vicious, ugly look on that old man Gallo's face as he gleefully talked about gutting me in public.

The cold, detached stare of Frost, like I was some kind of money-making machine for him to play around with.

Those are the men Erick's keeping me from.

And some part of me is happy he's doing it. If it weren't for him, they would've played out all those violent fantasies on me already. I would've suffered, and suffered in horrible ways.

But that suffering is abstract, and the suffering I'm about to go through is very real.

I eat and drink, thinking the whole time, trying to get my mind off my problems, trying to focus on the one thing I can control.

This painting.

It's my entire life now. I feel so intimately connected with each stroke, each spot, every line, like I came up with it myself.

"I owe you more. I know this isn't enough."

I jump and turn as Erick steps into the studio carrying more paint. He places the cans carefully down on my work bench.

"You're right, it's not enough."

"You'll have what you need. I promise."

"How about more time?"

"You were there, Hellie. You know what we're working with."

I nod, turning away. I'm just being difficult for no reason. I can yell and scream at him all I want, but nothing will change my situation.

"Did you know they were going to kill me?" I ask, not trusting myself to watch his face as he answers.

"Yes," he says.

"And you took me anyway? You knew they'd be angry about it."

"Yes, I did."

"Why? You didn't know me."

"I knew you."

I turn to stare at him. "No, you didn't."

"I knew you," he insists, hesitating. "Wait here."

"Erick, hold on. Where are you—" But he's gone. He strides out of the studio and I'm shaking my head. Typical asshole, just walks away when we're in the middle of a conversation like I'm supposed to dote on his every whim. Frustration rolls through me but I keep it in check. A few minutes later, he appears again, but this time he's carrying a canvas.

It's not a large painting. Three feet across by two-and-a-half long. Slashes of brightness contrasted by a traditional subject: two people standing in front of a lake. But their skin is bright pink, their hair down to their ankles, the water a strange and impossible cerulean, the sky itself beginning to twist like a hurricane. That bit was created in a manic-like state one night after a particularly shitty day at work. I'd know, because it's one of mine.

I can't believe he's holding it. The painting's called *Twilight Thunder*, and it was the best sale I've ever had. A thousand dollars, twice what I'd normally charge. The deal happened via Instagram, and I never learned the name of the man I sold it to—only that he had a local PO box.

"You," I say, my mouth hanging open. "How?"

"I fell in love with your work a long time ago." He places the canvas down on the table. "I should have told you sooner, but I didn't know how."

"Words usually do the trick."

He doesn't smile. "When I figured out that it was you we were looking for, I had a moment of panic. I thought to myself, I could let Gallo and Frost handle this. I could let them take her out. But what a fucking waste."

"Right, because I can paint, I'm worth saving?"

"Yes," he says. "Because you're beautiful. Because you can do something incredible. And because I didn't want you to die, not for something that you weren't involved with."

I should be freaked out. I should be angry. He kept this from me.

Instead, I'm flattered.

"What am I supposed to do with this?" I ask him, genuinely confused. "You knew me before this happened. You own one of my paintings."

"I told you I knew all about you. I wasn't lying. I'm showing you this now because I need you to understand that I'm not your enemy."

"No, of course not, you're just my kidnapper."

"Damn it, Hellie." His words come out like a growl as he walks toward me. Menacing, massive. Oozing raw, sexual rage. I back away until I run into the window, staring at him with an open mouth, unable to ignore my body's keening need.

He's gorgeous. Every inch of him like a sculpture made just for me. If I were given the ability to carve a perfect man from clay, my masterpiece would look like him.

And that scares me half to death.

"What do you want from me?" I ask, frustration and desire slamming inside my chest. "Am I supposed to thank you for locking me in this room and forcing me to work?"

"Yes," he says.

"Well, I won't. If you really cared about me and wanted to protect me, you'd find some way to get me out of this. You know I'm going to work myself to death over the next five days to get this thing finished. If you thought the first time was bad, this is going to be worse."

I can tell he hates that. His face twists in pain, but he shakes his head. "It isn't that simple."

"How? Why's everything so damn complicated with you?"

"They'll come after you sooner or later. If I tried to stall, or to hide you, or to simply help you disappear, they'd find out and they'd act. I can't risk starting a war for you."

"No, I guess not, which means I'm fucked."

He snarls, coming close. He pins me against the wall beside the window, showing teeth, his hand wrapping around my wrists and holding them down at my sides. I gasp, wriggling against him, but he's too big and way too strong.

"You're right, you are fucked if you keep resisting. I'm doing my best for you. I'm giving you a real chance at surviving this, and all you do is make my life hell for it."

"You think just because you owned one of my paintings means I should be thanking you for this? That won't happen."

"No," he says, very slowly. "But you should at least think about your assumptions. I haven't hurt you. I've treated you well. I've given you all of this and asked only that you don't get yourself killed."

"And that I paint for you."

"Yes, and that you paint. Which won't last forever. This is how you survive, Hellie. I need you to see it."

I can see. I'm not blind. I see a big man, a beautiful man, a man used to getting what he wants staring back at me with raw, undeniable want in his expression. I see that he is the only thing standing between me and a couple of psychopaths hell-bent on torturing me to appease their own bruised egos.

And I see myself tumbling down into a hellish nightmare, but unable to stop, and not sure I really want to.

"What are you going to do if I never believe you?" I ask very slowly, daring him.

He stares back. His face is inches from mine. Our lips practically touching. Excitement curls down my spine like a lazy cat stretching. Something dangerous passes over his expression, lust like melting steel.

"I can show you."

"How?"

"I want you to see, but maybe you need to feel."

I suck in a breath. "How are you going to make me feel something like that?"

"You need to know you're protected. You need to know you're safe. I have ways."

"Come on, Erick. We both know what you really want."

"And now you need me to say it out loud? You know what'll happen."

"Go ahead. Show me."

His grip releases on my left wrist and slowly moves up my belly, over my breasts, to my throat. He holds it there, hand around my windpipe. Not squeezing, but pressing.

"I want all of you," he says.

"This is how you show it?"

"Yes, Hellie, by proving that I could destroy you whenever I want, but never will, because you are mine to protect."

"Liar. You just want to fuck me."

His eyes blaze. "Yes. I do."

"Good. Admit it. No more bullshit about saving me. You just want to fuck me. Go on, stop pretending."

"You're right," he snarls. "I want to fuck you, Hellie. I want to fuck that filthy, bratty mouth of yours. I want to grip your hair and rip my cock into your tight pussy until you scream my name. I want to get you wet, lick your cunt until you moan, let you orgasm against my mouth. I want to punish those beautiful lips with my shaft. You've been nothing but a pain, and now I want to take you and show you what it's like to be all mine."

I gasp as he bruises my mouth with his, slamming our lips together.

Chapter 18

Hellie

He kisses me with a hand around my throat, and I kiss him back, just as needy, melting into the moment as his tongue invades my mouth and a whimper rips itself from my guts.

It feels good. Fuck, it feels so good to have this man take me, kiss me, dominate me, finally break some of the insane sexual tension that's always percolating between us. And the sick part is I want everything he said: I want his cock between my legs, his shaft in my throat. I want him to fuck my mouth and punish me. I want him to ruin me, leave me quivering, shaking, soaking wet and brainless. I want him to stop holding back.

I gasp as he turns me and lifts me up, throwing me down onto the work bench. I spread my legs as he slams himself between them, kissing me hard, pulling my hair as his other hand unbuttons my pants and dives down between my legs. No bullshit, not gentle, not playing games. His purr drives me wild as his fingers find my lips.

"Wet," he says, gliding his fingertips up and down my folds. "Fucking soaked. You stand there, all self-righteous, whining about how I kidnapped you, unable to realize that I saved your life, and all this time you're a messy slut for me."

"Erick," I gasp, shocked by his dirty mouth.

"That's right," he says, sliding his fingers inside of me. My back arches as pleasure rockets into my brain. "Messy fucking slut. You're soaking wet, dripping onto my palm, and you have the nerve to act like you hate me. Liar, Hellie, you devil girl, you succubus, you little fucking liar. You're dripping wet with lust. You want my cock. You want me to punish your filthy fucking mouth."

"Oh, god," I gasp, grinding against his hand. "Fuck, I want it."

"Messy little slut," he whispers, biting my lip, and drags me down off the table, forcing me to my knees as he takes off his slacks.

I'm losing my mind as I stroke his hard cock. He's big, thick, long, and pulsing with lust as I lick him, but that's not enough. He grabs my hair and pushes me down onto his tip, shoving himself into my mouth. "Touch yourself while you suck me, Hellie," he commands. "Right now, I want you to moan while I fuck your face and punish that dirty mouth. Do it, touch yourself."

I moan, my free hand between my legs. I'm buzzing with need as I start to tease my pussy, and he's right, it feels so fucking good. I suck him faster, messy, unrelenting, and he pushes himself deeper, holding tight to my hair.

I pull back, groaning like he wanted, stroking him.

"You're so fucking pretty touching yourself down on your knees," he says, bending down to kiss me.

I kiss him back. He drags me up by the hair, turns me around, and bends me over the bench. He drops down, yanks off my pants, and rips my panties aside as he licks me from behind, his fingers teasing. He turns me around and I wrap my legs around his head, sitting back on the bench top, his tongue sucking and gliding up and down my folds, rolling around my clit as I grip his hair tight.

"Incredible," he grunts, fucking me with his fingers. "I never knew a dirty little hell demon like you could taste like heaven."

"Erick," I gasp, back arching. "You're really going to tease me?"

"Until you tell me what I want to hear, god damn right I am."

"Fuck you," I moan as his fingers find that perfect spot and my skull melts. He rubs me like that before stopping again. "What do I have to say?" I'm begging now, pleading.

"Tell me to fuck you."

"Erick," I groan. "Please."

"I want you to say, *Fuck my needy, messy pussy, please, Erick.* Say it now."

"No." I glare at him, my face flushed, and only a tiny sliver of rational thought still remaining in my skull. "I won't."

"Then we're done here." He steps back.

"Asshole," I gasp. "Fuck me, you bastard."

He comes back, kisses me, fingers teasing slowly. "The whole thing."

"Fuck my needy, messy pussy, please, Erick, you piece of shit."

He grabs my hair, spreads my legs, and sinks himself inside of me.

I gasp, back arching as it burns and feels so fucking good I could scream. He's big, way too big, but he knows exactly what he's doing as he sinks deeper and deeper, my legs hooked over his arms. I lean back on the table on my elbow, staring at him with my mouth open. He kisses my neck, rips open the buttons of my blouse, and kisses my bra-covered breasts as he slowly fucks me deeper.

"You grip me like this pussy was made for only me," he whispers, grinding into me. I'm so wet and making these filthy noises, but I love it. "I don't know how it took me so long to find you, my hell girl, but you're everything I need."

He fucks me faster. I wrap my arms around his neck and push myself along his shaft. I'm gasping, moaning with incredible bliss, and when he bites my neck, and shoulder, and my lower lip, I can't take it anymore. I explode against him, coming so hard I stop breathing, and he doesn't hold back, he fucks me until I'm lying back on the table and sweating, but he's not done with me yet. He drags me back down, turns me around, my ass in the air, and spanks me.

I yelp in surprise, staring over my shoulder at him. "What the fuck?"

"That's for not trusting me." He spanks me again. I try to move but he grabs my hips and yanks me against him. "That's because I love turning your lovely ass bright pink." Then he sinks himself inside of me and I melt against him all over again.

He fucks me rough, his hand exploring my body like he's been holding himself back this whole time but is finally releasing every bit of pent-up desire deep into my pussy. I push back down his shaft and gasp with bliss as he takes me, ripping deeper and deeper. He grips my breasts, wraps a hand around my throat, pulls my hair, spanks my ass. I'm dripping down my thigh, moaning his name, using my hand to push off the work table and harder down his length.

Every inch, every thrust, it's too much. I'm losing myself as he leans over, his massive body dwarfing mine, and kisses me over my shoulder. It's the kiss that finally does it, that throws me over the edge for a second time. I come on his shaft, come as I moan into his mouth, and I feel him stiffen as he fills me from behind.

I collapse against him. He groans, holding me tight. We're spent, sweaty, half-naked, disheveled. The room's a mess. I hadn't noticed him knocking over paint cans and brushes, tossing materials around. It's like a hurricane went off, but I hadn't even noticed. I slide down to the floor and he holds me tight against him.

"I should clean this up," I say, but I don't move, and he doesn't let me go.

"Soon." He breathes deep against my neck. "You're a pain in my ass, you know that, Hellie?"

"Great thing to say right after fucking me."

"I know, but I mean it. This would be so much easier if I despised you."

"Too bad I'm such a delight."

"Really is a shame."

I smile to myself, and even though I know it's a mistake, I let myself enjoy this moment, feeling strangely safe and satisfied.

Chapter 19

Hellie

After we straighten up the studio and I take a shower, it's time to get to work.

Dread fills my stomach. I'm terrified that I won't be able to pull this off, that I'm way overestimating my painting abilities, that I'm a total fraud and everyone will find out—and I'll get murdered for it.

But I shove that aside and focus.

I start like I did with the first version, but this time, I know what I'm doing. I make fewer mistakes as I sketch out the base layer, getting the canvas prepped for the painting to come. I move with confidence, or at least pretending I feel confident until it starts to become somewhat the truth, selecting colors, brushes, laying it all out like a chef at his work station. Lunch appears at some point and I eat without thinking, my mind focused on the task ahead.

I feel myself start to sink into that work mode. It's like I've flipped a switch and now there's nothing else but what I have to do. I let myself drift, obsessive, intense, deeper and deeper, like a trance.

The mother first. The daughter next. The riot of light and dark, the smattering of color, the instruments, the father's muted back and lank hair.

A miracle happens every time I drop into this state. It's a rushing river, a never-ending motion. Ideas leave my hands like I'm shedding skin. I work late and go to bed for only a few hours, but I'm up early the next morning, working hard until coffee and breakfast appear. I don't know who brings it. I'm not sure it matters. Everything in my world narrows down to my workstation, to the canvas, to the paintings, to my materials.

This job will either save or damn me.

Only one thought intrudes on my focus. Erick, his mouth, his hands, his body against mine. His groans of pleasure, his hand as it slaps my ass. Erick's the only person who enters my brain that isn't a part of this painting, and I wish I could keep him out, at least for five days. He's a distraction, and worse than that, I don't want to be distracted by him at all.

He's the reason I'm in this mess.

But there's no way it'll happen.

Erick's lodged deep into my skull, lurking there even when I try to excise him away.

I paint.

I paint and paint and paint for an entire day.

More food appears, I eat it, I use the bathroom, and I paint. I sleep for a little while, wake up, paint. The sun rises, I eat, drink coffee, allow myself a short shower, and I paint.

I don't see anyone. I don't speak to anyone. I assume there are other people in the house—Marina must be bringing up my meals—but nobody bothers me.

Erick disappears. Not from my mind, but from my sight, from my tiny existence.

Two days pass. I'm getting delirious but I'm only dimly aware of it happening. During the third day, I finish the mother, and start on the daughter. I'm making good progress—it's a little bit slower because I'm making sure every brush stroke is accurate, constantly referencing a blown-up, hi-res version of the original.

Materials appear, brushes get cleaned, paints are refreshed.

It happens as if by magic. I don't question anything, I just keep painting.

My hands ache. My head feels like it might explode.

I get through three days and head into the fourth, making good progress.

The materials are right. The brushes, the strokes, even the canvas material. I'm not used to these colors and it takes a little while to build a sense for the way they spread and lay on the canvas, but soon it makes sense, it feels natural. I work, unrelenting, obsessed, like I'm slaying a dragon. Fighting it one inch at a time.

When this is over, I'll hate this painting more than anything in the world, but for now, I still love it.

I still yearn to be a part of it.

Coffee appears. Food appears. Someone tells me to take a shower, but I ignore them and keep on going. They make me wash off anyway, and I do it as if in a waking dream.

The fourth day ends.

The sun rises on the fifth and I'm running on three hours of rest.

My face is heavy.

My hands feel like muck.

The painting is nearly done.

I'm in the final stretch, performing tiny adjustments, scouring the entire thing to make sure there's not a single microscopic mistake. My face is so close to the canvas that I think I'm getting high on paint fumes. Maybe that's just exhaustion.

It doesn't matter—all I want to do in this entire world is finish the damn painting.

"You need to eat something."

I jump, turn around expecting Marina, and find Erick waiting at the doorway instead.

I rub my eyes, thinking it's a mirage. I haven't seen him in five days, not since this nightmare started, and I was beginning to wonder if my sick, overworked mind made him up.

Which is stupid, since he's the whole reason I'm doing this, and then I wonder if maybe I'm not doing anything at all and I'm actually at home in my apartment, and that's about the time I realize I *really* need to sleep.

"Where the fuck have you been?" I blurt out, unable to help myself.

Seems that reaching rock bottom also means losing all my inhibitions. Good to know.

"What are you talking about?" He looks confused as he walks toward me with a tray of food. Saltines, a big bowl of soup, some tea.

Precious tea. I snatch it away and chug it down, despite the heat, which makes me start doing that gasping fish thing where I'm sucking down air and blowing it out to cool my scalded mouth. He gets me water, which helps, and when I'm finally able to speak, I pin him with a sharp glare.

"I mean, I haven't seen you in days. Where the hell have you been?"

He still looks confused. "I've been here."

138

"No, you haven't."

"Hellie, who do you think's been bringing you food and dragging you off to bed? Who's been shoving you into the shower so you don't smell like a rotten pumpkin? Who's been making sure you're drinking water? Who's been encouraging you?"

I frown at him. Those are great questions. "Uh, Marina."

"I don't pay her enough to wash your back. My god, you're an absolute wreck. You really don't remember any of that?"

"I've been busy," I mumble, feeling stupid, because now that he mentions it, I actually do remember someone scrubbing me down and washing behind my ears, which is admirably thorough, but very humiliating. "That was all you?"

"Yes, Hellie. I haven't abandoned you at all. I've been right here, day and night, keeping you from killing your-self." He kneels down and stares into my eyes. "You're done, aren't you? Is that why you're with me again?"

"I mean—" I bite my lip, staring at the painting, and for the first time in maybe a few days, I can actually see it.

The whole thing. Not the tiny details, not the pieces I've been obsessed over for the last few hours, but the entire picture.

It's gorgeous.

And flawless.

He's right—it's like I've surfaced from somewhere dark and comfortable, like forcing my way out from a womb.

"You're finished," he says, squeezing my knees. "That's why you're coming back out."

"Back out of what? What the hell happened to me?"

"You were in the zone. It's actually kind of amazing. I've heard of people able to get into a flow state like that before—"

"Flow state?"

"It's that weird space where your brain's just gliding along totally engrossed in a task, to the point where there's nothing else in the world. Most people can't get there very easily, but I think you've been in a kind of trance."

My stomach growls. I cover it with both hands and groan. "I had no clue I could do that."

"I bet you've been doing it your whole life. Probably not to this extreme, but there also haven't been such huge stakes before."

"Well, I did use to spend all night studying when I was younger. And in college, at art school, I could stay in the studio for hours and hours and forget I was there." I take another sip of tea. This time, it's a more reasonable temperature. "Well, shit, I really *have* been doing it my whole life. I always thought that was normal, you know?"

"There you go." He holds out a hand and helps me up. "What do you say, are we really done? I need to call Frost in a few hours and tell him we're all set. Do you think it'll be enough?"

I step away from the canvas and feel myself cross some invisible barrier back into the world, fully present in the moment for the first time in days.

I feel like shit. My head's pounding. My stomach's a wreck.

I stare at what I've created, at the piece of art sitting on the easel, and there's no part of me that thinks anyone could ever tell the difference between this and what Vermeer himself made.

"It's perfect," I say, nodding slowly.

And it's true. Deep in my heart, I know I've done it.

Erick hugs me tight against him. "I'm proud of you," he whispers, kissing my hair. "Hellie, you gorgeous, talented girl. I'm so proud of you."

"I need to eat," I say as my stomach grumbles a second time.

"Go ahead, get some food." He sits me down. "I'm going to make some calls. When you're done, I want you to go right into bed and sleep, okay?"

"But what if you need me?"

"No, Hellie. Your job is over. Go get some sleep."

I shift in my chair and glance back at the canvas. I can almost feel it calling to me again. The last five days have been nothing but painting and more painting, a steady stream of creation, and it feels strange to come out of that. Back into the mundane world. Some part of me wants to go back in, to forget everything else, forget my troubles.

Except if I did that, I'd lose Erick again.

He'd disappear into the background noise of the room like he did last time, and when I look at him and he looks back with that gorgeous face and those adoring eyes, I don't want that to happen.

I want to be here with him for a while.

"Yeah, okay," I say, shoveling soup into my mouth. "I guess you're up now, boss."

He kisses me again before snapping a photo of the painting on his phone. I feel strangely possessive of it, but this is the point, isn't it? Someone will buy this painting for a lot of money and display it in their house—or store it somewhere as a way to launder some cash. Either way, that thing is no longer mine. It's no longer a work I made.

It's a Vermeer.

Erick leaves and I'm alone again.

I eat, and when I'm done, I barely make it back to bed before I crash.

Chapter 20

Erick

I carry the painting with both hands, moving through the crowded casino toward the poker room. Ren walks beside me, strolling along like there's nothing going on, though I know he's armed and ready to draw down on anyone who gets too close.

"How's the girl feeling?" he asks. "She looked like shit last time I checked."

"She's been asleep for almost twelve hours now. I think her body's a wreck."

"I'm not surprised. She put herself through hell."

"Five days of nothing but painting." I laugh to myself, still insanely impressed. I don't know anyone who could focus on a single difficult task for that long without going insane, but she was like a laser. It was beautiful, but a little terrifying—to her, the rest of the world ceased to exist.

She didn't even know that I was taking care of her.

Day and night. I watched over her obsessively, lurking in the hallway, listening to her work. She whispered to herself as she painted, though it never made any sense, not to me at least. I still loved hearing her voice, loved watching her move around, thumping in the dark, staggering in the daylight, making something incredible from nothing but color.

I made sure she ate, got her to drink, showered her that one time. I put her to bed and woke her up. I reminded her to use the bathroom.

And through it all, she had no clue it was me.

"I'm a little worried about all this." Ren glances at me, his frown deep. "She painted for five days and you did nothing but watch her."

"That's not true. I went into the office."

"Once. You went in once. What's it gonna be like if she's doing this all the time, huh? You've got other responsibilities."

I force myself to relax my jaw. He's right, and getting pissed won't help anything. "It won't be like this again. We'll go slower."

He snorts, looking amused. "You really fucking think Frost is gonna ease up? Now that he knows the girl can make something like *that*—" He nods at the painting, covered by a cloth. "—that's his golden goose. His damn cash cow. He's gonna keep on pushing her until she breaks down. That's his goal from the start."

"I won't let him," I say but a voice whispers that Ren's right. Frost wants money, and he wants the girl dead. What better way to do it than to torture her with her own art? It's actually kind of beautiful, but terrible all the same.

"Don't forget what matters," Ren warns.

And as we approach the meeting spot, I wonder what he means by that. If the family should be my focus, or if it's Hellie that means the world.

Frost is waiting with three of his goons near a few empty tables next to the poker room. It's a comfortable sitting room meant for the high-rollers, but it's currently empty and semi-private. A squirrelly-looking man with a bald head and a tweed coat shifts from foot to foot, staring around him like a monster might jump from the shadows.

"Erick, how wonderful," Frost says, shaking my hand. "That's it?"

"That's it." I turn the painting towards them, still covered.

"This is my art guy, Dr. Pedro Scratch."

"You go to med school, huh, Doc?" Ren asks, giving him a vicious smile.

"Ah, no," Pedro says, wilting somewhat. "I have a PhD in Art History from Yale."

"Great, I'll keep that in mind the next time I get stabbed."

Frost waves Ren off. "Pedro here is going to tell me whether this scheme's going to work. Isn't that correct, Pedro?"

"Ah, I can take a look, but—"

"Good," I say and pull off the cloth. "Have at it."

Pedro's jaw drops. He stares at Hellie's masterpiece for a solid two minutes, saying nothing, not even moving. Frost is entranced too, along with the goons. Even Ren shifts around to get a better look, and I catch a few random passersby craning their necks to gawk.

Pride swells in me. Pride and fear. I knew the painting was good, but maybe it's too good, and what Ren said is about to happen. Frost will see dollar signs, and nothing else will matter.

"It's incredible," Pedro whispers, looking up at me with panic in his eyes. "Are you sure this is a forgery? This isn't some kind of test?"

"It's fake," I confirm. "I watched her do it."

"Remarkable."

"Will it pass?" Frost presses.

"Any expert in the world would be fooled. If I hadn't been told, I would've assumed you had the real thing." He hesitates, frowning as he squints. "If these paints are all historically accurate, and they certainly look like they are—well, I don't see how anyone could ever tell. Remarkable. Absolutely remarkable."

I cover the painting again and Pedro looks visibly shaken as he sits down.

"Looks like we have a deal going," Frost says, accepting the painting from me. He passes it off to a goon who carries it gingerly away followed by Pedro. I briefly wonder if the poor art doctor knows too much, but it isn't my problem. "I'll get in touch with my buyer."

"Does Gallo know what to do?"

Frost looks guilty as he shrugs. "I didn't plan on mentioning anything."

I glare at him for a beat before stepping closer. "Bring Gallo in."

"He's useless. And kind of annoying."

"I don't care. Bring him in. We're not stealing from one of our own."

Frost grunts, not looking happy. "Fine. Now, if this sale goes well, I'll want another."

"You'll get another on our timeline."

"Not good enough." Frost stares at me and I feel a prickle on my neck. "I need another."

"She'll get at least two months per painting," I say, not backing down. "I'm not going to work her to death."

"Two weeks at most. If we can keep her working, imagine how much we stand to make. If they're even half as good as that—"

"One month. No more negotiating. She'll have her own choice over what she paints, and she'll get a month to do it. We split the cost of whatever materials she requests. And once her debt is paid, the girl goes free."

Frost's nose wrinkles. "I don't like it."

"I don't give a fuck. She's mine, and I won't let you use her until there's nothing left."

"Fine." He turns his back on me, his shoulders tense. "But I expect something good. See you next month."

I watch him go. Ren steps up beside me. "Should I say it?"

"You told me so. And I told you." I look at him. "I'm going to protect her."

"Yeah, good luck. Frost has it in for the girl."

"I thought that was Gallo."

"Nah, that old fuck's got a hard-on for murder, but he's always like that. He says what he means and you don't have to worry about surprises."

I let out a slow breath. "But Frost is different."

"Exactly."

Frost will sneak up on us. He'll play the game, make me complacent, and one day he'll hit when I least expect it.

"Keep an eye on him," I tell Ren as I head back to the car. "We need to make sure he's playing fair."

Chapter 21

Hellie

Waking up feels like dragging myself from a grave.

My throat hurts. My mouth tastes like garbage. I groan, roll out of bed, and stagger into the bathroom where I splash water on my face and drink straight from the faucet.

I drag clothes over my head and stumble downstairs in search of something to eat. My stomach's completely empty.

"I almost forgot about you," Marina says when I shuffle into the kitchen.

I slump down at the table. "Great to see you too."

"You've been busy." She brings over coffee and cream. "Hungry?"

"Starving. I'd like one of everything."

"Everything?"

"In the kitchen."

She laughs and pats my shoulder. "A big breakfast then. Coming right up."

I drink coffee and watch her work. It's nice, having nothing to do but sit and stare and let the caffeine bring me back to life. I'm feeling more myself when she piles the table with pancakes, waffles, eggs, toast, bacon, and sausages. I help myself, chowing down like a maniac, stuffing it all into my mouth as fast as I can chew.

"Easy there," Marina says, refilling my coffee. "Erick would be very upset if you choked."

"She's right," he says, coming into the room. I look up, bacon dangling from between my lips. He makes a face. "It would be a shame if you died because you couldn't control yourself."

I chew and swallow like a good lady should. "I can control myself just fine, thank you." I sit up straight, using my utensils, shoving half a waffle down my throat.

He laughs, kisses Marina's cheek, gets coffee, and joins me. Erick's sweaty, straight from the gym, and focuses on the proteins.

"I met with Frost. He had an art evaluator with him."

I freeze. Nerves jangle in my chest. I'm absolutely confident in my work, but feeling that way is different from someone actually looking at it. "What did he say?"

"He asked if it was really a forgery. He seemed blown away."

I relax slightly. Warmth floods my body again. "Come on, seriously?"

"I'm not kidding. You should've seen the guy's face, it was like he was witnessing a miracle."

Marina comes over and puts more bacon on the plate. "You ask me, it was a miracle. A wonderful miracle."

"Thanks," I say, cheeks turning pink. I've never gotten so much praise for my own work before in my life.

"Frost wants another one."

Those words make me drop my fork. I feel a headache bloom. The thought of painting another in five days— "I can't," I say, trying not to lose it.

"You have a month."

I groan, leaning forward. "A month?"

"I argued for two, we settled on one. Is that enough time?"

I nearly weep from relief. "A month is fucking great."

"You won't have to kill yourself, at least."

"Compared to five days, it'll be leisurely."

"Good." He seems concerned as he tilts his head. "I don't want a repeat of last time. I don't want you to go back to that place."

"I have to go there for a little bit." I poke at my food, staring at the fork. "It's how I work, you know?"

"That's fine, but not for sixteen-hour stretches. You'll work normal days. Nine to five, lots of breaks. Eight hours of sleep. An hour of exercise."

"Are you making my schedule right now?"

"I was about to pencil in some fun time, but maybe not."

I laugh, half with relief, and half with joy at the idea of this man taking care of me again. "You're such a hard-ass."

"Only because you're a pain."

"Please, you'd be nowhere without my skills." I wiggle my fingers in the air. "I got all the talent."

"You do," he says more seriously than I expected. "Listen, today, why don't you work on something else."

"You got something in mind?"

"No, I don't, but you should come up with something."

"You mean, I should make my own art?" The idea hadn't even occurred to me since coming here.

"I'd like that if you wanted to."

"You want me to paint... just for myself?"

He nods and sips his coffee. "Yes, I'd love it."

"Oh." I lean back, considering. "Huh. Okay. Are you going to sell it?"

"No, it'll be yours to keep, or I can find a buyer and the money will be yours."

"You're serious?"

"Very serious. I want you to be happy, Hellie. I don't want you to forget why you make art."

I shake my head, mystified. This gangster, this monster, the guy that freaking kidnapped me—doesn't want me to get burned out on painting.

He wants me to create my own stuff purely for the pleasure of doing it.

What the hell?

But it almost makes sense. He's been taking care of me from the start, even if I've been too oblivious to notice. Maybe this is part of him making sure I'm satisfied.

A warm feeling wraps around my guts. There are very few people in my life that have truly encouraged my painting, and now he's one of them.

Which is confusing, because I'm supposed to hate him. He's the enemy. He's the reason I'm in this mess.

"Alright," I say after a while. "I'll paint. If I want to."

"Good. I hope you do." He stands, a piece of bacon between his teeth. "Have a good day, devil girl." Then he's gone, and I'm left with a pile of food and no appetite at all.

Chapter 22

Erick

I t's late by the time I'm able to get back to the desert house. I've been busy as hell catching up on all the work I've neglected—running a casino isn't fucking easy, there's always a fire smoldering somewhere—but my mind's been squarely back in that studio.

Back with Hellie.

I head straight upstairs as soon as I'm in the door, pausing only to loosen my tie and check myself in the mirror. Since when did I become so vain? Since when did I care what I looked like? But I want to look good for Hellie; I want her to see me as something more than a killer that stole her from her life. I'm excited as I reach her studio door and knock once before opening it.

She's sitting on a stool in front of a painting. Her legs are crossed and her brush is up in the air. Paint drips from the tip. I watch as she makes a stroke, a quick slashing line of color, blue from top to bottom. I'm transfixed as she turns to me, wearing an oversized sweater, her hair in a messy bun, a smile on her lips. She's glowing as the sun sets behind her, and I'm struck by how beautiful she is, and how precious, and how easily I could destroy her.

"You're home," she says, her voice sounding stronger than it did this morning.

"I'm home," I agree. "You look better."

"I feel a lot better." She lets out a long sigh. "I didn't even know I needed that."

"Needed what?"

"My own work. A little time to express myself. It's like therapy."

I walk into the room and linger over her shoulder. The canvas is medium-sized and shows a blue sky, fluffy clouds, a cartoonish sun in the corner. A man's hammering in a fence, a man with huge arms, an oversized snout-like face, curly black hair, simple jeans, and a shirt. I vaguely recognize him.

"That's Ren," I say with a laugh.

She beams at me. "You figured it out."

"My god, what did you do to him?"

"I made him into a dog person." Her smirk is wicked. "He's stuck in hell building fences for suburban housewives for all eternity."

I look closer, and Ren-dog's face is twisted in an expression of pure horror. "He'd love this."

"Good. I'll show him when it's finished." She yawns and stretches, but she holds up her hands when I give her a look. "I took breaks. I swear. I even showered."

I lean down, pretending to sniff her. "Not bad."

"Hey, get out of here." She tries to push me away, but I grab her wrists and pull her up.

"You've had enough painting time. I don't need you turning into a zombie again."

"Easy there," she says, laughing, as she pretends to struggle. "No, please, let me get back to the paint. I need the paint. It nourishes me. You don't understand!"

"Oh, god, she's lost her mind." I dip down and lift her up over my shoulder. She yelps in shock as I carry her back to her room, her fists pounding against my back the whole way.

"Put me down, you psycho," she says but she's laughing and kicking. "Oh my god, you can't just lift me up like I'm nothing."

"Can and did." I dump her on the bed, grinning huge, my heart racing. "There. I saved you from yourself."

"You do realize I have to make more paintings, right?"

"Yes, but we'll set you on a schedule and manage things. I'm going to take care of you, little devil girl."

She's lying there on the bed, staring up at me, chewing on her lip, and my pulse is going crazy. I stare back, and she looks so small, so vulnerable, and I wonder if I'm fucking this up. I'm putting her to work, forcing her to pay off this debt, and yeah, she's damn good at it, and I am trying to make this as pleasant as it can be, but she's still my prisoner. She's still working for me to right a wrong she didn't commit in the first place.

If I cared, I'd let her go. I'd find her a place where she can be safe, far away from Frost and Gallo. Somewhere she can work without being disturbed, without having to make forgeries, without having to worry.

Somewhere without me.

I move forward, coming toward her. Aware, in every inch of my body, that I'm a selfish piece of shit. Aware that I'm going to break her, and in the process, I'm going to break myself.

"What do you think you're doing?" she asks as I pin her down against the mattress. She's still smiling, but she's also licking her lips, and her eyes take on a sharp, needy desire. "I thought you were supposed to take care of me. Not take me whenever you wanted."

"Consider this my way of de-stressing you."

"Interesting. How self-serving."

"You can go ahead and try to get away if you want." I lean down so my lips are inches away from her delicious mouth. "But I don't think you can."

I give it my best shot. He laughs as I struggle, writhing, fighting, kicking at him, and it's like trying to punch a crocodile in the face underwater. Not happening. Worse, actively counter-productive.

It only makes him want me more.

And it only makes me want *him* more.

My core's a burning mess of want, a hot desire searing me like a brand. It's been days since I've been touched like this and I hadn't realized how badly I needed it—until this moment.

"Almost strong enough," he says, bringing a knee up between my legs. I gasp, arching my back. His bulks keeps me pinned. "But not quite."

"What are you going to do with me now?"

"I haven't decided. Depends on whether you want to be punished or not."

"Does anyone want to be punished?"

"Some people do." His lips brush my throat. "You do." He bites my chin softly. "You like being punished, I think."

"You think wrong."

Actually, he's completely right, but I'm staying in character.

"Tell me you want me to punish you, devil girl. Come on, my little Hellie, moan it and maybe I'll give you what you want." His knee presses tighter against my soaking pussy, and I gasp in excitement and pleasure.

"How about you go fuck yourself," I say, grinning huge, and he knows I'm only trying to egg him on.

It works. He grabs me, turns me over onto my belly, and pins my arms behind my back. I squirm, not really fighting anymore but putting on a good show, as he peels down my jeans with one hand, the other pushing my wrists into the small of my back.

"It doesn't have to be about pain," he says, his voice husky with want. "It can be about pleasure too. It can be about feeling good."

"How about you let me pin you down and see how you feel about it."

"Gladly. Go ahead and try. You can ride my cock to your heart's content."

"Okay, I see how that might not work."

He hums with pleasure once my ass is bare. I give my back a little arch, raising my hips into the air, and he groans.

"Look at you, you're soaking wet." His fingers tease me as he keeps my upper body pinned.

My head's pounding with lust. "Just a physical reaction to stress."

"You're dripping down my palm. Don't you dare try to tell me you don't want this."

"The body wants what it wants, but my brain's telling me to run screaming."

"That might be fun. Should I let you go and chase you down?"

"If I'm lucky, I'll die out in the freaking desert."

He laughs and his fingers keep teasing my pussy. I lift my hips higher, getting a little greedy—

And that's when his palm slaps down.

I yelp in shock, dropping my hips back down.

My ass stings where he spanked me and heat grows in my cheeks and between my legs.

"That's for talking about escape," he whispers and spanks me again. "That's for having an ass worth marking. I want to leave a handprint on your lovely skin so every time you look in the mirror, you think of me."

"That's not the good thing you're imagining."

"Please, little devil girl." Another spank and another. I'm whimpering now, panting for more. It hurts and it feels good, and I'm all sorts of fucked up but I don't really care. "You love this. You're radiating heat onto my hand. You're dripping on your sheets. You want me. Go ahead and admit it."

"I'd rather jump off a roof. I'd rather—" Another spank. Another. I don't get to finish my sentence, and I'm not sure what I was about to say since my brain's a buzzing mess of pleasure and pain, but I bet it was hilarious and biting.

"You'll stay right here, right where I'm holding you, and you'll let me spank your ass until I've had enough." Another spank, this one so hard I release a low moan of pain, but before I can try to twist away, his fingers plunge into my pussy, forcing my brain into overload.

The signals get crossed. Pleasure's pain, pain's pleasure, and there's him in the middle of it all, my Erick, my kidnapper, the man that saw something in me and pushed me to my limits.

I never knew I could paint like that. It never occurred to me to try. Nearly killing myself to create art has never really been my style—I've always wanted comfort too much for that.

Erick took me there. He took me and showed me what I could be.

Just like right now, as he spanks my ass again and fucks me with his fingers. He's showing me how badly I want him, how badly I need him to make me hurt so he can make me feel even better. I'm writhing, hips wiggling in the air, and I hear his belt unbuckle, hear him growl with pleasure. I look back over my shoulder and he's stroking himself, staring at my dripping pussy like he's having a vision of heaven.

"You don't know what you do to me," he murmurs, and I feel the tip of his cock press against my gaping, aching entrance.

"Show me," I say, meeting his gaze.

He slides himself inside. I whimper, groan, and he fills me to the brim. Right as he bottoms out, he spanks me again, hits me hard enough to make me scream, and that's when he fucks me. Takes me rough, fills me deep. Makes my back arch, grabs my hair, kissing me over my shoulder.

My brain fries and I come in a mess as he kneels behind me, filling my soaking cunt over and over again.

Sweat drips down my skin. Aftershocks of orgasm rock through my spine. He doesn't stop—he hasn't had his fill. He turns me over, gets between my legs, and licks my sensitive pussy. I gasp, wriggling away, but he holds me by the legs and laps me up and down before getting himself into position again.

"You feel so fucking good," he says, the thick tip of his long cock slowly parting me in half. "Easy now, Hellie, nice and easy." His hips move back and forth. I pant, moaning as he takes off my top and licks my nipples, sucking them hard. Pleasure blooms again, damn my sensitive breasts. He licks, fucking me faster, and holds my hands above my head.

"Is this what you were thinking about while I was working?" I ask, loving the way he's looking at me as he rocks back on his knees, his cock sliding in and out, his eyes roaming my body.

"Yes," he says, voice husky.

"You wanted to fuck me? For five days, you watched me work, and that whole time this is what you wanted?"

"Yes," he says, moaning now. "I wanted to fuck you right there in your studio. Fill you up in front of your easel. Fuck you on top of that expensive fucking painting, ruin the whole thing, just to get you off."

"You're a bad man."

"I am a very bad man." He kisses me, his tongue in my mouth, then fucks me faster. "I am a very, very bad man, my devil girl, and you feel like the only good pieces of me all put together."

I arch my back and I'm grinding into him now, moving to a rhythm only we can hear. I pull him down to kiss me again as bliss blooms between my legs and we're going faster, pushing harder. I moan into his mouth, into his lips, and he bites my shoulder, bites my nipples, grabs my hips as he takes me deeper and deeper.

And I come first. I come again, back arching, mind going black like that flow state but better, more intense, like five days of hard work all boiled into ten seconds. He doesn't stop, keeps going, and I feel him fill me deep, coming between my legs.

He groans as he pulls me against his chest, his cock still buried between my legs. I wiggle, smiling to myself. I want to feel him there for as long as I can.

"Tell me again why I haven't been doing that every night?" he asks.

"Well, for starters, I've been forging an extremely expensive painting and have been basically unaware of my surroundings for the last five days."

"That's a fair point. Fucking you when you're like that wouldn't have been fun."

"No, I bet it wouldn't have." I push closer to him, wanting his heat, his warmth.

Wanting to feel this damn safety.

"I don't want to make you do it again," he whispers, which is the worst thing he can say, because he's going to.

We both know it.

"Even if that's true, don't say it again unless you plan on letting me go."

He grunts in reply. "Alright. I won't say it again."

"You can't just act like there's nothing weird here. Like you're not holding me against my will."

"I like to think I'm protecting you against your incorrect assumptions."

"I doubt it."

"What can I do to convince you, Hellie?"

"I don't know," I admit and realize it's true.

I keep doing this, tumbling down into this pit with him, only to find myself staring back out at the light, wishing I were somewhere else.

Somewhere free.

Except I'm here, which means I'm out of the reach of Gallo and Frost.

He really is protecting me—but I can't help thinking it's all for his own selfish reasons.

"I'm going to stay here a while," he says, breathing the smell of my hair. "If that's okay with you."

"That's okay," I answer, because it's exactly what I want.

Chapter 23

Hellie

I wake up and squint against the sunlight. My bed's cold, and it takes me a minute to realize Erick's gone. The covers next to me are messy and the pillow's got a big indent, which means he slept here, at least for a while.

With nothing else to do, I stay in bed for a while, staring at the ceiling, trying to figure out what the hell I'm doing.

Sleeping with Erick—both sex-wise and just the normal, regular old sleep thing—is a really bad idea.

It's bizarre and dangerous, and if I were remotely smart, I'd run away screaming.

Except the thought of stopping, of giving up one of the few things that have ever reliably made me feel good, is too painful to consider.

I haven't had many boyfriends over the years. Guys have come and gone, but none ever stuck around, and none ever made me feel the way I do about Erick. This love and hate, this pleasure and pain, he's all of it and he's so much more. He's adrenaline and fear, he's a hand spanking my ass and lips kissing my mouth. Silk and iron.

The man kidnapped me. There's no getting around that. He picked me up off the street, injected me with a drug, and dragged me out to the middle of the desert.

I haven't forgotten about that.

Only things are different. We're different—there's a bond between us, and it isn't only sex.

It's the way he takes care of me.

I get out of bed, wash up, dress in comfies and head to the studio. I pad quietly down the hall and check to make sure he's not around before I shut the door as softly as I can. The painting I showed him is still on the easel where I left it, but I bypass that and head to the racks of painting equipment.

It's down there, behind the big cans of paint. I fish it out from where I hid it—just a small canvas, two feet by two feet.

The colors are dark. Moody. Blues, grays, dark purples, blacks. It shows a man, shirtless, in dress slacks, standing near a window. The room is covered in shadow. The desert beyond is bright, a contrast to him.

But the figure is everything.

It's Erick, the version that lives in my mind. Beautiful and terrifying. Standing between me and freedom. Not quite here, his back turned to me, something held in reserve, but still fascinating.

I stare at that painting for a while, trying to decide if I want this man, or if I want what he can give me.

This studio, this space, all the money and privilege. Marina and her food, the ease of a life wanting for nothing.

I could stay here. What's there waiting for me out in the real world? That paint and sip job? A few friends? No father, no grandmother, no family at all, just an empty void where my life should be.

That's the worst part of this captivity.

I want to stay.

I shove the painting onto the easel. I crack open more paint and start to slash at what I did yesterday, covering it with reds and blues and violets, until it's an abstract mess, like a Jackson Pollock on methamphetamine. I stand back, breathing hard, hating Erick and wanting him all at once. Hating the painting, but amazed that something so beautiful could come out of me.

I hide it again before it can dry.

If he finds it and realizes what it means, he might use it against me.

And I can't let that happen.

Chapter 24

Hellie

We have dinner together that night. Marina makes chicken piccata and it's absolutely incredible. Erick opens a very nice bottle of wine. "Here's to the artist," he says, raising his glass.

I drink long, and a pleasant bloom fills my belly. "Here's to the man keeping me in life."

He laughs at that as if it's a joke.

After we're finished and Marina's doing the dishes, I follow him up to the studio.

"I hate to say it, but we'd better pick out the next painting."

"What happened to never making me do another?"

His expression darkens. "Not an option. You had a couple days off, but you only have a month for this one."

"Right." I take a deep breath and blow it. "A month should be okay, right?"

"You tell me."

"I think it's fine. Two would be better. But one is fine." I linger near the windows. It's dark in the desert. I can't see any lights—which means civilization is a long way off. My prison is all open space.

"I'm thinking since you started with the Vermeer, you could do this one next." He pulls the art reference book down and flips through it. "Sticking to my idea about the Gardner museum, this one was stolen in that heist, and it's similar to the painting you just did."

I shiver slightly and look over his shoulder. He lands on a portrait of two people—a man wearing black with a white ruffle at his neck, standing to the left, and a woman seated on the right, also with a white ruffle, wearing a dark-colored dress.

"Simple," I say, tilting my head side to side. "This one's by Rembrandt, right? You do realize it's pretty intimidating trying to forge these old masters. Vermeer nearly killed me. I think Rembrandt might finish me off."

"It's no different. You can handle this, and besides, you have more time."

"You don't think it's suspect, doing another painting like this? I mean, a Vermeer resurfaces, and now suddenly a Rembrandt too?"

"Maybe, maybe not. These were stolen in the same heist, so it would make sense if they were sold around the same time."

I tap my lower lip, staring at the composition, my mind already reaching down to that flow state, grasping at it like a plant craning for sunlight. "There's not a whole lot going on." I squint, trying to look into the dark shadows behind the seated woman. "Tough to see the details. It looks unfinished."

"Could be. You're the expert." He gazes at me. "What do you think?"

I pace away, pretending to consider, but there's no real choice. I could push him to let me do a different work, but that won't matter—no matter what, he'll make me forge one of the great masters, which means I'll have to push myself to the limits. Anything else wouldn't be worth the effort.

I stop and face him.

"I think this sucks."

"Fair," he says, not smiling, giving me that neutral stare.

"But I can do it."

"I knew you could."

"You have so much faith in me, but I don't really know why."

"You proved yourself already. Twice, actually."

"What if I got lucky?" I tug at my hair, straightening it. "What if this one isn't as good?"

"You'll make it good. You'll make it better now that you have more practice."

I glare at him and turn away. "What happens if someone figures out that these are fake? It gets traced back to me, doesn't it?"

"No," he says. "It gets traced back to me and Frost. Well, back to me, since I'm sure Frost will throw me under the bus the first chance he gets."

"And what will you do?"

He shakes his head. "Nothing."

"Sorry, you do realize this is fraud? I'm pretty sure forgery is a crime."

"Yes, you're true, but nobody will prosecute me. My family has too much power, and besides, nobody will care that I fleeced a bunch of rich assholes."

"That seems like a big assumption."

"If you're worried that I'll give you up, I promise you, I won't."

I suck in a breath through my nose and blow it out. I stare into the darkness, out at the desert, and imagine I can see the outcroppings, the mesas and the striated patterns in their rock faces.

"You remember when we started this and I refused because I didn't want to be like my father?"

He grunts in reply. "I recall something like that."

"Dad was always trying to get me in on his schemes." I close my eyes and smile at another one of his lessons. *Make them trust you.* "He taught me a lot, you know."

"I'm sure he did."

"But I saw what it made him. Bitter, angry, so smart and talented but always using his talents in the worst ways. He wasted himself because he couldn't fit in anywhere, and I've always felt that in myself."

"Is that why you turned to art?" he asks, and I'm surprised by the question. It's smart, already a step ahead of me, and I feel like he's seeing something he shouldn't.

"Maybe," I admit. "It was a way to express myself at first. Sort of therapy too. Dad's always been a mess, and when I was young, it really bothered me, so Grandma would buy me paints and paper and encourage me to make stuff. I'd spend hours drawing, painting, whatever, just to forget that my dad was locked up, or my dad was wanted by some nasty people, or my dad had gambled all his money in the casinos again. I hated him so much, and I loved him just as much, and I promised myself I wouldn't become like him."

"Now here you are." His voice is close. He's standing only a few inches behind me.

I stare at his reflection in the window superimposed above the vague outline of the landscape.

"Now here I am, forging art, something I bet he'd love."

"You're not your father."

"No, but I've crossed the line I swore I'd never cross."

"I pushed you over it."

"What's the difference? Here I am, on the other side."

"I'm not going to lie to you, Hellie. I don't know how long this is going to last."

I turn and face him. "Now you don't want to lie to me?"

"I never have."

"I feel like it was a kind of lie when you injected me with propofol."

He waves that off. "I never lied, only had to use creative means to convince you to come out here."

"Yeah, real creative, drugging me." I let out a long sigh. "I'm not even angry, and I should be. Just drained at the prospect of doing this again."

"Look at it this way. If you weren't here, you'd be back there, in the real world, doing your real-world bullshit. Would that be better? You'd have to scramble to make rent, to pay bills, to feed yourself, and barely have time or energy for your own art. At least here, you can work five hours on the forgery, and another few hours on your own stuff."

My eyebrows raise. "You'd allow that?"

"Hellie, I would love it if you worked on both." He reaches out and touches me. I don't flinch away, which scares me in a way I can't explain. His fingers brush my cheek. "Make art. Do this job. Eventually, you'll pay off your debt, and I'll convince Frost and Gallo to leave you alone."

"Will they?"

"I'll be very persuasive."

"What about you? Will you leave me alone?"

He stares and doesn't answer. I look back, afraid of what he might say. But the prospect of money lingers behind all this, in the promise he made to give me a fat payout when this is over, a percentage of the sales. I know my life is going to change—it already changed—and the old world is left behind.

"I'm not sure I can ever leave you alone." He wraps a hand around my throat. Gently though. He leans in, lips brushing mine. "Now that I've tasted you. Now that I've had you in my life, in my arms. I've washed you, fed you. Kept you alive. Fucked you until you screamed. I don't know if I can just let you go and never speak to you again."

"I bet you could if you tried real hard."

"Is that what you'd want?"

"Right now, I just want to go home."

"Pretend this is your home. It's better here, isn't it?"

I hate him for saying everything I've been thinking. He's right, but he's also wrong.

"If you're going to kiss me, then do it," I say, chin raising.

His hand remains on my throat. His mouth stays close.

"I want you to admit you like it here."

"And I want you to throw yourself off a cliff. We can't all win."

"You like it when I kiss you. You like it when I make you come."

"Yes, okay, fine. Should I pretend like I don't?"

"Yes." His smile is wicked. "At least fight me a little."

"Go to hell." I smile back sweetly.

He kisses me. I kiss him back, breathing in through my nose as his tongue invades my lips and his grip on my throat tightens. He holds me there against the window, the cold glass against my back, kissing me, tasting me, and I breathe him in, feeling his muscular body, the power in his fingers. This man, this beast, he could destroy me, but instead he's done nothing but keep me going.

The kiss breaks apart. He leans his forehead against mine.

"I won't force you to stay here forever, Hellie, but while you're under my roof, you will do the best work you possibly can."

"I'll try."

"No, don't try, just do it. Create like you've never created before. The forgeries and your own work. While you're here, take advantage."

I laugh and he steps away. He's entirely serious, which is so bizarre. "Why do you even care?"

"Because you may never get another shot at doing something great, and I think you have it in you. So fucking try."

He turns and walks to the door. I stare at him, head ringing. I look toward the painting hidden behind the cans and wonder if maybe he's right and I've already started.

But he doesn't leave. He pauses, shoulders tense.

He speaks one last time. "Tonight, come to my room when you're finished."

I stand stiffly, eyes wide with surprise. "Your room?"

"Yes. My room. You know where it is."

"I know, it's just, we've never, you know, gone in there."

"I want you to sleep in my bed tonight. I won't force you, but I will be waiting up. Don't make me wait too long." Then he leaves without another word.

Chapter 25

Hellie

Another morning, another empty bed. This time though, everything's different.

Erick's room is simple, even compared to my own. Bare walls painted gray. A desk with a tower computer, the multiple monitors all turned off. An ensuite bathroom, a walk-in closet, a dresser. The furniture is wooden and smooth, almost like he made it himself.

I'm sore in a good way. After working on another painting of him, this time an image of him standing in the desert, crawling from a ravine, I found him shirtless and reading a book. He didn't take long to put it aside, drag me into bed with him, and spend the rest of the evening taking what he wants from my skin and giving even more in return.

Yes, I'm sore, and I'm pretty sure I have a big old handprint bruise on my ass, just like he wanted.

I get up, dress, use his bathroom, and I'm about to leave when I pause.

I've been in this house for a while now. A couple weeks, if I'm thinking right, and I haven't had any contact with the outside world. My boss is probably worried, and I'm sure Nicky's wondering where the heck I'm at.

Erick never expressly forbade contact with the outside world, only I haven't had the chance—until now.

I walk to his computer, turn on the monitors, and find the computer is already logged in and tuned to webpages showing stock prices. Complicated charts with lines that make no sense bloom like strange clouds. I click out of them, pull up Chrome, and navigate to my email.

Nervous energy jangles into my knees. I keep looking over my shoulder, waiting for Erick to walk in and catch me. Instead, it's silent, and I stare at all the messages cluttering my inbox.

It's mostly spam. Gone for two weeks, and the only people that really care are the ones trying to get me to buy something. But buried in there are a few panicked messages from Nicky, wondering where the hell I am, telling me to call her when I get a chance.

I pull up a reply window and my hands hover over the keyboard.

What do I tell her?

I could give her the truth. Beg for help. Get the FBI and the freaking CIA scouring the desert. Erick Costa's kind of famous in the Vegas scene, which means someone's got to know where this place is. If I tell Nicky, she could get the process started, and I might actually save myself.

But what happens next?

Gallo still wants me dead. Frost probably wants me chained up in a basement somewhere churning out paintings. The second I'm released home, they'll find me, and my life will be much, much worse.

It's scary, how Erick really is protecting me, even though he's the one that drugged me and dragged me here.

Nicky, hey!!!! Listen, I am SO SORRY that I haven't gotten in touch until right now. I swear I'm okay!! I got this last-minute opportunity to go to this crazy intense art retreat up in Maine. No phones, no computers, I have to write this from an actual internet cafe like it's 1998. I'm fine! If I don't write again it's because I'm sitting in this gorgeous little cabin surrounded by nature doing yoga half the day and painting the other half. Please don't worry! I'm all good!

I hate that email. I hate it so much. It's all lies, and I don't want to lie to Nicky, but I've already crossed the line. Here I am, on the other side. My father's daughter, building her con.

I hit send and feel like I might be sick.

This is my chance to escape, but I'm not taking it.

I scroll more, ready to close this window and forget this portal to the outside world exists, when I see one more message.

It arrived five days ago and it's nearly buried under the advertisements.

I stare at the sender's name.

Danny Accardi.

My flesh and blood.

Good old Dad.

I click open like I'm throwing myself into a haunted house and read through his message three times before it starts to make sense.

Hi, Hellie, I know you're pissed. I know you're mad I did what I did and disappeared, but honey, things aren't what they seem. Are they ever with dear old dad? Honey, please, don't reply to this email, but we've got to talk, and it has to be in person. Meet me off the Strip in the Coconut Gorge casino. Go all the way back to the pai gow tables. I'll be at one of those. Meet me seven days from this message at 6pm. You got it, kiddo? I love you, Hellie. I'm sorry too. See you soon, I hope. Dad.

I blink away the tears. Fuck Dad. Fuck him. And fuck him for sending that damn email. That came in five days ago, which means he wants to meet in two days—which isn't going to happen. There's no way Erick will ever let me, and I can't tell him about this anyway, because then he'll catch Dad and do terrible things, and I just can't.

Even though I'm so pissed at my old man, I won't let them torture him.

Which means I'm screwed.

I can either try to run away and make that meeting.

Or I let it go and I'll never find out what the hell Dad's talking about.

I delete the email without replying. Tears stream down my face. Angry tears, frustrated tears. How am I going to get to Coconut Gorge in two days without anyone finding out?

Because if I'm followed—Dad's dead.

I log out, clear the history, pull his windows up, and make it look like nobody ever sat at the computer.

Then I go to the studio because there's nothing to do right now but think and paint.

Chapter 26

Erick

I walk the floor of my casino with Ren by my side. I try to do this at least once or twice a week—but lately, I've been distracted by the gorgeous painter girl I have working her ass off back in my house.

She's everywhere for me, from the moment I wake to the moment I fall asleep and everything between.

"Quiet day," Ren remarks as a group of young men wearing business suits all cheer around a craps table. "Wonder how much damage they're doing?"

"We'll get them in the end." I pause near one of the bars and signal for a drink. "Want something?"

"I'm fine." Ren gazes into the crowd, always looking for threats. Take the man from the streets, but the streets don't ever leave the man. That's why he's my number two —paranoid to the end, and I love him for it. "I meant to tell you this earlier, but you seemed like you were worried about other things. I figure now's a good opportunity."

"You're keeping things from me now?" My whiskey arrives and I take a long sip. Drinking on the job's almost required for me. I'm the damn boss, and people want to see me acting like it.

"Not if I don't have to, but you've been busy with other projects." He glances over. "You've been coming in less and less. Spending more time out there." He nods in the general direction of the desert. "I've been picking up your slack around these parts."

I bristle at his tone, but I keep it cool, because he's right. Ren's been stepping up and I appreciate him for it.

"I've been making sure this plan comes together."

"You've been lusting after your houseguest."

"Easy," I say, eyes narrowing.

"That's what I mean." He jabs a finger at me. "A comment like that never would've bothered you before."

"Hellie's different. Things are different."

"Yeah? Why? Tell me what it is about this girl, and maybe I'll understand why she's worth putting yourself through all this shit."

I open my mouth to tell him off but stop. Ren's always had my back, and if he's doing this now, it's because he cares.

Why is Hellie different?

It's a reasonable question from his perspective. I've been with plenty of women over the years, but I've never cared about one the way I care about Hellie.

Why is she worth it?

"She's got something," I say, straining to find words. I take another drink. I've never been good at expressing myself. I'm the quiet one in the family. Maybe that's why I like her—Hellie oozes emotion, while I keep them locked down tight. "It's her focus."

"She can paint. I'll give her that. But why her?"

"She's beautiful. She's clever. She likes to fight, which I appreciate. But it's more than that. It's the way she can get sucked into her own little world and make something better in ours. You know how many people can actually add instead of subtract? Everyone's a taker. Everyone wants to get what they're owed. There are so few people who give anything, and Hellie gives. In her art, she gives it all."

Ren grunts. "Alright. You're selling it."

"I don't need to convince you of shit, okay? I'm telling you what I'm thinking, that's all."

"Fine. I understand you." He crosses his arms, but some of his combative attitude fades. "I heard from Frost's people a couple hours ago. The sale's done."

My eyebrows raise. "And you didn't tell me right away?"

"Like I said, you've been doing other shit. You didn't get in until an hour ago, and you wanted to go for your little walk right away."

He's got a point, but fuck, he's also doing this on purpose. "What did they say?"

"Everything went the way it should. No surprises, no problems."

"The money?"

"Accounted for, allegedly. They say our split is coming shortly."

"I don't like that 'shortly' bullshit."

"We'll get it, don't worry." He stands up straight, dropping his arms, one hand going to his hip, right where he keeps a pistol tucked under his shirt. It's like one second, he's relaxed, at ease, and the next he's a pitbull on alarm.

I follow his gaze. Across the casino, four men walk toward us, three of them big goons in black suits and sunglasses, all of them packing heat under those oversized jackets.

The man in the lead is Gallo.

"Great," I say, throwing back my drink. As he gets closer, I move forward to greet him, which I can tell annoys Ren. He wants me to stay back, but that's not the kind of leader I am. "Alberto. Nice of you to come say hello."

"You motherfucker," Gallo snarls at me, his wrinkled face bright pink. "You piece of fucking shit, how *dare* you cut me out—"

187

"Not here." I stare him down. "Not on my fucking floor."

Gallo seethes, but he's a casino owner too and he understands better than anyone in the world. After a beat, he nods once, and I gesture for him to follow. He falls in beside me, and we're followed by Ren, who cuts us off from the three big thugs, none of whom look happy about the arrangement. Nearby, I spot more of my men shadowing us, making sure things don't get out of hand.

I talk as we take the elevator to my floor. "I understand you're upset. I told Frost this was a bad idea."

"She stole from all three of us." Gallo glares at me. "What's keeping me from getting my pound of flesh now? You realize Frost wants to go to war, right?"

"You're getting a cut. There won't be violence."

"Not according to my sources."

"Your sources haven't spoken to me yet. I'll straighten this out."

We step into my office, but Gallo grabs my arm. He stands too close, and I can smell his aftershave.

"I barely trust you, Costa, but at least you're from a good family, an Italian family. You've got a foolish American name, but I can forgive that, we're American now. Frost though? He's slime. He's an investor, a jumped-up banker playing at being a casino owner. There's no honor in that man."

I stare at Gallo until he releases me. I'm aware of the irony in this old gangster calling Frost *slime*, but a part of me agrees. Gallo may be violent and bombastic, but he's got a code and he follows it, whereas Frost does whatever the fuck Frost wants for whatever reason he chooses. There's order in Gallo's world. There's only money and the bottom line in Frost.

Gallo understands relationships and taking care of his people.

Frost understands balance sheets.

"We're going to make this right," I say, walking to my desk. Gallo remains standing near the door. Outside, his men lurk glaring at Ren, who ignores them.

"You'd better. If you don't, I'm going to find that girl, and I'm going to do what I've wanted to do from the beginning."

"Don't threaten her." I give him a long look. "She is under my protection. Going after her is going after me, and you know my threats are not empty."

He laughs, a raspy and ugly thing. "What the fuck is with you and this girl, Costa? You've been protecting her from the start."

"She's useful."

"There are plenty of useful people in Vegas. This girl's more than useful to you, and I'm starting to think you're fucking her. That's it, isn't it? She's got a great body and you want to keep her around, huh?"

"Watch your mouth."

"Alright, I can see you're getting upset. I respect you enough to back off. But listen to me, Costa, I will not be treated like this again. Make sure Frost understands, and if that motherfucker can't get it together, I'll make him pay too."

"This isn't the old Vegas anymore. You can't walk around threatening to murder people."

"I said my piece. Don't forget it." The old man turns and leaves. I watch him and his people storm off, wondering what sort of nightmare I've found myself in.

Ren sits down in a chair across from my desk and crosses his legs. "That went well."

"Get Frost on the phone. Contact his people or whatever you do. Make him understand that Gallo is a part of this deal whether he likes it or not. Gallo needs a cut."

"I suspect that won't go well."

"I don't care. It's happening."

Ren doesn't move. He keeps studying his fingers. "Is she worth this? You realize Gallo's going to make a move sooner or later, right? Either against you or against Frost. Once that happens, a real war's going to break out. Is she worth that?"

I stare at him, heart hammering in my throat.

"Yes," I say.

"Good." He gets up, wiping his nails on his pants. "I hope so."

Chapter 27

Erick

The day is a mess. Gallo's people are pissed, Frost's people are a pain in the ass, and in the end, I have to threaten to withhold future paintings to get the whole matter resolved. I'm in the middle playing peacemaker, when I'd rather start shooting to make this all go away.

"I never wanted the fucking prick to cut Gallo out in the first place," I say to Hellie that night. We're in the studio, and I watch as she does some work on the forgery, mostly testing paints and getting a feel for the overall shape. "I told him not to do it, and he goes ahead and does it anyway, which makes me look complicit."

"That sucks."

"Now I'm soothing egos and trying to get this mess sorted. Meanwhile, we're running a multi-million-dollar art scheme and any little thing could fuck it up. Gallo could run his mouth and ruin this if he wanted, and I'm not totally convinced he won't just to piss off Frost."

"Oh, yeah."

"Here I am, complaining about it to you instead of doing what I really want to be doing, which is breaking knees and slamming skulls into walls until people do what I say. I miss the old days sometimes. When I first started, I didn't have to worry about playing politics. I only worried about who had more guns."

"Rough."

"You're not listening, are you?"

"Huh."

"Hellie." I stand and walk to her. "You're not listening to me."

She frowns as if she's only just realizing I'm there. "I heard you. Gallo got cut out. Frost is an asshole."

I grunt, head tilted. She's been strange since I got home earlier tonight, and I can't figure out why. Short answers, no interest, like she's trying to keep herself distanced, or like she's got something else on her mind.

I chalked it up to work on the painting, but that's not it. She's barely doing anything, and I can tell her head's not in it.

"What's going on?"

"Nothing. Just working. You're distracting me, you know."

"You're done for the day." I take the paintbrush from her hand and toss it on the floor. It leaves a brown smear as it clatters away.

She looks outraged. "That was the perfect color, asshole!"

"You'll be fine. Tell me what your deal is."

"I have no deal." She gets up from her stool and storms away, grabbing the brush from the floor and putting it back in the can. "Maybe I'm just sick of chatting with my kidnapper about his day. Maybe I don't want to hear about your feelings."

"No, I don't think that's it."

"Did you stop to think that maybe I still hate you? And maybe I'm sick of pretending?"

"Nope, definitely not it."

"You're such an asshole. How can someone be so arrogant?"

"Because we've been through this already and nothing's changed." I walk to her, forcing her to back up to the window. It's a familiar position. One I very much enjoy. "Let's skip the game and go right to the part where you tell me what's wrong."

"Nothing's wrong." She lifts her chin defiantly.

She's lying. I don't know why, but she's holding something back. Something is definitely wrong—and I can't tell if it really is the kidnapping thing, which is frustrating since I thought we were past that by now. If that's not it, I have no idea why she'd be in this shitty mood.

"Is the painting too difficult?" I ask softly. "We can find something else. The Gardner stuff—"

That pisses her off. "The painting is fine. I can handle the stupid painting."

"Are you sure?"

"Don't start questioning me now." She shoves at me. I knock her hands away and grab her before she can run.

Her mouth opens in a gasp as I pin her to the wall.

"Tell me what's wrong."

"Nothing's wrong. You're pulling my hair."

"You're right, I am pulling it. I'm also going to spank your ass pink and raw unless you start talking. What's the matter?"

"I'm tired, okay? I spent half the day working on my own stuff and half of it working on this forgery, and I'm exhausted. You think I'm some kind of robot, but I'm not."

I stare at her. My heart's racing. Her throat bobs as she swallows, and I'm positive she's lying, but pressing isn't going to do anything but make her retreat further into more stories.

I decide to change tactics.

"You're right, you aren't a robot." I run a thumb down her lips. "You need to destress. You need a release. You need to be treated like a woman with a body."

"Erick," she says, warning. "I'm not in the mood."

"Liar." I pull her hair tighter. "I'll spank you until you're begging me to fuck you."

"Can't we just leave it at I'm not in the mood? Do you really have to keep prying?"

"You're worth the effort." I kiss her neck. She lets out a whimper. Yes, she wants this as much as I do, but there's still something bothering her. "You can tell me. You know that, don't you? You're safe here."

She closes her eyes, breathing fast. "You drugged me. You stole me. I'm just supposed to forget?"

"No. Don't forget. Think about why I did it and how I've been treating you. You know what would've happened if I hadn't been the one to grab you first. Frost and Gallo would've come for you no matter what, and your life would be much worse if they'd gotten you first."

"I know. I know. I just—"

I kiss her chin, her throat. "You just what?"

"It's a lot. What we're doing. It's really a lot."

"I understand."

"Do you?"

"Better than anyone else."

"I'm afraid that might not be true. I'm afraid—" She doesn't keep going. I tighten my grip in her hair, pulling her chin up.

"Tell me what you're thinking."

Her eyes meet mine. There's an intensity in her expression, a shadow of her incredible focus. I could sink into that gaze, dive deep into the depths of her and never resurface again.

I want to do it too.

If anyone could make me lose myself, it's Hellie.

"This thing between us. It scares me." Her voice is small. But the way she looks at me drives a spike of need into my core.

My heart hammers. My throat swells. It's the first time either of us has admitted that there's something more going on here—something more than fucking, more than pleasure.

A connection.

Forged in this fucked situation.

But pure in a way that never could've happened otherwise.

"It doesn't scare me."

"No?" She almost laughs. "It should. We're enemies, right? I should hate you? And my dad stole from you, so you should hate me."

"I don't. And you don't hate me, either."

"No. I don't. Which is why this is so wrong."

"Why does it have to be? You and I mesh, Hellie. Tell me why you're so scared."

"Because I have feelings for you, okay?" She blurts the words out like she's forcing them past her lips, and as soon as they're in the air, her eyes go wide with surprise, shocked at her own admission.

I stare at her, heart racing. Heat between us like burning silk. I release a soft groan as my chest swells with something—pride, joy, I can't even tell, it doesn't matter.

All I know is I want her, and she wants me too.

I kiss her. Fuck talking. Fuck explaining. I kiss her deep, slow, tasting her, drinking her in, and she returns that kiss, because she wants me. She feels something for me the same way I feel something for her. I hold her tight, hands on her hips now, and I can't stop myself as I undress her, shoving her back onto her work table, my hand slipping between her thighs.

She's so fucking wet. She's panting my name as we fuck slowly, staring into each other's eyes. She rides me, her lithe, gorgeous body graceful and perfect. Sweat drips down her skin, and I lick it up. I suck her nipples, tease her pussy. She makes these heavenly noises as she sucks my cock, going deep, her spit rolling down my shaft.

I admire her, that beauty, that poise. I fuck her deep, spank her until she screams, until she comes in a frenzy, and it still isn't enough.

She has feelings for me.

I go down on her, lick her until she's grinding her mound into my mouth. I fuck her again, foreheads pressed together, needing more, dripping with need. "Hellie," I whisper as she comes a second time. "My beautiful Hellie." And I come inside of her, deep inside of her in a flare, in an obsessive release of pure bliss.

I have to carry her back to my room. She's nearly catatonic. "Hellie, Hellie," I whisper, kissing her once she's under the covers. I hold her in my arms. "Hellie, there you are."

"I shouldn't have said anything." But she's grinning. "Now you have the wrong idea."

"And what idea is that?"

"You think we're going to do this." She touches my chest. Then touches her own.

"No, darling girl. I think we're already doing it."

"You're wrong though. I'm your captive, remember? We can't have a relationship while you own me."

"Do you want me to free you?"

"We both know you can't. We're way beyond that."

"You're right."

"Then don't offer something you don't want to give."

"I won't again."

"Good." She closes her eyes. "You want to hear something sick?"

"Yes. I do."

"I like it here."

"That's not so bad."

"But it's actually worse than bad. It's psychotic."

I stroke my thumb across her cheek. "I like that you're here."

"Yeah, because you get to fuck me, and you seem to enjoy that."

"Yes, I do, very much so."

"It's not just the sex, although I enjoy that too." She grins at me, almost shy, but it fades. "Everything makes me want to stay. The studio, the food. I know I'm a prisoner, but I also feel free. I do nothing but think about painting all day long for the first time in my life, something I've always wanted to do. Even back in art school, there was always something else, some distraction. Here, it's just... painting. And it's amazing."

"But you're still my prisoner."

"Yep. Still your prisoner."

"How do we fix that?"

"I don't know."

We lapse into silence. I understand her hesitation, but it's not like I can let her go—and she doesn't want me to. Even if I did, Frost or Gallo would scoop her up. If I said she was free, it wouldn't mean anything, because her freedom is effectively gone. This house is the only safe place in the world for her right now.

Her breathing gets measured. She snuggles closer. "You're falling asleep," I say.

"Should I go back to my room?"

"No. Stay. But you might want to eat."

"I'm fine. I'll eat, I don't know, at some point. Just hold me and let me sleep, okay?"

A stronger man would drag her from bed and feed her.

Instead, I kiss her and let her drift.

Chapter 28

Hellie

Yep, there is something massively wrong with me.

I mean, who the hell in their right mind admits to their freaking captor that they have feelings for them?

The guy is my warden. He's my freaking kidnapper.

And I have feelings for him.

I didn't say that to distract him from the real reason why I was being distant—although that was a bonus.

I told him because it's true.

He feels the same. Maybe he didn't say the words but I felt it when he kissed me. I can feel it, every day, when he stands and watches me paint with that intense admiration, that pure joy in his eyes, like he can't believe his luck. An artist, working just for him.

No, not just an artist—me, Hellie Accardi.

Erick's up and gone early the next morning. I spend more time in his bed, lounging around, feeling sorry for myself.

Dad's email said to meet him in one day. I have one day to figure out what I'm going to do.

I could tell Erick. Some part of me wants to. But Dad stole a lot of money, and while I think Erick has feelings for me, I don't think they're strong enough to keep him from murdering my old man.

Which means that would be sentencing my father to death.

I have to keep my mouth shut. I hate it, but it's my situation. Erick might be into me, and we might have something real, but that doesn't mean he could pass up the chance to catch my father.

Would that be so bad?

Dad did feed me to the wolves. He robbed those casino barons and ran off, knowing full well they'd come after his family—which means me, since there's nobody else.

Dear old Dad deserves to be shot in the head for that.

After everything, I still love him. I can't help it. He's all I've ever had, aside from Grandmom. Despite everything, I don't want my father to get murdered, even if he kind of deserves it.

I get out of bed, shower, get dressed. I have other options. I could skip the meeting entirely, chalk it up to bad luck and bad timing, but there's something about the message that's bothering me.

The email is a huge, huge risk.

The fact that he sent it at all means this meeting is important.

Dad needs to tell me something—and he's risking his life to do it.

Even coming to an off-Strip casino is a massive gamble. Dad's good at getting around unnoticed, but still. He could've disappeared overseas somewhere, ran off to Indonesia, Singapore, freaking Siberia. Instead, he's coming to Vegas, or he's still in Vegas, and he wants to talk.

I need to go if it's even remotely possible.

Which leaves me with one final option.

Escape.

The problem is, I don't *want* to escape. All the reasons I'm enjoying myself here still remain. The comfort, the time, the focus on my art. Hell, even Erick.

If I tried to get away, he'd be heartbroken.

I still don't see another option.

I head downstairs for breakfast. Marina's there as always. She brings me coffee and a newspaper, one of my only connections to the outside world. I try to read it, but mostly I'm thinking about my shitty situation. A plate of eggs and toast appears, but Marina doesn't walk off. Instead, she looks down at me, one hand on her hip.

"Erick asked me to ask you if there's anything you want from the store tomorrow."

I blink at her, surprised. "Uh, I don't know. I didn't realize I got a say in that."

"Normally, you don't." She scowls. "I like to do shopping myself, but he insists. Says you seem down, and maybe some comfort food will make you happy again. I told him, I cook you comfort food. You want comfort, I can comfort. He insisted. Here we are."

"Thank you," I say, trying not to smile. "Anything I want?"

"Anything but canned soup. You want soup? I'll make soup. You want chicken noodle? I'll make chicken noodle soup so good you'll take a bath in the stuff. Canned soup is banned from this house. It should be banned from the world."

"Oreos. Please."

"Fine. Little sugar cookies. I can do that." Her scowl deepens. "Anything else?"

"No, that's okay." I hesitate a second. "What time are you leaving?"

"Morning," she says. "I'll have quince in the refrigerator for you. Coffee made and ready. But I go early, get back early."

"Sounds good to me."

"Fine. Tell me if you think of something." She softens as she returns to her stove. "Canned soup. It should be illegal."

"I agree," I say, grinning to myself.

A plan takes shape. It's a stupid idea. I'll get myself killed if I actually try to do it. But I'm desperate and out of options, which means a stupid way forward is better than sitting around doing nothing.

Chapter 29

Erick

That night, after I get back home from work, I make Hellie put on hiking shoes and a hat. "We're going for a walk."

"A walk? Why the hell are we going for a walk?"

"Because I want to show you my land. Unless you want to stay up in here longer?"

She makes a face at the canvas. There are barely any marks, still only a vague sketch. "Fine. Hike. Let's go."

I lead her out the back door and toward the hills. "Recognize this?"

"Sure, from my escape attempt." She makes a face. "That was unpleasant."

"It'll be cooler now that we're near sunset, but still hot. You know that story about it getting freezing in the desert at night? Not around here."

"It goes from unbearable to slightly bearable."

"Exactly, but dark." We take a path I know by heart that winds through an outcropping of rocks and up to the top of a low rise. "Here. Look."

I gesture into the distance. The desert spreads out like sheets on the earth, pocked with a surprising amount of color. Lights and darks, browns and blues and greens, all of them mixing together to make this strange, alien landscape.

"Beautiful," she says.

"Do you want to know why I moved out here?"

"Sure. I'd like that."

I take her hand. She holds onto mine, looking surprised, but doesn't argue as we start to walk again. I take her on a circuit I've walked a thousand times in the past. I don't tell her, but this is where I used to go when I needed to think. There's nothing like the quiet of the desert to quiet my brain.

"I come from an intense family. The Costa family. How much do you know about them?"

"I know the rumors. Connected to some shady people."

"Go ahead, say the 'M' word, I know you want to."

She laughs lightly. "Okay, fine. Everyone says you're mafia, which I know is true, but I don't really know what that means, you know?"

"It means, the casinos are only one piece of my business. We import things, illegal things, and we sell them on to distributors. We're wholesalers, but we deal in weapons, drugs, anything that can't be purchased through legitimate avenues."

"Okay, so you're rich and you're shady. Got it."

"I bought this house because my life has been speeding past me for a very long time. Ever since I was young, I've always had this feeling that the world is spinning faster and faster, my days are getting shorter, stretched thin, there's never enough of it. I felt overwhelmed, exhausted, like I couldn't catch my breath. Until I started coming out to the desert for these long drives."

She looks up at me. I try not to return her gaze. I don't want to get lost in her eyes right now.

"This place calms you down," she says.

"It took me longer than I'd like to admit to figure that out, but yes. That's when I purchased this house. This place is my refuge away from that life, away from the Strip, from my family, from my enemies. It's the one place in the whole world where I don't have to be Erick Costa, where I can just be whoever I am when the baggage of my name isn't applied. I can be myself."

"I'm jealous of that, you know. Not many people get a place like this."

"You're right, and I try not to take it for granted. When your father stole from me, and I realized you were in the crossfire, I had to make a choice. I could leave you for Frost and Gallo, or I could steal you myself. I couldn't take you to the casino though, that would be stupid. No, there's only one place in the world where you'd be truly safe and where you couldn't escape."

"Here." She cocks her head. "You didn't want to bring me here, did you?"

"No, I really didn't. I've never brought a woman here, not once. There's only ever been me, Ren, and Marina in this house, plus the doctor now too, I suppose. Other than that, this place has been all mine. Bringing you to this house has been very intimate for me, in ways you probably won't ever understand, but I need you to know I don't regret it. I don't regret it at all."

She stops walking. The sun's beginning to set, turning the sky pink and purple, a beautiful, lush mixture of smeary color. "I didn't know that. I figured this was just your house."

"It's more than my house. Giving you a room, building that studio for you, it took a lot from me. At first, it was like losing something, but now I realize I was wrong. Bringing you here, letting you into my life, it was adding something bigger."

"Thank you," she says. "I mean, not for drugging me and kidnapping me, but for sharing all that."

"I have feelings for you too, Hellie." I stare into her eyes and pull her against me. "I didn't say it last night because

I was overwhelmed, but I'm telling you now. I feel what you're feeling."

She chews her lip. It's adorable, and sexy, and I'm thrumming with want for her. We're alone here, sandwiched between two mesas where nobody will find us, and I can't stand the idea of not kissing her.

"Will this ever be over?" she asks. Her voice is tiny. "Will you ever let me leave?"

"Yes. I will. Our plan is going to work."

"Okay." She takes a deep breath and let sit out. "I believe you."

"Good." I kiss her gently. Softly at first. Exploring her reaction. She responds with a soft moan and pushes herself against me as the kiss blossoms and blooms.

Tongue her in mouth. Lips on hers. Tasting her, drinking her. I pull her back with me until I'm leaning against a rock wall, her hips on mine. She's breathing fast as I pull up her top, pull up her sports bra, find her nipples. I kiss them, lick them, bite her neck, bite her lower lip. I fist her hair and lick her teeth, wanting every inch of her body, of her mouth.

"You could at least wait until we got back," she says, panting as I slip a hand down the front of her yoga pants.

"I don't think I could wait if I tried."

"Shit," she says with a groan as my fingers slide up and down her slit. She's dripping wet, like I knew she would be.

"You really do like me, don't you?" I bite her earlobe.

"Like? Are we teenagers now?"

"We are. You like-like me. And I like-like you too. Especially when you're bent over getting fucked."

"Oh, now you're just being filthy."

"And you love it." I slide my fingers inside, making her gasp. "Come on, Hellie. Say you like it when I talk dirty."

"I like it," she says, giving me that unfocused, needy stare. "I really, really like it."

I tease her there near the rocks before getting down on my knees, her yoga pants removed, her top tossed aside, until she's in only her hiking boots. I lick her pussy, making her gasp and shudder, breasts shaking. We're exposed, in the elements, but this is my world—and I want to share it with her.

"Hellie, my Hellie," I whisper as I fuck her with my fingers. "My delicious little Hellie. If you scream while you come, do you think anyone will hear?"

"I fucking hope not," she says, digging her fingers into my hair. "I also don't care."

"I didn't think you would." I lick and suck her clit faster, fingers sliding in and out. "Go ahead. I want to hear you.

Don't be fucking shy, you filthy girl. Don't pretend like you're not my dirty, dirty fucking girl. Come for me."

"Yes, Erick," she gasps, back arching. "Fuck you, yes, I'm so close."

I stroke my fingers in and out faster, faster, licking her clit the whole time, until she finally releases—a beautiful, perfect, slick and lovely release, and I don't stop until she's a quivering mess, leaning up against the rocks for support.

I stand, cock hard. Unable to resist her like this, so lovely and vulnerable. I turn her around, running my hands down her flanks.

"Beautiful," I murmur. "Hellie, you are truly incredible. You're perfect for me in a way I never dreamed about." I grip her hair. I position my cock against her dripping entrance.

"You're only saying that because you want to get in my pants." She grins as she leans back against me, my shaft between her legs. She grinds her hips, moving back and forth, and kisses me over her shoulder. "Looks like you don't need to keep working at it, you know."

"I'll never stop working at it." I push her forward, make her hips arch, and slide myself inside.

I fuck my Hellie. I go deep and feel her, groaning in her ear. If she's nervous or embarrassed about being in public, out in nature, she doesn't show it. She's wild, uninhibited, at least when I'm fucking her, and I love that. She doesn't hold back, not when it comes to our pleasure.

Her pussy floods with heat. Her core contracts and tightens around my cock. I can't take it and growl into her ear, more beast than man, as she comes again. I share her orgasm, filling her with my own. It's intense, heightened by our mutual understanding, by the feelings we can't escape.

We dress as the darkness rushes toward us. I hold her hand as we walk fast back toward the house. I didn't get to show her everything—the vistas, the intense loneliness of being in the middle of an enormous space with no other humans in sight—but we can do that another time.

"Sleep in my bed again tonight." We reach the property but pause before going inside.

"I figured that went without saying."

"I'm saying it. Sleep in my bed every night."

"Alright. I can do that." She gets on her toes and kisses me. "I really do have feelings for you."

"I believe you."

She gives me a long look, one I don't understand. It's almost melancholy. But she covers it with a smile and drags me inside, already chatting about what wine we'll have with dinner, and how late I'm going to keep her up, and the moment passes.

Chapter 30

Hellie

I wake up early the next morning, afraid I screwed up my timing, but it's still dark outside.

I scramble over and check the clock: a little past five in the morning. The bed's empty, which means Erick's awake and down in the gym getting in his workout; he'll be there until six at the earliest, sometimes later depending on the day. I sit in bed, staring at the ceiling, taking deep breaths, trying to decide if I'm really going through with this.

If it works, best-case scenario, I get to meet my father and find out what he wants. We'll talk, he won't get caught, and then—

And then I'm free to do what I want.

I could run. Get out of Vegas, hide somewhere Frost and Gallo can't find me. But the thought of doing that makes my throat itch like I'm allergic to the very idea.

I could call Erick, admit I ran away, tell him everything, and hope he brings me back.

Except I have no clue how he'd react.

Maybe I could sneak back into Marina's car somehow, or ask a cab to drive me out here, except I don't know where here is and there's no way I'll get to the meeting with Dad and back in time.

Basically, I'm screwed. I have no exit plan, and no matter what I come up with, there's some terrible downside.

I have to trust that Erick won't be angry. Better to ask forgiveness than permission, right? Some voice in the back of my head keeps saying I'm being stupid, Erick's not the type to forgive and forget, but I get out of bed, take a quick shower, throw on comfortable, lightweight clothes, and try to push that from my mind.

First stop, the studio. I click on some lights and leave a note taped to the door: *In the zone, do not disturb until lunch. I already ate and I have tea!* I have no clue if that'll work, but it'll probably buy me enough time.

Next stop, downstairs.

I sneak along the steps, listening at every landing. This early, the house is silent. Marina's probably in the kitchen cooking breakfast. The home gym is in the back of the house, and Erick listens to loud music as he lifts. Ren's not here, and there aren't any other guards since there's nowhere for me to run.

The path to the garage is wide open.

I slip out the door. It's cool and dark. Tools are hung on a very neat pegboard above a well-used workbench. It's a long space, more workshop than anything else, though there are a few vehicles parked in the bays. A vintage Mercedes, a black truck, a new Ferrari, and a sensible Nissan Altima.

It's not hard to guess which one Marina drives.

I peer in through the windows of the Altima. It's a basic sedan, a few years out of date, but kept very neat. The biggest tell is the cross hanging from the rearview mirror: Marina's Catholic, but Erick's nothing, meaning I'm at the right place.

I take a deep breath. It smells like oil and old wood. I stare back at the door, and this is my last chance. I could go back inside, head into the kitchen, ask Marina for coffee and eggs, and forget all about this.

My dad's email keeps playing in my head. Why did he write that? Why did he take the risk? Unless it's important, there's no way he'd come back and risk himself, not for me anyway. For all he knows, I'm already dead, but he sent the message and set the meeting.

I have to go. I don't want to, which is the worst part. I should want to face my father, tell him off, hear what he has to say and let him know what I really think of him—that in the end, he's a selfish asshole that only ever cared about himself, leaving me as an afterthought at best. I want him to understand how he basically put a death sentence on my head, and that I'm only alive because Erick's a decent man and didn't want to murder me.

Instead, I'd rather remain here in comfort, with nothing but my painting and Erick, the only two things I really want right now. I need him like I need my art, but having them together means I'm completely satisfied.

It's strange how when this all started, I would've killed for a chance like this. Instead, I'm reluctant to take the risk.

But in the end, I walk around to the back of the car and pop open the trunk. It's unlocked, because why bother locking it? There's nobody around. I steady myself before climbing in, and I take one last look at the garage door, then yank the trunk lid down and shut myself in.

Darkness falls.

The only sound is the pounding of my heart.

I'm supremely uncomfortable, but at least I'm not very big. I have to shift my weight and contort myself before I find something vaguely comfortable, but eventually I start to relax as I realize that I'm here for a while, because I have no clue when Marina's actually going to leave.

A thousand things rip through my head. The note won't be enough—Erick's going to check on me anyway, and he's going to find the studio empty. If that happens, he'll realize something is happening, or he'll panic and think I'm in trouble. Either way, he'll tear the house to pieces to find me, and Marina won't be going anywhere.

Or maybe Marina has those reusable bags and she's going to find me hiding in here before she even leaves, which would be a freaking nightmare. Or she'll spot me when I try to get out once we make it into town, which could be even worse. Or I'll suffocate in here because I'm not getting any air, or I'll die of heat stroke out in the desert since this trunk isn't air-conditioned, or I'll fall out mid-drive and get run over by a semi.

Dozens of ugly deaths and failures torture me as an agonizing amount of time passes. I try not to check my watch, but it starts to become compulsive as I count the minutes. An hour, two hours. I start to wonder if Marina's ever going to leave and if I'll be in here for nothing.

I want to scream.

Until I hear a sound. It's a door opening nearby, followed by voices, muffled at first. They get louder as people come near.

"Yes, yes, I'm sure, leave her be." Marina's voice, sounding harried. "She's happy when she's working, yes? If she has food and tea, she's fine, let her work."

"I don't know. She's not good about taking care of herself when she gets like this." Erick's voice. He sounds worried.

"Stay out of there, okay? Leave her alone. Now, I'm going to the store, and I'll be back in a few hours. When I get here, I'll check and bring her food, okay?"

He sounds slightly better. "Alright, that would be a huge help."

"No problem at all. Go to work. I'll make sure she's okay."

"Thank you, Marina."

A car starts nearby. Not the one I'm in. A door opens, the garage door grinds upward, and tires crunch on gravel.

A minute later, Marina climbs into the front seat. The shocks groan, the body shakes on the springs. The radio turns on, tuned to a Top-40 station, and Marina hums along as she backs out.

Then we're on the move.

Fuck, it's bumpy. I shouldn't be surprised since it's a freaking desert road, but still, I'm practically getting thrown around like a piece of luggage. I have no clue how she hasn't heard me thumping around yet, and I do my very best to brace myself, but it's not helping that much.

Then it gets hot.

Like, really hot. I knew it'd be warm, but holy shit, I'm sweating like crazy and getting jostled and I'm pretty sure I'm getting cooked in this stupid thing. I don't know what I was thinking, getting in here to begin with, running away from Erick when we finally made a breakthrough together last night.

He cares about me. He has feelings for me in the same way I have feelings for him, and here I am, running from it.

Risking something good for a father that doesn't deserve my devotion.

I'm aware that this is a massive mistake.

As I'm thrown around, I keep thinking I should yell out, tell Marina I'm here, explain to her the situation and hope she takes pity on me and drives me back to the house. Maybe she won't even tell Erick, since she knows he'll be really pissed and hurt.

Erick. His lips. His arms. The way he looked at me in the desert during our walk. He opened up, told me his story, gave me a piece of himself and it was a beautiful moment, something special, something I cherish.

Here I am, running from that.

This is wrong.

I don't want this.

I need to turn back—forget my father. Whatever he has to say, he can screw himself. He's the one that got me in this situation, not Erick, not anyone else.

I'm about to start shouting and kicking when the car slows and comes to a stop. The radio turns off and the engine dies, and I'm sitting there like, what the hell is going on?

There's no way we're at a grocery store yet. We've only been driving for ten minutes max, and the whole time it's been bumpy as hell. Marina never even reached a paved road.

Why are we stopping and why is the engine off?

My heart starts racing. An ugly feeling enters my guts. I'm on the edge of freaking out when a voice speaks.

"I'm going to open the trunk now."

I freeze. I can't move. I can't think.

The trunk pops and light floods my eyes. I groan, covering them, cowering away from the blinding sun.

A shadow looks over me. It resolves into the outline of a person, then their expression coheres.

Ren frowns at me, shaking his head slowly, disappointment clear in every inch of his body.

Chapter 31

Hellie

This can't be happening.

Ren? Here? Now? I don't understand—I never heard him, not earlier when Marina and Erick were talking, and I was paying attention to every little thing.

"Where did you come from?" I ask, too bewildered to say anything else.

His lips twist in disgust. "Get out."

I hesitate, and he reaches in and drags me free of the trunk. His grip on my arm hurts, and I stumble, nearly fall, as I get my legs under me and look around, blinking against the sudden brightness.

There's only desert.

We're in a small clearing surrounded by ridges. Rocky pathways wind into the mountainous terrain. Cacti, scrub brush, brown grasses, not much else.

Marina's leaning against the hood of the car, smoking a cigarette. I can't read her expression, but if she's upset with me, she doesn't show it. If anything, she seems bored, like this happens all the time.

"What's going on?" I ask, confused and still trying to get my bearings. Why is Marina just looking at me? Why are we in the middle of nowhere?

Then my brain starts to break out of my panic.

Ren knew. Somehow, he knew, and he caught me.

Now he's going to kill me.

That's why we're out here in the middle of nowhere.

"I really hoped you were smarter than this," Ren says. "I really, really hoped, but I couldn't be sure. There was always the possibility, and here you are. Like a mouse to some cheese."

"Please," I say, backing away. "This was a mistake. I knew it was a mistake, I just—"

"Don't start pleading. I really fucking hate when they plead." He rubs his forehead, teeth clenched together. "Erick's going to be upset. Really goddamn upset."

"I wasn't trying to run. I swear, I wasn't, I was just—"

He looks up. His eyes sharp. "If you say one more word, I swear I'm going to make you dig your own fucking grave, then I'll bury you alive in it."

I close my mouth, hands sweating. Head spinning. I'm going to die out here all alone, and Erick's going to think I tried to stab him in the back.

Oh, god, Erick. The thought of him finding out about this hurts more than anything else.

Marina sighs. "Ren, don't be dramatic."

"She's pissing me off."

"You dangled this in front of her. Can you really be surprised?"

"Erick's going to be."

"So what?" Marina takes a drag of her cigarette. "He likes her. I like her too."

"She tried to escape." Ren paces back and forth. "Fuck. Fucking fuck. I really hoped you wouldn't be so goddamn stupid."

"I'm sorry," I say, my voice small.

"Don't apologize to him, dear," Marina says, but she doesn't sound kind about it. "You'll have to apologize plenty to Erick. But, Ren, you don't have to bother, and it won't help."

"Oh." I look down at my feet. "Oh, shit."

Erick's going to find out about this. Erick, the man that told me he has feelings for me, is going to find out that I tried to escape.

I tried to sneak out behind his back.

I lied to him.

And it's going to kill both of us.

"Don't act like you care," Ren says, his voice cold. "How long were you playing him for? From the start?"

"I don't know what you're talking about."

Ren sneers. "Play dumb all you want, it won't help."

"You tested me, didn't you? Both of you." I look from him to Marina. "Did Erick know?"

Ren snorts. "Of course not. You think he'd be okay with testing his precious artist girl? Fuck that. This was all me."

"He roped me into it." Marina shrugs. "Offered money. I said you weren't so stupid and I figured it wouldn't hurt. Guess I was wrong."

"Shit." I lean my head back against the car. The early morning desert sunlight burns into my skin. "What do we do from here?"

"I take you back to the house, throw you in your room, and lock the door from the outside." Ren comes toward me, hands clenched.

"You're not going to kill me?" A sick kind of hope fills me. I'm surprised this isn't my final resting place, but now it means I have to face Erick and see the look of hurt in his eyes.

Marina laughs sharply and flicks away her cigarette. "No, he's definitely not, because Erick would kill him next."

"The *cook* is correct," Ren says. Marina flips him off. "I am not going to kill you because my boss and best friend would be upset. However, I am going to tell him you took my fucking bait like a starving little minnow. God, how stupid can you be? Marina just so happens to be going to the store? Her car is unlocked? The halls are all empty?"

I could cry. Now that he's saying it, I can see how everything aligned perfectly. But one problem—

"You didn't send me the email?" I blurt out, unable to stop myself.

He looks confused, head cocked to the side. "What fucking email? Jesus, Hellie, don't tell me you've been getting online too. Erick's going to lose his shit. You've been very, very bad. What fucking email?"

I shut my mouth and say nothing.

It was a test. Marina, the car, everything, it was a test, except one thing.

He didn't send the email—that was really from my dad.

Which means I can't say a word unless I want to get my father killed. Once they know he's around, they'll tear the city apart to find him. I can't take that risk.

"Hellie," Ren says, getting in my face. "Don't piss me off. Tell me what email."

I stare him down. I've been really dumb up to this point, blinded by my need to get out and see my father, but now I'm starting to think.

"Hellie." His voice drops lower. "Tell me, or I am going to make you tell me."

"No, he's not," Marina says. "He's not going to touch you."

"Shut up." Ren's glaring at me. He slams a fist into the car. "Tell me what email."

I shake my head slowly and keep my mouth glued shut.

The moment hangs there, tense and thick, and I'm terrified he's going to hurt me. Marina lights another cigarette and seems bored of the whole thing.

Ren pulls back, cursing as he kicks a rock, sending it clattering away. I relax slightly and hug myself, rubbing my arms, still shaking from the adrenaline coursing through my veins.

"You are going to talk when we get back," Ren says, rounding on me. "You're going to tell Erick everything. You'll admit you tried to escape. You'll tell him about the email, whatever the fuck that is. And when it's done, you'd better hope he doesn't murder you himself. Now get in the fucking car."

I climb into the back seat. There's no way I can tell Erick about my father's message. No way in hell. Marina gets behind the wheel and blasts the air conditioning; it feels like heaven after that damn trunk. Ren gets into the passenger seat and says nothing as Marina navigates the clearing, gets back onto an unmarked path, and returns to the house.

I'm fucked.

No other way to say it. I'm totally fucked.

Erick's going to be so hurt when he finds out about this.

I hope I can explain. If I'm lucky, I can make him understand—

But I can't tell him about the email.

If I do, he'll know my father's still in Vegas.

Erick will hunt Dad down, and despite everything, I still can't let it happen.

I bent my morals once already. I agreed to help Erick make these art forgeries, and hell, it turns out I'm really good at it. But I never wanted to do something like that, never wanted to be a con artist and a criminal like my old man.

I have a chance to be better.

I can do something my father would never do.

Which is to keep my mouth shut. I can protect him in a way he would never protect me.

Even if it means ruining something good with Erick.

Chapter 32

Erick

"**Y**ou did fucking *what?*" I stare at Ren, seething with rage. We're in the kitchen of my house. He called twenty minutes earlier and told me to get back home, something important happened with Hellie. I raced back here, only to find out that he created some elaborate scheme to test her loyalty.

And she fucking failed.

"I dangled bait," he says, holding his hands up like he's got no part in this. Like it isn't his fault. "I didn't force her into anything. I didn't coerce or trick her. All I did was have Marina mention the shopping trip, and I made it so that Hellie's exit path was clear and easy. I let her do all the hard work."

I shake my head, not understanding. "She wanted to go to the store?"

"No, Erick," Ren says. His voice is soft now, which pisses me off. Like I'm some child. "She was hiding in the trunk. She wanted to escape."

"I don't believe this." I look to Marina as she stands off to the side of the room, avoiding eye contact. "Tell me the truth. Did this happen the way Ren's describing it?"

"Everything he says is true." She doesn't look happy about it. "Don't be too hard on the girl. This isn't easy on her."

"Stop," I say, digging my fingers into my palms. "She really tried to escape?"

"Yes," Ren says. "She had her chance and she took it. I'm sorry, Erick, I really am. I know you like the girl, but she's lying to you. Whatever you think you two have, it isn't real."

"He doesn't know shit," Marina cuts in. "Just because she tried to run—"

I hold my hands up. "Shut up, both of you." I take deep breaths, pacing back and forth. "Where is she right now?"

"Up in her room," Ren says. "I have her locked in for now."

"She has food and tea," Marina adds, as if that helps.

I turn away. "I'll talk to her."

"Wait." Ren doesn't move, but I hesitate and let him talk. "I get it, man. Shit's complicated with her. But do you really trust her? I mean, really, after all this? We drugged

231

her. We kidnapped her. Do you really think she wants to be here after all that?"

"We saved her life," I say, even though the words sound pathetic now.

"We did, but does it matter? We still kidnapped her, and now you're forcing her to make art forgeries, even though she doesn't want to."

"It's not like that."

"Isn't it? Yeah, she's good at the painting shit, and maybe she even enjoys it, but we still drugged her and forced her to work for us. How the fuck can you trust her? How are you even remotely surprised that she tried to run? Brother, you gotta open your eyes and understand. She's our prisoner."

"Why are you doing this?" I can't look at him. I'm too angry, and I'm worried I'll do something stupid, like beat that sympathetic fucking look off his face.

"I need you to see clearly. You've been compromised since the second she walked into our lives, and I'm worried that you're going to make bad decisions because of her. This shit with Gallo and Frost is serious. You barely avoided an all-out war once already. You think Gallo's done? You think Frost isn't going to try something again? I need you, Erick. I need you on your game, not lusting after your prisoner."

I slowly turn and stare at him. "Fuck you."

"Yeah, fine, you're pissed, but I'm still right."

I walk away. If I stay a second longer, I might strangle him.

But part of me knows he has a point, or at least he has good reasons for concern. I hate those reasons, despise them with every fiber of my being, but I understand them at least.

We drugged Hellie. We kidnapped her. That doesn't change.

He's right about Frost and Gallo too—they're going to be a problem no matter what we do to keep them in check. I need to be actively involved, not chasing after Hellie.

That doesn't excuse what he did. Ren never should've tested her without my consent. He stepped over a line and he will be punished for that shit.

I reach Hellie's room. The bolt's closed on the outside and it breaks my heart, seeing her locked down like that. I can't open it yet—I take a second to compose myself, trying to come to grips with what's happening.

Hellie tried to run away.

After everything, after yesterday, she tried to escape.

I opened up to her, gave her a glimpse of the man beneath the gangster, and she bolted the first chance she got.

It kills me, thinking about her trying to escape right after I told her that I have feelings for her.

She manipulated me from the start.

I unlock the door and go inside.

Hellie's sitting in a chair near the window, her knees pulled to her chest, her eyes red from crying. I stand in the doorway, my heart fucking broken, watching her for a long time. Everything we've done together floods back: kissing her, fucking her, taking care of her. This is my Hellie, and I thought we had something real.

She looks back at me, tries to smile, but it fades.

"Is it true?" I ask. "You tried to escape?"

"Yes," she says. "It's true."

I want to ask a dozen things. Why, how, what did I do wrong, why now? Except I can't make any of it come out. I continue looking at her, searching for that feeling from the night before, trying to hold on to that little bit of goodness in my life.

The feeling's still there. The connection, the need. It's still there, and that's what kills me the most.

I feel like I've been dumped into the desert with a rock crushing my spine. My body's numb, my brain's gone haywire.

She betrayed me.

She tried to run after all this.

Even knowing Gallo and Frost are out there and both of them want to kill her, she still tried to escape.

The first chance she got, she took it.

Despite everything. Despite the night before when I admitted how I really felt.

She tried to run away.

If it had been the first week, if it had been before everything we said to each other, I might be able to find way past this.

Right now? I don't think I can ever forgive her.

"There will be new rules," I say, struggling to keep my voice steady. It takes more effort than I like to admit. "I can't trust you anymore."

"Okay. I understand." Her voice is flat, like it's coming from someone else. She looks defeated, slumped over, small.

"We still have a job to do, despite your escape attempt."

"I get it."

"There will be new restrictions. Hellie—" I shut my mouth with a click. I want to stride across the room, drag her to her feet, and kiss her hard until her mouth bleeds.

I want her to understand what this means. I want her to feel how this feels.

Instead, I'll keep going the best I can.

She betrayed me and there's no coming back from that.

"I know," she whispers. She's blinking away tears.

Crying? Why the fuck would she be crying?

"Stay here until someone comes to get you." I turn and move to leave because I don't think I can handle this. I'm too raw.

"It wasn't because of you," she says before I can go. I don't turn around to look at her. That doesn't help—it anything, I feel worse. If I stay right now, I'll say something I might regret, I'll do something that will make me hate myself, and I don't want that. "It wasn't because of you," she repeats softly.

"Doesn't matter," I answer.

I walk away and lock the door.

Chapter 33

Hellie

I cry a lot that first day. Erick doesn't come back. The look on his face as he turned to leave the room haunts me. It was so pained, like I stabbed him in the guts and kept on twisting the knife.

He doesn't come back. He doesn't ask me to explain. Food appears, carried up by Marina, who at least seems a little sympathetic. "Is he okay?" I ask her that night once dinner arrives. "At least tell me he's okay?"

"Erick Costa is a very strong man. It'll take more than you to break him." She gives me a sad smile and leaves.

That doesn't make me feel better.

I barely touch my food. I'm stuck in the room with nothing to do, my head going crazy, alternating between hating myself and hating Ren, even though I know it isn't Ren's fault.

He's Erick's best friend. He's loyal to the Costa family above all else, and can I really be angry with him for testing me? I fell into the trap willingly with a big smile on my face.

I'm the one that tried to run.

I made that stupid decision, and it'll haunt me for a long time.

To kill time, I take a long, hot bath. I try to relax, but I keep seeing Erick's face, twisted in agony and rage and heartbreak.

I did that to him.

For a good reason. Not because of him, but because of that email, even though he doesn't know that and I can't ever tell him.

From his perspective, I tried to run because I wanted to get away from our relationship.

I debate telling him the truth. Over and over, I question my decision. If I tell him about my father's email, he might actually understand why I did it. But no matter how I look at it, I keep coming back to the same facts. I can't tell him, I can't risk my father's life, I can't stoop to that level. I have to save myself and my father, even if it means losing Erick.

I try to sleep. It doesn't go great.

The next morning, breakfast arrives, but I don't recognize the guy that drops it off. He has big, dark eyes, dark hair, and glares at me like I'm an annoying hamster. "Eat, shower, dress. You have work in a half hour." He leaves again, locking the door behind him.

I don't understand what he means, but I follow his instructions anyway. Thirty minutes later, at exactly seven in the morning, the door opens again. It's the same guy—broad, built like a bull, more shoulders and back and chest than head and neck, with arms like wrecking balls—and he gestures for me to follow. I walk after him to the studio.

"Work," he says jabbing a hand toward my painting. "On the job. No other stuff. Boss's orders."

"Wait." I look around in a panic. "Not my own art?"

"No. On the job. If I catch you doing anything else, I have instructions to lock you in your room. If it keeps happening, we'll start taking away comforts." The big guy leaves, closing the door behind him.

Something clicks. A lock slams shut.

I stare at the room. It's as I left it, nothing changed, except I'm stuck here with that forged painting, the beginnings of a false Rembrandt, staring at me from the easel.

I take deep breaths. I try to gather myself together. But it feels like I'm sinking, when suddenly, in a complete blind panic, I rush to the rack of paints and fish around behind it, looking for the portrait of Erick I hid there.

It's gone. I check all over, but it's not in this room.

I slump onto my stool, feeling like I've been drained of everything. I stare at the canvas, at my job, but there's no spark. There's no excitement. Only dread. Only terror.

I don't know how long I'm sitting like that before the door opens. Marina comes in with lunch. Tea and tuna sandwiches. "Eat and drink," she says. "Yell if you need the bathroom. Tony will take you."

"Alright." I don't even look over.

"Try to work." Marina's voice is almost kind now. That hurts even more. "You feel better when you work, so try to do the job, okay?"

"It doesn't feel the same anymore."

"No, I'm sure it won't, but try anyway. You'll get through this if you can keep on working."

She leaves. The door locks. I eat, drink some tea, and look at the canvas.

I can paint.

There's that place in me still, that zone where the world disappears, and I don't want anything more than to escape into it. I can hide there, throw myself into the canvas, into the job.

Nothing hurts in that place, in that flow. There's only the art.

No Erick. No Dad. No failures.

I sit down on the stool. I pick up a brush.

Marina's says I'm happy when I work, but she's wrong about that.

I'm not happy—I'm just not here.

Chapter 34

Erick

I stay far away from the house in the desert and sleep at the casino. I have a condo I barely ever use, and it feels empty, bereft of warmth, barely more than a space to drink too much and pass out until morning. I want to go back to that place—I want the smell of wet paint, the taste of a wooden brush between my teeth, Hellie's laughter, her deep breaths, her rolling eyes and her moans. I want it all, crave it like my heart needs blood.

Instead, I refuse to go back.

My days drift. Ren updates me on Hellie's progress. He never mentions her by name—she's only ever *the girl* or *the painter*, but I still can't help but picture her, feel her lips against mine, her hair wrapped in my fist, her thick, dark, wavy curls against my nose as I breathe in her smell. I hear her whimpers, her laughter. I taste her still. Every day.

I can't shake her, even when I try.

Work isn't enough. It's all I have but it only dulls the edge. Drinking helps, but only for a little while. I still wake in an empty, cold bed, wondering where Hellie's at —only to remember that she betrayed me, tried to run away, and manipulated me into feeling something for her.

That's what hurts the most. She said she didn't want to be anything like her father, but now I can't see what's true and what's a part of her game.

Days pass like that. One morning, with a particularly nasty headache grinding in my skull, Ren intercepts me on my way down to the office. "I got a call from Gallo's people, they want a meeting with you and Frost later this afternoon."

"What do they want?"

"Don't know, they didn't say, but it can't be good." Ren hesitates. I can tell he's about to mention Hellie—he always gets this guilty look on his face before he does it. "The girl's fine, by the way. We have that place locked down tight."

"Good. Make sure it's guarded. I don't want her getting away, and I don't want anyone getting in either."

"You don't have to worry about it. I've got it under control."

I grunt in response. My relationship with Ren hasn't been good since he pulled this testing shit, and even though I understand he did it for the family, I still don't like it.

He did it behind my back knowing I wouldn't like it.

I've always valued Ren's independence. He's clever, works hard, and is very loyal. Maybe too loyal.

Except this time, he crossed a line, and I don't know if I can go back.

Though I can't blame him for Hellie's choice.

Later on, after another agonizing afternoon hating myself, I'm in the back of a black SUV heading over to another neutral location. Ren's with me while Wolfie's driving up front. Nobody's talking and I prefer it that way. The tension's heavy, almost unbearable, but why the fuck should that matter? Ren doesn't deserve my friendship right now. He betrayed me the same way Hellie did.

"We just gonna sit in this silence, bro?" Ren glances over. "You good with that?"

"Works for me."

"You can't ignore it forever," Ren says as we get close to our destination. He's looking at me across the seat. "You can't pretend like it's fine."

"I'm not pretending."

Now the motherfucker wants to talk? How convenient for him—we're trapped in the damn car together. Bastard's smart. Picked his ground to have this stupid battle.

"I get it, you're pissed. You don't like that I went behind your back. But, Erick—"

"I don't want to hear your excuses." I stare at him. My eyes narrow. My hands shake. He wants to talk? Alright, we'll talk. "I had something with her. I know she fucked up trying to run, but I still don't believe everything was fake. I can't believe it."

"Why not? The girl's the daughter of a con man. She learned some shit from her father."

It's like he knows exactly what's been running through my head these past few days.

Hearing it out loud nearly kills me.

"She's not like that," I say, but what if she is?

"Maybe, maybe not, I don't know. I just don't want you to keep dragging yourself through this shit."

"I'm not dragging myself through anything. Hellie's back at the house. She's paying off her debt. When she's done, we'll let her go, and I can forget she even exists." I hold up a hand before he can speak. "But don't think I'll ever forget what *you* did."

Ren's jaw works. I can tell that pisses him off. "I've always been looking out for you, bro. I've always had your back. Now you're going to act like I'm the one who turned on you?"

"That's exactly what I'm going to do. You've had it out for Hellie since the second she showed up. I don't know what it is, maybe you're jealous, maybe you really do think I was distracted by her, but either way you did your best to make sure you fucked things up to get your way."

"That's not how it went down." He sounds exasperated as he leans away from me. "I was just trying to see if she was for real, and if she was, I planned on leaving it alone. I *wanted* her to pass, don't you get it? I wanted her to ignore her opportunity. It killed me when she climbed into that fucking car, because I knew it would hurt you so much. I was pissed, man. I didn't want this to happen."

"I bet you didn't. I'm done talking about it and I don't want you to bring it up again. We're colleagues. That's all."

I can tell Ren's not done, but the car parks. I get out and stride into the hotel with Ren on my heels. One of the porters spots me and waves for me to follow him, and I find Gallo sitting with Frost at a bar in the far corner of the casino.

"Strange place to meet," I say, taking a chair next to Frost. I wave at the bartender and ask for their best whiskey. Time to wipe that conversation from my mind. Ren hovers nearby, staying out of the way, but watching closely.

"I wanted to make this brief." Gallo's expression is grim. "I heard a disturbing rumor this morning."

"Your doctor finally tell you that swollen pathetic lump between your legs is actually a cancerous lesion?" Frost asks, grinning. The asshole's already trying to start shit.

Gallo doesn't take the bait, lucky for me. "Danny Accardi's been spotted in town."

Frost's smile disappears. I sit back, stunned into silence. Danny Accardi? Hellie's father? There's absolutely no way. Here, in fucking Vegas, the one place in the entire world he shouldn't be?

"That makes no sense," Frost says before I have the chance.

"My intel is good." Gallo shakes his head when the bartender asks if he wants more. I sip my whiskey, savoring the burn, trying to make sense of this. But any way I look at it, there's no reason for the old man to still be around. "He was spotted last night. Apparently, he grew a beard and he's real skinny, but it was definitely him."

"Why didn't your guys grab him?" I ask.

"It was an associate of my family, not a member. By the time the guy made the call to my people, and my soldiers showed up, Accardi was long gone."

"Well, fuck." Frost laughs to himself. It's mirthless, too surprised to have any humor. "What's that crazy asshole doing here? I thought he'd be long gone."

"I have no idea, but we can catch him now that we know he's around." Gallo stares between us, looking grim. "This shit with the paintings is alright. The last payment came through, even though you tried to fuck me."

Frost grunts. "Get over it. As if you wouldn't have done the same."

"But we can work together on this one," Gallo continues, ignoring him and staring at me. "We can tear this city to shreds, and if Accardi's really still here and laying low, we'll find him, but only if we pool resources. We can get what we really want and forget about the girl."

Forget about the girl... easy for Gallo, easy for Frost.

But for me?

"I can do that," Frost says. "Costa?"

I don't know what to say. I'm still too stunned to process. Hellie's Dad, here in Vegas, the root of all our problems. If we can catch him, get all the money he stole back—

Then there'd be no reason to hold Hellie anymore.

I could let her go and be done with this nightmare, and she wouldn't be in danger.

"Yeah," I say slowly. "Yeah, we can find him. I'll help."

Except I don't know if I want to, because I'm not sure Hellie would ever forgive me.

Not that it matters at this point. I can't forget she's the one who tried to run. She's the one who ended whatever we started together. She made her choices, and now I have to make mine.

Find her father. End this mess.

Let her walk free.

Even if I'm angry with her, even if I feel like she betrayed me, at least I can give her this much.

I can give her some freedom.

Chapter 35

Erick

I step into the house in the desert feeling conflicted. I haven't been here in nearly a week at this point, but I can't keep avoiding it forever, especially not now.

It's cool and dark, but it smells incredible. Marina's making my favorite—a simple spaghetti Bolognese. It's pure heaven in my mouth, that woman's freaking sauce. I'll have some later though—I don't have much of an appetite at the moment.

Soldiers are posted throughout the property, some walking outdoors in the heat, most hiding in the shade. I nod at the few I recognize, make sure I stop in the kitchen to say hello to the best cook in the whole fucking city, aware that I'm stalling before I do the one thing I actually came here to do, before forcing myself to climb the steps to the second floor.

She's in the studio. Her personal guard Tony's in the hallway, but I dismiss him. If I'm going to see her, I want privacy, because I'm not sure how I'm going to handle this interaction.

I pause outside of the door, gathering myself, before heading inside to face her.

Hellie's on her stool in front of the easel and doesn't look over as I enter.

The painting looks incredible. I draw in a surprised breath. She's made a ton of progress. It's still rough, but coming into shape, and I'm even more impressed than I was the first time. It's like the more she does this, the better she gets, and she was pretty damn good the first time around.

I wait and watch her for a little while. I let myself forget about the betrayal and focus on the way she moves. On the girl herself, the reason I fell. Her wrists, her fingers, the way she brushes her hair back. Paint stains her sweats, her shirt, the sleeves rolled to her elbows. Her hair's tied back and held in place with a clip. Her lips press together, her eyes squint, and each mark she makes is considered for a moment before it appears.

Her entire world is that canvas. I marvel at her beauty, at her confidence, at her talent. It's seductive, what she can do; I'm still drawn to her, despite everything. I wish it were otherwise, but I still want her, still need to taste her lips and feel my fingers dimpling the flesh on her hips. If I could turn off this part of me, I would. That would make my life so much easier.

Instead, she's a constant, low-level hum in the back of my mind. Always there.

"Hellie," I say, and when she doesn't react, I repeat her name louder.

She jumps and looks back. Her mouth opens, her eyebrows raise. Fuck, those eyes, I missed those eyes so much. I missed the way she looks at me.

"Erick. When did you get here?"

"Just a second ago." I decide not to tell her that I've been watching for nearly a half hour now. I don't want her to know what I'm feeling. I don't want to give her the chance to use it against me. "We need to talk."

"Right. Okay." She puts her brush down and turns to face me, the spotlight of her attention shifting in my direction. It's seductive, that attention. I want more of it, but I'm also terrified of the way it makes me feel. Too vulnerable, too seen. "What's wrong?"

"How do you know something's wrong?"

"Because you've been avoiding me for days and I just figured you wouldn't show up unless you had to."

I stop myself from flinching. She's right—it's obvious what I've been doing, but I don't like that she can see through me. I keep wondering if she's going to find a way to con me again, but the moment I feel myself going there, I try to push back against those assumptions, try to make myself remember how it felt to be with her, how real it was, and it's all a fucked-up mess. I could stand here looking at her all day, listen to her talk, watch her work, but I'm here for a reason. I make myself focus.

"We found your father."

She doesn't move. Total stillness, like a pretty creature in sight of a predator. "How?" she asks.

And it hits me.

All at once, like a kick to the chest.

She's not surprised.

There's no shock in her eyes.

Only fear and concern, which means—

She knew he was still in town.

I stare at her, trying to get a read on this situation, and feel at a complete loss. It doesn't make sense. I'm positive she didn't know where he was when she first came in— she was mad enough at the time to have turned him over without much prompting— and she hasn't had any contact with the outside world since she's been here. There's no way she should know anything about her father's location.

Unless I'm missing something.

"Gallo's people spotted him." I step closer, one hand pressed against the work table to steady myself. "You knew, didn't you?"

Her mouth shuts. Her lips press into a line. I can tell she's struggling with something. Fucking Hellie—I know her now, know her better than I ever expected I would.

And I can tell she's trying to come up with a story.

"I can't say." Her voice is tiny. Like she's embarrassed.

I close my eyes and take a steadying breath before opening them again. Another connection clicks into place. A stray problem I'd almost forgotten about. "The email."

She touches her hair, and I know it's true. That's her little tell, her nervous gesture. Even though she shakes her head, I can see right through her.

"I don't know what you mean."

What a shitty fucking liar.

And suddenly, I can't imagine this girl played me. It slips into focus, everything that happened on that day. Hellie can't lie to me, she's terrible at it, which means all that other stuff about having feelings for me, all of that was true.

There's no way she could've faked it.

Con man father or not, that isn't Hellie.

But she does know something now, something she's been keeping from me. I steady my heart and move closer, aware that I have to be careful. She may be a bad liar, but there's still something happening here.

"Ren told me you said something about an email. I asked you about it that day, but I was too angry to follow up, and he never mentioned it again. But you checked your email, didn't you?"

She shakes her head. "I don't want to talk about this."

"When you were in my room, you used my desktop, didn't you? I leave it logged in all the time because it tracks my stock portfolio and it needs a dedicated connection to keep everything up to date. You used that, didn't you?"

"Please don't make me say anything. Please, Erick."

"What did you see in your email, Hellie?"

"I can't tell you." She jumps to her feet and stalks away. I let her go. There's no sense in rushing this. "You'll kill him."

I let out a long breath. God, this makes so much sense, and I hate myself for not seeing it sooner. "That's what this is about?" I ask, keeping my tone soft, trying to find a way to put her at ease.

"I know I should hate my dad, okay? I get it, I should despise him for doing what he did and leaving me here to fend for myself. But he's still my dad, and even if I want to write him off, I just can't. I'm not that kind of person. I don't want to be like him. So I can't tell you, because I know what you'll do if you find him, and I can't be a part of that. I just can't."

It all makes sense. Her father reached out to her. That's why she mentioned email—she thought Ren might've faked that too as part of his little plan. But when she realized he hadn't, she kept her mouth shut.

Because her dad's in town and she's protecting him.

"Tell me where he is." I advance on her.

She shakes her head. "I don't know."

"Tell me what he said."

"I can't. And I won't."

"I'll check my computer. I'll hire an IT specialist to dig the email out of memory. You know I can do it."

"Maybe, but that was a week ago, so I doubt it." She looks at me, hands spread. "Please, don't make me a part of killing my own father."

I hold her with my stare, looming over her. Relief fights with anger. She tried to escape, she kept this information about her father's secret—but she wasn't manipulating me the whole time.

Some part of me softens, and a strange kind of hope blossoms.

If she wanted to escape because she was trying to protect her dad somehow—

Then what she said that day was true.

It really wasn't about me.

"We'll talk more later," I say, walking to the door, afraid that if I stay then this feeling will wither and die, and I don't want that. I need to hold on to it for now. "Keep working."

"What are you going to do?"

"I haven't decided yet, but this doesn't change anything. You still need to paint."

"Erick—"

"Don't, Hellie. Not yet. I believe you, but I'm not ready to forgive you."

She turns to her work. "What if I don't want you to forgive me?"

"You do."

"What if I just want you to promise not to kill my dad?"

"We both know that's a promise I can't keep."

"You could try."

"Hellie. He made his choice. It's not only up to me, and there's too much at stake. If I helped your father, and Gallo and Frost found out, the whole city would go to war. It can't happen."

"Right." She lets out a long breath and slowly sinks onto her stool. "He's as good as dead."

"Has been since the day he stole from me. Keep working, Hellie. You're doing great."

I leave. There's no reason to linger. It'll only torture her more.

But now I know her father is definitely in the city, and he contacted his daughter. I don't know why or what he wants, but if I find him first, I can put this together.

I can fix this nightmare, but only if I keep holding on.

Chapter 36

Hellie

Erick's visit leaves me pretty fucked emotionally for the next couple days. I keep expecting him to show up and explain what's happening, but he doesn't bother. Which makes things so much worse. My father's out there somewhere, and I don't know if he's living or dead at this point.

Instead, I resort to begging my stupid, mute guard Tony for information, which doesn't go well.

"Please, pass a message on to Erick, Ren, or Marina. Please ask them for any information about my father."

Tony stares like he doesn't speak English. He's just a giant wall of muscle and zero brains. Or maybe the guy's a genius and knows better than to open his mouth.

"Come on, I know you understand me. Just pass the message along okay? I need to know what's going on."

He grunts. That's the best I'll get. That's basically a full conversation, coming from Tony.

"Great, thanks, nice talking to you."

He grunts again, which I assume is his native tongue for *get back to work* or *I will break your knees*.

I do as I'm told, or as I'm grunted at, even if it's freaking hard. My intense focus seems to fail me as the days drag past.

I'm not sleeping well. Most nights, I stare at the ceiling thinking about Erick, and about my father, and about my life before all this happened. Could I have gone on like that, going to that awful job day after day, getting home too late and exhausted to work on my own art? Barely scraping by, never flourishing, not happy but not sad, just existing.

Sometimes I wonder if this is better.

If Tony actually does what I asked, I don't get any reply— not from Erick, not from Marina, not from Ren. It's still total silence, and I'm expected to paint under these conditions, despite this crippling anxiety.

My father's out there, and Erick knows about it. Right now, the city's crawling with Costa soldiers hunting for any sign of my old man, and there's no way he can stay hidden under these circumstances.

Dad screwed up. I don't know how or why, but he got caught, and if Gallo's men are the ones that saw him, that means everyone knows about it. Gallo has no reason to keep it a secret.

It's a race now. Only a matter of time.

I should've just told Erick what the email said at the beginning, but I couldn't. That little bit of information might've been enough to use against him, and Erick said it himself. My father is not worth saving, not if killing him will avoid a gang war. Showing Erick the email would've been like handing over my dad, and I just couldn't do it.

It's easy calculus for him. But for me, it's agony.

I'm a mess. A total wreck. I paint and paint, and the forgery's coming along on schedule, but whenever I'm not actively working, I'm lying in my room and feeling like shit.

I wish someone would come explain what's going on, but anytime I complain, Tony just glares at me like I'm a hungry mosquito and he's ready to swat me dead.

The big useless bastard.

I keep going. I throw myself into the work like during that first painting and practically spend all day and night in front of the easel. I paint and paint until my hands cramp and I can't paint anymore, but I keep going anyway. My head's spinning, my fingers are chapped and bloody from washing them all the time, and the man and his wife begin to take shape. Light and shadows, black and white.

I obsess over contrasts, over paint colors, over facial expressions. It takes me three whole days to get the wife's nose correct.

But soon, it's nearly complete, and my dread grows with each brush stroke. It takes some effort to identify the feeling, but soon it's clear that I'm afraid to be done, because once I'm done, I won't have anything left to distract me.

Day and night, I'm obsessing. The floor, the chair, the strange map thing hanging on the wall. The frills, the cloaks. The glove dangling from the husband's hand. His pointy little chin hair. Until one morning, I step back after an entire night of doing fine details, my eyes red-rimmed and bloodshot, my hair a mess, paint caking my fingertips, sick from putting on the little finishing touches to make it look as real as possible—emulating brush-strokes, reproducing small mistakes—until I realize there's nothing else to do.

It's like a chasm opens under my feet.

There's a loud knock then the door to my studio opens.

I jump and turn, heart racing.

Erick stands on the threshold. He's carrying a tray with tea and toast. "I brought this. Tony said you haven't slept." He puts it down on the work table and stares at the painting, stopping short. "Is that it? Are you finished?"

I follow his gaze, chewing on my lip. I want to lie and say no, it needs more, but there's nothing else, and I'm sick of keeping things from him. No more lies. No more holding back.

"That's it. I'm done."

"Incredible." He steps up beside me. I'm overwhelmed by his presence and shocked that I can still feel like this, even after everything we've been through. Tall, athletic, muscular. His usual spicy scent makes me dizzy. His eyes squint in concentration, and I love that look, those lips, the small dimple on his chin. Even his thin, scruffy beard. I want him close, I yearn for his nearness, and his heat is like a salve for all my pain.

"I think it's good." I don't know why I'm nervous. "I mean, I hope it's good."

"It's more than good. God, I can't tell the difference." He laughs softly and looks at me. "You're a marvel. You really are."

I pour myself some tea and take a few big sips. "I'm glad you're happy with my work."

My tone seems to knock him back into the room. He shakes his head, turning away from the painting, and meets my gaze.

"Congratulations, Hellie. I am extremely proud of you."

"I thought you hated me. I thought I betrayed you."

"You did. But no, I never hated you. And I realized something over the last few days. I realized you had a good reason for what you did, even if I wish you had gone about it a different way."

"Did you find the email?" I ask, my voice a whisper.

"It took a while, not as long as you thought it would, but yes."

I clutch the teacup tightly. "I'm sorry."

"I understand. You were protecting him. I get it, even if I wish you could've been honest with me."

His tone makes me flinch. "I couldn't tell you. He's my dad."

"Family matters. I understand that."

"It was never about escaping you." No, because I wanted to be with Erick more than anything. It's sick, but I still do.

"I believe you, my devil girl."

I shiver at the nickname. When I first came here, I hated it. Now, hearing that name on his lips again, it's like I'm waking up from a bad dream.

"Now what?" I ask, afraid of the answer, but desperate for something.

He gestures toward the door. "Your father would like to talk to you."

I stare, trying to make sense of the words, but they don't click into my brain, like they're all jumbled up. "My father... wants to speak with me?"

"Yes, he'd like that very much."

"How?"

"He's waiting downstairs."

Then it clicks like a mountain cracking in half.

Dad's here. He's here, in this house, because Erick used the information in that email to find him.

I double over. I drop the tea cup and it crashes onto the floor. Suddenly, my night of no sleep hits me, and I think I might pass out.

He's there. Erick catches me and guides me to a chair. Big, strong hands, a soft, soothing voice. I'm too weak to fight him. I lean forward, face between my knees.

"Did you hurt him?" I whisper.

Erick crouches by my side, one hand on my thigh. "No. I promise. You can ask him yourself."

"Why not? I mean, why didn't you just hand him over? I don't get it."

"You'll see. Come talk to him, Hellie."

"I'm nervous this is another trap." I lift my head, staring into his eyes. He looks so beautiful. So sincere, like he really does give a damn about me.

"No games. No tests. This is just me and you." His fingers dig into my thigh. "I should've believed you from the start. We should have talked about it, and I'm sorry we didn't. But it's okay now. Come downstairs."

"I'm afraid."

"You don't have to be." He stands and holds out a hand. "Come on. Come see your father."

I hesitate, but I take his big palm, and I follow him.

Chapter 37

Hellie

E rick takes me to an empty guest room at the back of the house. It's sparse, simple, with only a big bed and a chair shoved in the corner.

Dad's standing near the window. He's looking outside, his hands folded behind his back. I recognize him from the way he stands with his shoulders square and his chin up like he's taking on the entire world. But the moment he turns around, my hand comes up to my mouth.

He's thin. So much thinner than I've ever seen him. Gaunt, emaciated, his eyes sunken. His hair's gray and short, and his beard's gone wiry and long. His gaze is still sharp and blue, but his hands are gnarled, his knuckles swollen, and his clothes hang off him like they're two sizes too big.

"Hi, honey," he says, smiling broadly. "How are you, Heloise?"

"Dad?" I step into the room. Tears threaten and I struggle against them. Erick remains near the door, watching. "You're seriously here?"

"I'm here." He spreads his arms, as if for a hug, but I don't get closer. He lets his arms drop after an awkward moment. "It's not often a big crime lord like Erick Costa invites me to his home. I couldn't turn him down, you know?" His eyes shine like he knows it wasn't really an invitation.

Dad. After all this time. There he is, standing in the flesh.

I finally rush over and give him a hug. It's so strange, he's all skin and bones, which shocks me. He laughs gently as I pull back and wipe my eyes, the tears finally winning. "Are you hurt?" I ask.

"I'm fine," Dad says, his smile sadder now. Like he's not telling the full truth. "All things considered, Erick's been easy on me."

"He deserved at least a beating," Erick grumbles.

Dad laughs. "That's very true. At least."

"I don't understand what's going on." I look between the two men. "Are you two going to explain? Why are you acting like you're friendly?"

"You can talk." Erick steps through the door. "I'll be nearby if you need me. I can't hear what you're saying, so you'll have to yell."

He shuts the door.

I shake my head in shock, trying to comprehend this situation. Erick has Dad, and Dad stole from Erick, and Dad should be extremely dead—but he's not.

Instead, Dad's standing in this room, and he's alive.

"What's happening?" I ask as he walks over to the bed and sits down with a sigh like it was hard for him to stay on his feet for long. His breathing is labored. He was always in such good shape, and seeing him now, like this, it's disturbing.

"Well, I got caught. Lucky for me, I got caught by Erick, instead of by Gallo or Frost. Those sadistic fucking pricks."

"I'm sorry, that was my fault. I opened your email on his computer—"

He waves that away. "The email was a stupid risk. I was trying to find you in person, but you disappeared, and I heard the rumors about you getting snatched by Erick, and I got desperate."

"I guess the rumors were true. Erick really did pick me up."

"So it seems." He sighs and closes his eyes for a moment as if gathering himself before looking at me again. "Are you okay?"

I laugh, trying to figure out how to answer that. I was drugged and kidnapped and forced to paint, but I'm also the happiest I've ever been, or at least I was before Erick and I got into that ugly fight when I tried to escape. Now

I'm mostly confused and tired, running on no sleep, basically dangling over a chasm.

"It's complicated," I eventually say. "But I'm physically fine."

"Good. That's good." He leans back and looks tired. "I have a lot to tell you."

"Why did you need to meet? Why the hell are you still in Vegas? You should be long gone by now. Everyone assumed you were on some tiny island somewhere hiding out."

"I never left. Running was an option, but it never came to that. The plan went so fucking wrong."

"What plan? Dad, what were you thinking, why would you steal from the casinos? You know what they're going to do to you."

He nods slowly, still smiling, but it's sad now and an ugly dread fills my guts. "Listen, hon. I've known for a while, and I guess I should've told you, but you've always been sensitive. I didn't want you to suffer along with me, you know?"

A horrible, ugly pit opens under my body. I feel like I'm spiraling down into the dark.

"What are you talking about? You know what?"

"Heloise, I've got cancer, and it's the bad kind that doesn't go away."

I don't know what to say. His words pound in my ears. I'm trying to make sense of it as I stare at him in total shock, but suddenly his appearance makes sense.

He looks sick.

It's the worst I've ever seen him, and I've seen my father in some bad states over the years. Drunk, strung out, scared for his life.

But this trumps it all.

"Daddy." I walk over and sit next to him. He puts an arm over my shoulders as I try not to cry. "I'm sorry. I didn't know, I would've helped or done something."

"It's alright, Heloise, it's okay. I made peace with it a while ago. We all gotta die sometime, right? This is my time."

I lean my head on his shoulder. "What kind is it? Is there anything we can do?"

"Started in my lungs, but now it's all over. And no, trust me, I tried. Doctors say I've got a few months left at best, but the way I've been feeling lately, I think they're a little optimistic."

A sob breaks out from my chest. I can't hold it back anymore. The sick irony kills me. I get my father back, only to find out that I'm going to lose him for good.

He holds me while I cry. I wish I could be stronger for him, but it's my dad. He has always loomed large, a massive presence in my memory, immortal and incredible, and he still has that magnetic weight about him even looking like he's half the size he used to be. But his smell is the same, his hands are the same, he's still my father, and he's here right now. Eventually, I get myself under control.

"What I don't get is why you're doing all this," I say after a while of just sitting with each other. "If you're so sick, why wouldn't you spend your last time with me instead of pulling off another job? You don't need the money, right?"

His grin is bitter as he rubs my shoulder. "Here's the thing. That last job, that money, I had this grand idea for what I'd do with it, but I got fucked."

"Fucked how?"

"I don't have a dime, Heloise."

I laugh but he's not kidding and my grin fades away. "Seriously?"

"I had a partner." He grimaces as if something hurts. "I hate working with partners. Still hate it. But I needed one for this job, because I was too sick to pull it off alone." He pauses to catch his breath and I'm caught between hating him for doing something so stupid and loving him so fiercely it breaks my ribs. "He took everything. Screwed me hard and left. He knew I couldn't do anything to stop him, not in this state, and he didn't give a damn. Rob an old cancer patient? That's just another Tuesday for a guy dumb enough to go up against the casinos."

"Dad. You're a thief too, remember. You're just as dumb."

"Right. But I'm a thief with morals."

"You stole from my high school science teacher. Remember that? You took his wallet during a parent-teacher conference."

"Did I get away with it? I don't remember that at all."

"No, you got caught. And you don't remember because of all the pills you were on that time."

He smiles fondly. "I could use some of those about now."

"Dad."

"Right, I get your point, but *my* point is this. I have no money, Heloise. I can't pay back Erick and the other two even if I wanted, which I really don't, because fuck those rich bastards. They're still fine, aren't they? I don't see them fucking suffering."

"Dad."

"Okay, I'm staying on track." He takes a deep, rattling breath, and I imagine I can hear the sickness inside his lungs. It's ugly, crinkling like tissue paper. "I can't hand my partner's identity over. That's another problem. Because once I do that, I don't have any leverage anymore, and anyway, I don't know where he's hiding. All I've got are guesses and they might all be wrong."

"You can make a deal." I glance over toward the door. Erick said he's not eavesdropping, but I can't help but wonder. "He'll listen to me. I can negotiate something for you."

"There's no way the other two are gonna listen. Costa might go for that though. So far, he's been shockingly soft on me, which I guess is your doing." Dad's lips press together. "What's the deal with that?"

"Complicated," I say, feeling uncomfortable. My dad's never been shy about boy stuff but still, it's a little weird. "But he really will listen to me if you want me to talk to him."

"Frost and Gallo are the real problem. Even if Costa cuts me some slack because of your *complicated* relationship, the other two sure as hell won't. I'm in a bad spot, my girl."

I nod slowly, staring at him. "Why did you email me? Why did you reach out to begin with? You might still be hiding if you hadn't."

He laughs, coughs, laughs again. "Desperation."

"You never do anything when you're desperate. That's one of your rules, remember?"

"I'm dying, sweetheart, and some part of me wanted to be with my daughter one last time. Rules don't matter in the end. I figured, I'm screwed anyway, I might as well try to see if I can't be screwed and with the only person that ever gave a damn about me."

"Dad—"

He holds up a hand, his face serious. "No, listen to me, because I don't know if I'll ever get a chance to say this again. You were the best part of my life, kid. I really mean that. I've done a lot of bad shit as you're well aware, but spending time with you always made me feel like a better man, and if I've got any regrets, it's not being around you more especially when you were little. I'm sorry I was a shit dad and a generally awful person, but I do love you. I always loved you, Heloise."

He gets me crying again, the asshole. I hug him, and mumble how I love him too and he wasn't so bad, but we both know it's not true. He really was a terrible father, barely around, barely involved, and half the time too fucked up or into his own problems to pay attention.

But there are those glorious days still burned into my memory. The days where he taught me things, where he showed me how to spot a mark in a crowd, how to catch the eye of the pickpockets, how to stand at a craps table and laugh at the dice, how to live, how to be bold and big and loud. That was my daddy—a glowing monstrosity, a black hole, a diamond. Even mixed in with all the bad things, I still see him like a brightness in my mind. It hurts, that light, hurts me all the time, but I'd never give it up for anything.

"Alright, I'll talk to Erick." I wipe my eyes with my sleeve. "You don't have to say anything else, okay? I'll see what he thinks and we'll go from there."

"Sure, Heloise, sure. But can you promise you'll be back? Before the end, I mean."

"Dad—"

"No, don't get upset, I just mean I want to spend a little more time with you. Hear about what you've been up to this last year."

"Yeah, okay, I promise I'll be back. I won't be gone long, okay?"

"Good." He grins and squeezes my hand. "Love you. Hey, come on, what'd I teach you about crying?"

"Don't ever do it?"

"Nah. I taught you crying's great for getting out of trouble, but always be in control of it. Remember?"

"I remember. You made me cry in front of cops when I was six years old so they'd let us walk away when you had a bunch of stolen cash in your back pocket."

"Damn right I did, and you were amazing, kid." He kisses my hair. "Get going before you start bawling your eyes out again." I notice that his eyes are wet too, and I wonder if I finally touched something in the cold con man's heart, but I doubt it. Danny Accardi only ever cries when there's some benefit to it, and there's no benefit now.

I get up and walk to the door, glancing back only once. My skinny father still fills the room.

Chapter 38

Hellie

"I don't want you to kill him." It's not the best way to open a negotiation, but it's true.

Erick paces across his room. I'm sitting at the end of his bed, watching him. This is the only place he says we're safe to talk freely, and I wonder who he thinks is listening.

"I'm sure you don't."

"How do we keep him alive?"

"According to him, he doesn't have much time left anyway."

"You know what Gallo and Frost will do to him. Either he can spend his last days here with his daughter or we can turn him over and those two will come up with some terrible way to kill him painfully and slowly." I spread my hands, feeling desperate and sick. "There's got to be some way."

"Sure, there's a way. He can give back the money then shoot himself in the head."

I glare and get to my feet. "Why are you being an asshole?"

"Because your father's got some game going and I don't know what his play is, but you're falling for it."

I scoff, staring like Erick's lost his mind. "I get why you think that, but my father can't fake the way he looks. Seriously, Erick, go down there and just *look* at him. He's sick."

"Maybe, but we have a serious problem. The fact that I brought him here and haven't told Gallo and Frost yet is damning enough. Keeping him alive any longer than necessary is begging for a war."

"Why can't you hide him here? Nobody would ever know, and he can have peaceful final days."

His face twists, and I can tell the idea of letting my father live is distasteful to him.

"Sooner or later, word will get out, and do you have any idea what Gallo and Frost will do if they learn I have both you and your dad? They'll start killing people, that's what. It'll be very, very bad."

"I can keep painting. I'll paint every single day, as many paintings as they want." I'm desperate and I know this isn't a real solution, but I'm trying to come up with anything that might work.

"I won't let you do that." He stops, his voice softening. "Hellie, listen to me. Your father knew what he was doing when he stole from us. He understood, and he got fucked in the process. I don't feel sorry for him, and I don't feel any pity. I hate how it's hurting you, but I don't see how there's a good solution here."

I throw my hands up in frustration and turn away. I finally got my father back after a year of barely seeing him, after weeks of wondering if he had abandoned me for dead, after days of worrying he'd get caught by the wrong people—he's finally here, in the flesh, and it doesn't matter.

He's still going to die.

"It isn't fair," I say, feeling like a stupid little kid. Power-less and tiny.

"I know. You're right." Erick's voice is closer, like he's standing only a few inches behind me. I shiver but don't turn around. "I'm sorry, devil girl, I really am. I can give you a couple days with him if you want, but after that, I have to tell the others."

"Two days." I take a deep breath and turn around. He's there, my Erick, my big man, looming, his lips pressed into a deep frown. "We can come up with a solution in two days. A way to save everyone."

"Hellie—"

"We can at least try. I know it's unlikely. I know it's pathetic. But I can't help myself."

He sighs and nods slowly. "Alright. Two days. This is against my better judgment. I want him dead as much as Frost and Gallo do, but I care about you more than I care about your worthless father. We'll try to come up with a solution, but if we can't think of anything that could actually work, I have to talk to Frost and Gallo."

"Fine. Okay. I can work with that."

He doesn't move. He remains so close, staring down at me with this piercing, probing expression, like he's trying to see inside of me, trying to see deep into my body. I look back and shiver, feeling like I'm tingling from head to toe. I've missed this—missed his body, his stare, his desire.

"I want to give you everything, Hellie." He's speaking quietly, and he comes closer. I don't try to run away. I don't want to move—I want his hands on me so desperately it hurts. "I don't want to kill your father, even though he deserves it. Because of you. Do you know how many men I've shown mercy to over the years?"

"I'm guessing single digits."

"Try none. I've never shown mercy to a thief, no matter what, regardless of their reasons. Your father is the first I've ever considered saving."

"I should be honored."

"You should." His hand comes up. I whimper as his touch tingles against my cheek. "I missed you."

"I missed you too." I stare into his eyes. "You're not angry anymore? That I tried to run away?"

"You were going to see your father."

"Yes, I was."

"Did you mean what you said before? Everything you said?"

I grab the hand on my cheek and lean into it. "Yes," I say. "I meant it. I still mean it."

"I meant it too. I feel things for you I never planned. Things I didn't think I was capable of feeling, and it has me ruined, Hellie. But I like it."

"I like it too."

"Where do we go from here?"

I kiss his fingers. I pull him closer, kiss his wrist, his forearm, and he moves down, bringing his lips to mine, wrapping his arms around me.

"I don't know, and I don't care. Right now, I just want this."

Our mouths touch. Softly at first, then harder, then so deeply his tongue invades my mouth and I'm all his, he's all mine, and everything rights itself. His taste, his smell, the feeling of his warmth, all of him.

I tumble into that kiss. I groan as he moves me back to the bed, pushes me down, kisses my neck. His words are honey, sticky and lovely, as he takes off my top, his hands on my chest, on my hips, tugging off my sweats. I arch my back, let him undress me. He does it slowly, worshipping as he goes along.

"I missed these hips, this skin, the way you gasp when I touch you right here." He kisses my hip bone and I whimper, biting my lip. "I missed your mouth, your tongue, your stiff, pink nipples." He moves up, sucks one, licks and bites it, and I tug at his hair. He sighs, smiling as he rolls his tongue around my sensitive areola. "I missed the way you grab my hair when you're feeling overwhelmed. I missed overwhelming you, my devil girl."

He moves down between my legs. I groan as he kisses my inner thigh, licking up and up, toward my soaking, burning core, and he doesn't stop. No more teasing, no more taking it slow. He shoves my panties aside, tongues me from top to bottom, rolling his stiffened tongue around my clit.

"I missed your taste," he says, growling as he laps me up. His fingers slide inside my pussy and I'm breathing hard. "I missed making you feel good, Hellie, god, I missed that so much."

"I missed you too," I manage to say even though my brain's currently melting into a puddle of goo inside my skull. "I missed you so much."

"I refuse to leave again and I refuse to let you go. Can I keep you, Hellie?" His fingers slide deeper, fucking me in and out. "Can I have you?"

"If you keep doing that, yes, you can have all you want."

He chuckles, sensual and gorgeous. He licks my clit, fucks me with his fingers, going faster. I grab his hair and hold on, moaning his name, overwhelmed, exhausted, terrified, more turned on than I've ever been in my life, and he doesn't stop. The beast, the monster, my kidnapper, my everything, he licks, sucks, slides his fingers in and out until I'm twitching, moaning, back arching, coming with his name on my lips. I come hard, groaning, and sprawl back when he's finished.

A thin sheen of sweat covers my skin. He stands back and undresses.

I watch him do it, at a loss for words. Eyes unfocused, a lazy smile on my lips.

Muscular chest, rounded and defined. Stacked abs that continue on forever, down into that lovely sharp V of his pelvis and his hip bones, his waist tapered, his ass tight and muscular. His tight thighs, ripped and thick, and calves rounded and lean. Everything about him, from fingers to his shoulders, screams sex. He crawls into bed, and even though I try to scurry away, playfully making my escape, he catches me and pins me down on my belly.

"Lovely devil girl," he whispers as he kneads my ass. His hands move between my legs, cupping my pussy. "This is mine now. I'm staking my claim."

"Is that your psychotic way of asking me out?"

"I don't ask."

"Now you're getting all macho and controlling?"

"Hellie, I swear, I'll lock you in that studio for another week until you're begging to suck my cock if I have to."

B. B. Hamel

"Oh, honey, tempt me with a good time, go ahead."

He laughs, bites my shoulder, and spanks my ass hard. I gasp, back arching, a purr escaping my lips. "Fuck you, asshole."

"Don't act like you hate it." His hand cups my pussy again. "Now say it's mine."

"Uh-uh, no thanks."

Another spank. Harder this time. I moan, sensitive skin tingling.

"Say it." He cups my pussy. I'm so wet I could scream.

"Nope."

Another spank. Another cup, holding tighter. This time, I grind my hips into his hand.

"Say it, Hellie. You're mine. This pussy's mine. No matter what."

"Give you license to do whatever you want? I know better than that."

"You're going to kill me, girl." He spanks me once, twice, three times. I let out a sharp yelp, but that hand's back, this time rubbing slowly. I work my hips, grinding harder, and fuck, it feels so good.

"Seems like you're going to kill me first," I say, breathing hard, "with all this spanking."

"If I wanted to break you, I would. No, you just like it when I get you real close, right up to that edge, and then—"

Another spank. I gasp as he pulls my hair and lifts my hips into the air—

His cock presses against my dripping entrance, bare and slick for him, and he slides inside me.

Fuck, that stings, it stretches, and it feels so fucking good I could scream. I am screaming—moaning his name.

He fills me. Goes deep, right to the edge. One hand on my hair, the other on my hips, my face down in the sheets. He keeps me there, and I rock slightly, slowly, wanting him to fuck me so badly it kills.

"Say you're mine," he commands. "Or I will keep you right there. I'll spank you raw and red with my cock filling your tight little cunt and I'll call you all sorts of nasty names until you finally give in."

"What kind of nasty names?"

"First, I'll call you my dirty little slut."

"Oh," I say, whimpering as I try to move my hips, but he holds me in position. "That's very mean."

"I'll call you my soaking, dripping wet little cunt."

"Filthy. You're a bad man."

"No, darling. You are the filthy wet slut that loves to suck my cock, that loves to ride my shaft, that wants to do nothing but grind her little cunt up and down my body. You, lovely girl, are filthy."

"You make that sound like a bad thing, but I think you like it."

His hand tightens in my hair. I'm trying to grind into him but he won't let me move. It's driving me insane, this need for friction.

"You're my little fuck toy. Do you understand? I want you in my bed, every day, your legs spread and wet, waiting to be filled. I'll come in your pussy, in your mouth, all over your lovely tits, and you'll thank me for it. I'll spank you until you scream, until you're dripping, and I'll make you lick your own pussy from my fingers while I fill you to the brim. Do you want that, dirty girl?"

"Yes," I say, losing my fucking mind.

"Good. Tell me you're mine."

"I'm yours," I moan, knowing I've lost but not giving a damn. "I'm all yours, Erick, please—"

He slams into me once. I gasp, crying out. He slams again, again, fucks me, reaches around to rub my clit with his fingers as we start to grind into each other, and I'm gone, totally lost, exploding into him as he takes me. Hands on my breasts, in my hair, fingers in my mouth, making me taste myself as he fucks me faster, takes me like a monster. He feels so good, and yes, god, yes, I'm his toy, his slut, his dirty girl, his filthy Hellie, and I want him to fuck me until I'm nothing more than bliss. He gives me more, gives me every inch of him, hammers me into the bed until I come, fuck, I come so hard I'm gasping into the sheets unable to form words anymore. He growls in my ears, more beast than man, both of us sweating, and pulls back once my orgasm passes. He turns me, slides his cock in my mouth, makes me suck him and lick him, until he finally finishes on my tongue. I swallow him, every drop.

We're a heap of bodies on the bed. I'm breathing hard and barely conscious. He pulls me against him and holds me tight. "I missed you," he whispers.

"You missed fucking me."

"I absolutely did, you're right. But I missed you too. And I'm glad you finally said it."

"Does it count? If you tortured it out of me?"

"Oh, it counts even more."

I'm grinning to myself, eyes fluttering shut. I've barely slept over the last day, and after that, I'm basically out of energy.

"You're right, it counts."

"All mine," he whispers, kissing my neck, and I nuzzle in closer to feel his warmth and let myself drift.

Chapter 39

Erick

I watch Hellie sleep for a while. She's exhausted and she needs rest, which is why I'm quiet when I slip out of bed. I shower, clean myself off, and get dressed before heading to the back of the house. Tony's standing guard and he grunts once, his way of saying everything's as it should be. I dismiss him, knock, and step into the room.

Hellie's father is right where we left him. He's sitting in the chair now, paging through some random thriller novel that he found somewhere. Probably hidden away in a drawer from years earlier. He looks up and lowers the book.

"Mr. Costa," he says. "I was waiting for you to show up."

"Danny." I remain standing, and he doesn't move. "Your daughter doesn't want me to kill you. I'm not sure I have much of a choice in the matter. What do you think?"

He laughs. The bastard seems delighted as he tosses the book onto the bed. "We always have choices, Costa. You just have to think them through."

"From my perspective, you made your decision already. You committed suicide the second you chose to go through with your plan to rob me, Frost and Gallo. If we're talking about thinking things through, your plan seems very short-sighted."

"I can see why you might think that."

"Did you really imagine you'd pull it off?"

"I did." He smirks at me, the arrogant bastard. I don't know what Hellie sees in him, but this is her father. We're blind to our family sometimes, a problem I can see in myself. "But here we are."

I step closer. "What really happened?"

"I don't know what you mean."

"You claim your partner backstabbed you, but I don't buy it. You're a con man, Danny. You always have an angle. What really happened?"

"I'm a sick old man now and my days of playing every side are long gone."

I don't believe him. It'd be stupid to think anything that comes out of this man's mouth remotely resembles truth, but I don't have much of a choice at the moment. Hellie cares about him, which means I'm stuck.

"I need information. If you want a shot at breathing past the next two days, I need everything you can tell me about where the money's at."

"Can't do it. The second I tell you, all my leverage is gone. Sorry, Erick, but we need a deal first."

"Here's the deal. You tell me everything. Names, dates, addresses, bank account numbers, everything you can about you and your partner's little heist. Then I let you live here for a couple days, and we hope Hellie comes up with a way to save your ass from Frost and Gallo. That's my only offer. Take it or I'll end this stupid little game and kill you myself."

Danny considers. There's nothing to think about though. I'm not bluffing—Hellie will be upset, but she'll get over it one day, and I despise this guy on multiple levels. He was a shit dad to Hellie, and he fucking stole from me. It takes all my willpower not to strangle him right here.

"She really is special, isn't it?" Danny smiles as he looks away toward the window. "Even when she was little, she was always so damn smart."

"I gotta wonder how a girl like her came from a piece of shit like you."

"Probably got most of her mother's good genes. And she was raised by her grandmom, a really fantastic person. Honestly, Heloise is lucky I wasn't in her life more than I was. I probably would've fucked her up."

"More than you already did."

He grimaces but doesn't argue. "Alright. I'll tell you some things, but not everything. I need to hold a few key bits back. You understand."

"Fine. I'll send in my partner, Ren. He'll get it all sorted."

"Great." Danny looks back, considering his next words. "It's not an act, is it? You're not trying to pull something over on me, are you? The great Erick Costa is in love with my daughter."

"Yes, I am very much in love with Hellie, but she's not your anything. You're just the scum that brought her into the world. I'm the man that'll take care of her."

"I hope so." He's smiling huge now, which pisses me off. "I really do."

I leave the room. Fuck him. I got what I wanted, and if I stay any longer I'm afraid I'll hurt the guy, which won't be good for anyone. I head downstairs and find Ren in the kitchen eating my Bolognese with a bit of good red wine.

I sit across from him. Marina brings me a helping. "Smells like heaven," I say and she pats my shoulder.

I eat and drink. Ren doesn't say anything. We go on like that in silence for a few minutes, and I do my best to focus on the meal, but there's too much left unsaid, and I'm sick of not saying shit. Everything's complicated when I keep my mouth shut.

"I was too hard on you." I grunt the words out. I'm not a fan of being wrong, much less of apologizing.

"Were you? Hadn't noticed."

"Don't be a prick." I jab my fork in his direction. "You still fucked up."

"I know."

"Alright. We good?"

He laughs, shaking his head. "Look, Erick. I've known you for a while. You're my best friend and I realize that's pretty much the best I'm going to get in terms of a resolution, but seriously, you're crazy as hell."

"I know." I shovel some pasta in my mouth, chew, swallow, take a big gulp of wine. "Food's good."

"Really good," he agrees.

"I've got Danny Accardi upstairs still. He says he's got information about the money he stole. He's got a partner somewhere, but I can't be sure where the guy's hiding or who he is. I want you to take everything he's offering and run with it."

"Understood."

"Hunt down anyone involved. Bring them all in. Accardi wasn't alone, and I doubt it was only one guy helping."

"Wide net?"

"Wide as you can get it. Full autonomy. Do what you got to do and let me worry about cleaning up the mess."

"Understood." Ren finishes his wine and shoves back from the table. "Glad we're back, bro."

"Yeah, alright, don't start crying on me." I say it with a smile and he laughs as he walks away, hands in his pockets, ready to do his job.

I go back to eating. Hellie's on my mind. I want to get back in that bed so badly it hurts, but I'm starving. Marina comes over, refills my glass, and gives me another small helping. Before she walks back to the stove, she bends down and kisses my cheek. "Good man," she says, patting my shoulder. "Very good man."

"Ah, get out of here," I say, not looking at her, but I can feel her smiling as she walks off.

Chapter 40

Hellie

I sit on the back porch with Dad. It's early in the morning and not too hot yet. The overhead fan spins lazily, and the sun reflects off the rocks, stretching out into the desert. Dad drinks coffee and stretches his legs. I sip tea, cupped in both hands, enjoying the comfort and the warmth.

It's beautiful, and I don't want to ruin it by talking, but we've been silent for a half hour and there's too much to say. I'm afraid I'm running out of time.

"It's beautiful." I glance at him, gauging his response. He smiles and nods.

"Gorgeous. Makes you wonder."

"Yeah? Wonder what?"

"What's out there. All the stuff we're missing. It's a big world, honey. You can spread yourself out a bit, you know."

My eyebrows raise. "Is that your sideways attempt at commenting on my relationship with Erick?"

"Nah. Never."

"Dad."

"Alright. You want me to be straight?"

"Please, go ahead."

"The guy's a criminal. You could do better."

I laugh and punch his arm. "Coming from you?"

"I know, but hey, takes one to know one. But in this case, Costa's on a different level. His family, they're like an octopus with tentacles big enough to cover the whole ocean. Do you understand what you'd be signing up for if you really got into his life? It's not just this house, hon."

"I have a vague idea," I admit, looking out at the landscape. I can picture wealth, power, danger. Though all I want is this place, the art studio, and my gorgeous husband in my bed. "It's hard to imagine, all that other stuff."

"Just think about it, that's all. Don't get drowned by him. Don't get sucked in too deep."

"You worried about me?"

"Yeah. I am."

"Funny coming from the guy that abandoned me to these people." I try to say it lightly, but the bitterness comes out anyway.

Dad's silent for a minute. His lips are pressed tight and his eyebrows are knitted down. It's his thinking face.

"I get why you think that, but it wasn't my intention." He speaks slowly like he wants to be sure he's understood.

"I'm sure. You didn't consider what would happen to me when you bailed, did you?"

"I had contingency plans. I had ideas." He leans his head back and sighs. "Alright, if I'm honest, I fucked up."

"There you go. I'm glad you said it." I take a sip of tea, not used to this version of my father—he's never been able to admit to his mistakes in the past.

"I'm sorry, Heloise. I didn't know they'd go for you, but I should have."

I consider my father. He's sunken, and shrinking every day, pieces of him disappearing. Soon, there won't be any of him left. "You've always been that way. Only thinking about yourself, never planning for anyone else. I've known you long enough that I'm used to it by now, but it still hurts."

"I'm sorry, Heloise. I really am. But I'm here now, and I want to do right by you."

"Only because you have to be here. Anywhere else, and you'd be dead."

Another grimace, and he goes quiet. I take a few breaths to calm myself. Getting mad at him won't help, and I don't want to spend our last days together pissed off. This isn't fixing anything.

My dad's an asshole. He's a piece of shit, most of the time.

But he's still my dad, and he's dying, so I might as well get over it. I said what I wanted to say, stood up for myself a little bit, and now I can move on.

Dad clears his throat and looks at his fingernails. "My partner's name is Saul White. That's the one bit of information I held back from Costa. My partner's actual name."

"Oh." I tilt my head, frowning. "Why are you telling me?"

"You can choose what to do with it. Tell Costa, keep it to yourself, I don't care. It's yours now. I'm done. That's all I have left to give you."

I chew my lip. Dad's always got another angle, but I can't read this one. Maybe just trying to make peace between us, I don't know.

"We want to help you. At least, I want to help you, and Erick's going along with what I need for a while."

"You two really care about each other, huh? This isn't some Stockholm syndrome thing?"

I laugh, unable to help it. "I mean, it might be that, or it might've started out that way. But no, it's real."

"You're happy?"

"Yeah, Dad, I'm happy here. I'm happy with him. He appreciates me and he loves my art. It's kind of amazing."

"Good. That's really good."

"I don't know what'll happen between him and me, I really don't, but I feel like I've been too scared to take real chances my whole life. You know what I mean? I watched you do nothing but take risks, and it sort of scared me into being good."

"Probably for the best. My life hasn't been all that amazing, if I'm honest. Lots of pain, lots of hurt people."

"True, but I think I went too far. I was hiding at that paint and sip place, working for crappy money, barely creating art for myself because I was just too scared of failure. But I'm not scared of it anymore."

He nods and looks content. "I'm happy then. Sounds like you're in the right place."

"You did the right thing too, reaching out to me."

"At least it gave us a little time to say goodbye, huh?"

"Sure, Dad. I'm glad we got that."

"Me, too, hon. Me too."

We lapse into silence. I sit with my father, staring at the landscape, finishing my lukewarm tea, feeling sad, angry, strange, but comfortable. It's good, having him here, and it's good to talk about Erick with someone. I've kept that all to myself, and now it's out in the world, which is a strange relief.

I don't know how I feel about my father, and I don't know how to save him. If there's anything I could do to give him more time, to let him die on his own terms, I'd do it. Even if that meant painting another dozen forgeries, even if it means giving up a piece of myself, I'd make it happen.

But I can't think of any way to save him. Not without causing a war.

It's awful, but I try to push it from my mind. I try to be present, with him, enjoying what we have left. Even if my dad was an awful father and was nothing but trouble, I still love him, despite everything. He tried, in his own twisted way, he really did try.

"Hey, Dad? I love you."

"Love you too, kid. And I really am sorry for all this."

"Yeah, I know. It's okay. I mean, it's not, but I'm in a forgiving mood."

"Lucky me."

Another comfortable silence before he starts to reminisce about the old days. About the time she took me around the Strip, through the casinos. We talk and tell old stories and I make him laugh so hard he nearly coughs up a lung, and then we talk some more. I'm grinning and crying by the time Erick appears behind us.

"Mind if I borrow her for a few minutes? It's important."

"Please, go ahead," Dad says with a sigh. "I could use a break. Hell, I could use a nap."

"You sure?" I ask, looking at Erick, who stares back with a serious intensity.

"Positive. Go on, talk to him. I'll be around." Dad leans back in his chair and I get to my feet.

Chapter 41

Erick

"I hate taking you away from your dad, but I don't want this to wait much longer." I lead Hellie away from the back yard and toward the garage. "This is something I've been thinking about a lot lately, and I think it's past time."

"Sorry, are you about to change my oil or something? Why are we going into the garage?"

"You'll see." I open the door and step down. The lights come on, and I take Hellie's hand and gesture toward the truck parked in the last spot.

She walks over. It's a smaller, black, four-wheel-drive. Good in the desert, and brand new. "It's nice," she says. "But so what? You got a new truck."

"This is yours." I dangle the keys from my finger. "Hellie, you're free."

She frowns at the truck then frowns at the keys and finally shakes her head. "Sorry, is this some kind of trick?"

"No trick. You're free. There's no reason to keep you captive anymore, and hell, you haven't been a real captive in a while."

"Except for that time I tried to run away and you got really pissed."

"Okay, good point, but I'm ready to move past that now."

She chews her lip, thinking, and walks around the perimeter of the truck. "This is really mine?"

"Yes, it's really yours. I'll have Marina take you down the path tomorrow. There are some tricky spots, so you'd better only leave and come back during daylight, but once you know all the twists and turns, you'll be fine."

"I can leave whenever I want?"

"Whenever you want." Which feels strange to say but it's true. I'm not keeping her captive anymore. I'd like to lock her away in my room and never let her go but that's not a reasonable way to have a relationship.

And I'm ready for something more with her.

Something real, something not contingent on keeping her locked up in the studio painting until her arms fall off.

"I'm having trouble making sense of this. Why now, why all of a sudden?"

"You know why." I walk to her, forcing her to back up until she bumps into the truck's bumper. "Hellie, it's time I stopped pretending like I own you. I don't even want that anymore. I want this to be real, and it can't be anything more than a fantasy unless you're free to make your own choices."

"Which means you're giving me a truck?"

"It's more what the truck represents, but yes, I'm giving you a truck."

She takes a slow, deep breath, and blows it out with a laugh. "Thank you."

"You're welcome."

"Seriously, I mean it. I probably would've been content staying here forever, living in that studio, eating whatever Marina cooks, but now you're reminding me that there's a world outside this place."

My guts twist. I don't want her to leave. The truck's there because without it, we can't have an actual relationship—and I want that with her—but the idea of her using it, of her driving back to the Strip or deep into town, scares the hell out of me.

I don't know what Gallo or Frost might do to her.

But at this point, I can keep her safe. I'll post guards, make sure she's watched and protected at all times if it comes down to that. And if she leaves, decides she doesn't want this with me, then I'll still make sure nobody touches her. That's the least I can do.

"If I'm honest, that's what I want too. I want you to stay here forever, paint as much as you like, sleep with you at night, see you in the mornings. I want you around all the time, but that's not how relationships really work, right? You can't be a prisoner, and now it's time to get rid of the bars and the gates, and let you go free."

She tilts her chin up to me and leans forward, pressing herself against my chest. I bend down and kiss her gently. God, this girl tastes like heaven, and I'll never get enough of those lips.

"That means a lot." She blinks a few times like she's trying not to cry. "Can I admit something?"

"Go ahead."

"It never really occurred to me that we'd get here. I sort of figured we'd just, you know, keep on going."

"I want to be with you, Hellie. I want you to be mine."

"But what does that mean?"

"My partner. My everything. I'd say girlfriend, but the word feels so inadequate."

"I understand." She's talking quietly and looking at me through those long lashes of hers. "You're sure about this?"

"I'm very sure."

"You're not going to yell and stomp around if I drive into town?"

"I might yell, but I never stomp."

"Sure you don't." Her palms press against my chest. "I want to be your partner too."

A thrill of excitement runs through me. Why is this so hard? Why can't I just tell her what I think, how I feel? I kiss her, hold it longer this time, and lean in to whisper in her ear.

"I love you, Hellie. I am very much in love with you, and now that you're free, it only makes me love you more."

She kisses me harder. Her tongue in my mouth, her taste on my lips, fuck, yes, she's everything I've always wanted, and so much I never knew could feel this right.

"I love you too," she says once the kiss breaks apart.

Those words light up every nerve in my body. It's like I'm burning for her, glowing with need. It's crazy, this feeling, this overwhelming want, but I can't stop myself. I run my hand through her hair, grip it, fist hard, and kiss her tight until she whimpers into my mouth.

"All mine," I say with a growl.

She grins, nodding slowly. "All yours."

"We'll make this public. I'll make sure Gallo, Frost, and all the other casino owners understand that you are officially off-limits."

"What a gentleman."

"You'll have to meet my family." I scowl a bit at the idea. "My brothers especially."

"I'd like that."

"I'm not sure that's true. I have three, and they're all assholes. Especially Conlan."

"I want to know everything there is to know about you. I want to be a part of your life, even if that means meeting your asshole brothers."

I laugh and hug her against me. So warm and soft, so perfect. "Alright, devil girl. We can really do this."

"There's only one thing." She pulls back, searching my face. "My dad."

"Your dad."

"What can you do for him?"

I shake my head slowly. "I don't know yet, but will you trust me if I say I'm working on it? You may not like the way things play out."

"I trust you," she says and kisses me gently. "Just please, help him if you can."

"For you, I'll do absolutely anything."

I hold her like that for a while longer. She stays in my arms, content, breathing deep and slow, but eventually I release her. She kisses me then goes to spend more time with her father, since the days are short, and he doesn't have many left. I don't know how I'll keep him a secret from Frost and Gallo, but I meant what I said—

I'll do anything for that girl.

No matter how distasteful. I can stomach sparing her father if it'll make her happy—and it helps knowing that he won't live long anyway.

I pat the back of the truck before heading inside.

Chapter 42

Hellie

D ad and I have a strangely normal afternoon considering he's dying and I was just freed. The idea of having my own truck feels bizarre, but the weight of the keys in my pocket keeps reminding me that it's real.

Everything is real.

We have dinner with Erick. He's on his best behavior, although I can tell he'd rather kick my dad in the face than have polite conversation. We listen to Dad tell stories about his conning days, and Erick even laughs a few times, before Dad finally excuses himself for bed. "I'm old and sick and can't hang like I used to. Love you, kiddo. And thank you for not putting a bullet in my head, Erick."

"Goodnight, Dad." I hug him and see him off.

Erick grunts at me and puts an arm over my shoulders. "He's charming."

"He'd better be, considering his occupation." I smack Erick's chest. "Come on, I want to do a little work."

"Work? On what? You finished the painting."

"On another painting I've had rattling around my head for a while." I lead him upstairs and into the studio. He stands awkwardly as I arrange the space, getting the lighting just right, and place a chair next to the window, black with night-time dark. "Sit down and don't move."

"You're going to paint me?" He seems surprised by that.

"Who else would I paint? Sit down."

"I don't know." He hesitates, not moving. "You're not going to ask me to strip, are you?"

"Not yet, but if you don't do what I say then we just might turn this into a nude."

He smirks at me but he perches in the chair. "If only you could be so lucky. My cock wouldn't fit on the canvas, it's much too big."

I roll my eyes. "You're a disgusting man, Erick Costa."

"And you love it. What am I supposed to be doing here?" He puts a fist under his chin. "Should I look pensive and deep?"

"No, please don't."

"How about strong?" He sits up straight, arms over his chest, puffing himself up.

"Even worse. Just sit."

"I don't know how to just sit now that I'm thinking about it."

"Fine, then don't think."

"How am I supposed to not think about thinking?"

I set up my canvas and my easel and start picking out paints. I lean towards blues, cool colors, sharp ones.

"Why don't you tell me a story while I work?"

"I'm not much of a storyteller."

"Yes, I'm aware. How about you tell me about the first time you came to Vegas? You're not from here, right?"

He smiles, glancing away, and that's the look I want to capture. I sketch it as fast as I can before it disappears.

"No, I'm not from here. I was born and raised in Jersey. Casinos are in my blood, in the Costa family. My father built our empire, turned it into a massive operation, and now we have hotels all over the world, from California to London. When Dad passed, my older brother Adler took over as the Don of our family, and the rest of us took a piece of the empire."

"Don is the leader, right? That's like a mafia thing?"

"Yes, it's a mafia thing. You watch movies, right?"

"*The Godfather* is basically all I know about mob stuff."

"That's not a bad way to think about it, except we're more like a business these days. We have our illegal operations still, but the casinos and the legitimate businesses are extremely profitable to the point that the illegal stuff is more of a liability than anything else. Adler's been slowly phasing it out, although that's difficult, since the family's bigger than just the Costas. We have soldiers, captains, lieutenants, dozens of associates, and they're all pushing their own agendas."

"Sounds like a lot."

"It's a lot," he agrees, leaning back in his chair. His relaxed posture is so masculine and powerful, like he can sit there and own the room without even trying. It's impressive, this aura he has, and I try to capture that in quick brush strokes.

"Are you nervous about bringing me into all that? My dad warned me about it, you know."

"He was right to." Erick's voice softens and his gaze goes distant. "If I had my way, you'd stay here in the desert house and never get anywhere near the Costa family, but that isn't reasonable. You're smart, talented, and beautiful, and I'm not concerned about you fitting in, but yes, some aspects of your life might be dangerous."

"You mean, someone might grab me off the street and drug me?"

"Yes, exactly."

"Been there, done that."

"Good. I'm glad you're already hardened to it." He's silent for a moment. I focus on his jaw, on his lips, on his eyes. The background is all darkness, shades of blue so dark it's nearly black. He's the only bit of light on the canvas.

"Tell me something nice now. You're getting too tense."

"Yeah? What's nice?"

"Tell me how you want to fuck me tonight."

His eyebrows raise. "You want me to talk dirty to you while you're painting me? You don't get much work finished if we go down that road."

"Very good point. Maybe I shouldn't rile you up."

"Too late, devil girl."

I grin at him and he smirks back, but at least his shoulders drop and his hands stop clenching the armrests. "Think you can hold that pose for, I don't know, an hour?"

"Doubtful. I'm having some very filthy thoughts, Hellie. I don't think I can sit still for much longer."

"Try. Have some self-control."

"No, self-control is for weaker men."

"Oh, now you're a big, strong bad boy, huh?"

"Damn right, and don't forget it."

I laugh, making more fast marks on the canvas. "I like it when you look at me like that."

"Like what?"

"Like you're going to get up, walk over here, grab me by my hair, drag me into your bed, and fuck me senseless. It's a very nice look."

"I bet you like it. When did you get so dirty, devil girl? I feel like I've corrupted you."

"Painting makes me relax. I guess I just say whatever comes into my head when I get like this."

"You're drunk on art."

"Wow, yeah, it is sort of like that, isn't it?"

He laughs and sighs, glancing toward the windows. "I love your work. It's beautiful, you know that? It shows something in you, a deeper layer that I feel like I'd never reach without you bringing it out on the canvas."

"You think so? I always like to imagine I'm digging that layer out and revealing it in others."

"You could be doing both."

"Oh, look at you, an art theorist now."

He chuckles, I grin at him, feeling good and relaxed. I paint for a little while in silence, getting sucked into that deep focus again. It becomes less about teasing and flirting, and more about creating. That flow, moving through my hands, translating into paint. Erick comes into view, a figure of lights and darks, glowing in front of a dark background, a contradiction and a smear, gorgeous and dangerous. A threat and a promise of deeper pleasure.

But I'm torn from my zone when someone knocks at the door. It flies open and Marina steps into the room, breathing hard. "Erick. The truck."

Erick gets to his feet. "What's wrong?"

"The truck," she repeats, looking panicked. She glances down at me, her hands coming to her face. "He took the truck."

I drop my brush. Paint splatters on the floor.

Chapter 43

Hellie

Erick makes calls. He has dozens of guys searching in town for any sign of Dad or the truck. Ren gathers a little posse, and they drive around in Jeeps with big spotlights, combing the nearby desert in case the truck is just a diversion.

I sit on the couch in Erick's office, leaning on my side with my knees pulled to my chest, feeling empty and confused.

"Why would he do this?" I ask, staring at the floor, seeing nothing. "We were trying to help him. Why would he skip out again?"

"It's in his nature." Erick stands at the window, palm against the glass, glaring into the night.

"No, that doesn't make sense. He's sick. He wasn't faking it."

"Are you sure?"

"I think so, I mean—" I stop myself. Am I actually sure he has cancer? Dad can fake a lot of things. I've seen him do it before. But he's so thin and gaunt, and he looks so sick. "I never saw any paperwork."

"Even that can be faked." Erick's fingers curl. "I'm sorry, Hellie. We'll try to find him."

"What if we didn't?"

He glances back at me. "Hellie."

"What if we let him run? Maybe this is his way of taking the decision out of our hands. He knows there's no real way for you to save his life. Gallo and Frost would find out about him eventually if you tried to hide him here. I've been racking my brain trying to come up with a solution, but there's nothing. What if this is his way of making things easier for us?"

Erick's quiet. He's considering, but I don't need him to agree. I know what he thinks of my father, and he isn't wrong. Dad's a con man, a liar, a cheat. Anything he does always has an ulterior motive, and those motives always lead back to him, back to whatever he needs and wants.

But for once, I want to pretend like my father's doing something hard that benefits everyone but himself, even if that goes against his character.

"We'll find him," Erick says at last. "And if we don't, I don't know what'll happen. I hope he doesn't stumble right into Gallo's or Frost's hands."

"I hope so too."

It's a hard night. Ren's men come and go, updating when necessary. The phone keeps ringing and Erick talks quietly, giving orders. Nothing happens, nobody's found. Marina brings tea and snacks. She's haggard, exhausted like everyone else, but she won't go to bed, not even when I tell her to. "I'll be here for you," she says, patting my arm.

I'm a wreck. I drift in and out, lying on that couch. Erick drinks, glares, talks. Eventually, the sun starts to come up, and I'm ready to stumble into bed for a few hours of sleep when Ren appears in the doorway.

I know it's bad news before he talks.

"We found the truck," he says. "Needed sunlight to do it, but we found it."

"Where?" Erick comes around the desk, his shirtsleeves rolled to his elbows, clothes rumpled.

"You'd better come see." Ren glances at me. "Maybe she should stay behind."

"No," I say, leaping to my feet. "No, I'm coming."

Erick stares at me before nodding. "Alright. Let's go."

Ren leads the way. We get into a Jeep and follow a twisting dirt road. I understand why Erick wanted someone to show me how to navigate it before trying to drive it myself: there are false turns with multiple steep drops into ravines.

B. B. Hamel

"We chose this place because it's hard to reach," Erick says over the noise of the Jeep's engine. "Lots of dangerous shit just getting out here. There's a reason it's a fantastic prison."

I give him a hard look. "No need to remind me." Though he's got a point and I'm glad I never indulged in my escape fantasies, because it's all desert and steep drops all over the place.

"We have enemies, Hellie, which means this place has to be secure. That's another reason why I want to keep you out here."

That makes more sense to me. I don't say anything as Ren slows the Jeep and rounds a corner. Ahead, more Jeeps are parked, forming a blockade across the path. On the left is another steep drop, a cliff that ends in nothing, and I understand that we're high in the desert mountains at the top of some massive mesa.

Ren kills the engine and we get out. Men stand around, all of them looking grim, and I feel sick. This is bad—this is horrible—and my mind's moving too fast to process everything around me.

"Maybe you should stay back," Erick says, putting a hand on my arm, but I shake him off and walk to the edge.

Down below, there's a twisted shape. It's blackened, and the rocks are scorched all around it. I stare, brain refusing to make sense of what I'm seeing, until Ren speaks.

"If I had to guess, he went over driving too fast in the middle of the night. It's not hard to do. He would've died on impact, nice and fast, if that helps at all."

Then I understand. Down below is my truck. My new truck—now a twisted mass of metal and burned-out parts.

"No," I say, horror grabbing me by the throat. Tears fill my eyes. "No, that's not real."

"I'm sorry." Erick tries to pull me away. "You don't need to see this."

"No," I say and try to fight him. I'm out of my mind, struggling, thrashing. I just got my father back, I wanted another day with him, there had to be another way—but he can't be down in that ravine, down in that destroyed truck, burned beyond recognition, dead on impact. "No, please, no, this can't be real."

"I'm sorry." Erick drags me from the edge. I'm not thinking anymore, I'm reacting on instinct, screaming in sorrow and mourning and rage.

"Why did you do it? Why did you try to run!"

Erick holds me tight. His big arms pin me against him, keep me from doing something stupid like running to that edge. I want to see Dad one more time, tell him I loved him, but the selfish bastard stole a truck and tried to run away, and all his games finally caught up with him.

Now he's dead. A burned corpse in the desert.

"Come on, we'll go back." Erick wrestles me into the Jeep. "It's okay, Hellie, it's okay. I've got you."

"It's not okay. It's nowhere near okay." But I lean into him and I sob against his chest as the Jeep starts up and turns around, driving slowly to the house in the desert, away from my father's body, away from the ruin he made himself. A terrible end, almost a fitting one.

Another con gone wrong and my father will never lie again.

Chapter 44

Erick

We can't drag the truck out. It'd be impossible, and anyway, there's no reason. It stays down there, a gravesite for Hellie's father. She visits three times over the next two weeks. She sits at the edge and stares down at her father's remains, saying nothing, only staring.

His funeral's on a Tuesday. Since there's no body, there's no casket. Only a big photograph of Danny Accardi smiling out at the crowd. There are more mourners than I would've guessed: old gambling buddies, old girlfriends, old marks and partners alike. It's as if all of ancient Vegas comes out, all the card sharks and call girls, the dangers and the freaks. They all miss Danny Accardi, even if he screwed them all over more than once.

I stand in the reception line with Hellie. She leans on me, her eyes red and swollen from crying, but she smiles and shakes hands with the visitors and listens to their stories about her father. Some are funny, some are tragic. All of them make her cry and laugh and cry some more. I keep her upright the best I can, and when it's time for the priest to say a few words, I sit her down in the front row.

Two men stand in the back of the church, waiting for me. I kiss her cheek and whisper in her ear, "I'll be right back. I love you."

She nods, numb, and I walk off.

Frost and Gallo are waiting outside in the church court-yard. A fountain stands surrounded by desert shrubs. It's dry and dusty.

"Can't believe that many people came out for a fucking shit like Accardi," Gallo says.

Goons lurk at the edges of our meeting. My people, Frost's people, Gallo's. All keeping an eye on things, but there's no more animosity.

"I agree," Frost says. "But he was charming, after all."

"Fucking doubt that." Gallo sits on the edge of the foun-tain with a grunt. "Alright, Costa. How's the girl? She good?"

"Holding up. Mourning her dad. Confused about the way it went down." I gesture, shrugging. "You know how it is. Life can be random and weird."

"Ain't that the truth." Gallo shakes his head. "May Accardi rest in peace. Eh, fuck that, may he burn in hell, that thieving fucking rat. Got what he deserved in the end."

Frost shakes his head in disgust. "We're at the man's funeral, for fuck's sake."

"Whatever. Fuck him." Gallo waves a hand in the air. "Go on, tell Costa why we're here and let's get this done."

"We want to hammer out a deal," Frost says. "Now that Accardi's dead, it's unlikely that we'll ever recoup our losses from him. Which means we need to come up with some alterative solution."

"To save fucking face," Gallo says, grunting in anger. "Although I want the damn money back too."

"You understand." Frost wipes a hand down his face. "What else can we do?"

I glare at the men. Coming here to a funeral to negotiate is shameful, but I'm not surprised. I keep my voice level and low, trying to avoid conflict if I can, at least while we're at the damn church.

"Here's my offer." I stare from Frost to Gallo. "Hellie's mine now. She's more than a captive."

"We heard," Frost says with a tight smile.

"Good for fucking you, but that doesn't help me." Gallo keeps on glaring like a sour fish.

"She's not going to work for you two anymore. You got the second painting and you sold it for a good profit. Keep that money, split it between you two. Tell everyone that covered your losses."

Frost snorts. "It's not even close."

"Then fucking lie," I say, staring him down. "I'll back up any story you decide to tell, but Hellie is mine."

Frost and Gallo exchange a look. Frost speaks first. "Here's the problem. You had Accardi and you didn't tell us. He died trying to escape your compound, and you do know that looks bad, right?"

"Looks like you were fucking hiding him," Gallo says with a snarl.

"What do you want?" I ask, crossing my arms. "You two want to keep pushing this mess and make it worse? We can do that. We can go to war if that's what you want."

"Nobody wants war," Frost says quickly, ever the sensible businessman.

Gallo laughs, hoarse and ugly. "We'll gut you, Costa, you little shit."

"Insult me again, old man, and I will kill you. It would make my life easier, stomping your skull until it cracked."

"Gentlemen," Frost says as Gallo gets to his feet, looking outraged. "We can be reasonable here. The money from those two forgeries was good. Why don't you have her paint one more? That'd get us close to breaking even at least, assuming you don't take a cut."

"No. Hellie doesn't work anymore."

"Give us something, Erick." Frost spreads his hands. "You did hold Accardi back."

I take a slow breath and let it out. I was waiting for this, and I knew they'd make these demands. I still don't like it, but I made some plans at least.

"Here's what I'm offering," I say, looking between them. "This happens one time. You turn me down, you complain, you do anything I don't like, and it's war. Fuck you both. My offer is simple. I pay half of what's missing from my own coffers. You two split it. You won't be perfect, but fuck you, I don't care. Then you leave Hellie alone, and you stay far away from my businesses, and if I catch either of you sniffing around my turf, I swear there will be bodies. Understand?"

Gallo sneers. "You must really like her, huh, Costa?"

"Shut up," Frost says. He nods at me. "Alright. That's reasonable."

"Fuck, no, it isn't, he hid that lying, thieving fuck from us! I never got my fucking revenge!"

"Seriously, Gallo, keep bitching and I'll help Erick burn your organization to the ground." Frost takes a breath through his nose and shoves a hand at me. "You got a deal. Wire me the money and this is over."

"Fine." I shake his hand. "Gallo?"

"Fuck you two." He gets to his feet. "Fine. Deal."

I shake the old gangster's hand and it's done. I turn away and head back to the funeral. "See yourselves out and don't ever come around Hellie again," I say, not bothering to wait for a response.

Once inside, I sit back down next to her. She leans against me, and I put an arm around her shoulders. I hate the deal I cut out there, but feeling Hellie against me now, being there for her, holding onto her, it's all worth it. The problems with Frost and Gallo are over. Danny Accardi is dead.

Now it's time to move on with our lives.

Just Hellie and me, nothing else.

Chapter 45

Hellie

Months pass by like water down a river canyon rushing past our house in the desert. I mourn my father, and while I never quite get over his horrible, violent ending, I can at least accept that he's gone.

And it helps that I'm starting a new life. Each day, I wake up in bed with Erick, eat breakfast with him, go for hikes around the desert, spend some time in the kitchen chatting with Marina, and eventually end up in my studio for hours on end. I paint more than I've ever painted in my life.

At first, everything's a portrait of him. Erick in different moods, different colors, but soon the landscape starts to infect my work and the desert itself becomes a character on the canvas. It's the most productive period of my life— and the sort of gift I never imagined I'd have, the one thing all artists crave more than anything else, time and space to do nothing but create.

Erick watches me when he's not at work. He spends hours on the weekends with me, sitting back and reading books, watching movies with his headphones on, all while glancing up and tracking my progress. Before him, I never would've let someone sit in on a painting session, but it feels natural to have him nearby, and I find my work's even better when he's looking, like I'm trying to make him proud with every brushstroke.

We sleep together every night. He's insatiable, and I find myself waking up in ways I never dreamed about. His hands on my skin, his mouth on my lips. It's obscene, it's beautiful, and I'm more physically satisfied than I ever imagined I could be.

I keep in touch with friends and have lunch with Nicky a few times, but I find myself retreating deeper and deeper into that house in the desert, hiking more in the early mornings and around sunset, throwing myself into my relationship with Erick. Telling him stories about my father, stories about me. Listening to his own stories about his hard childhood, about the stress of his work juggling the legitimate and the illegal aspects of his life, and it seems to help. He's looser, happier than he was when we first met.

Around seven months into my stay at the house in the desert, Marina brings the mail and there's a letter addressed to me. "Don't know who sent it," she says with a shrug as she places it down in front of me during lunch. Erick's down at the casino for the afternoon. "No return address."

She says something else, but I can't hear her. I stare at the envelope, at the handwriting on the front listing my name, Heloise Accardi, and the PO Box Erick uses to gather packages and letters since no delivery driver in their right mind would ever come out here. That handwriting, cramped and intense, more of a scrawl than actual letters. The handwriting I've seen a thousand times since I was a little girl, handwriting on notes, on lists, on forged documents.

Slowly, I rip open the letter, and unfold it.

My heart races into my throat as I sit back, unable to move, and read.

HELOISE, YOU'RE PROBABLY PISSED. I DON'T BLAME YOU, *sweetie, I really don't. I'm so sorry it came to this, and by the end of this letter, I hope you understand and can forgive both of us. At least, forgive Erick, because he did it for you, even if it hurt for a while.*

I'm not dead. Well, I will be soon. As of this writing, the last doctor I spoke with gave me weeks. He's some Caribbean quack so who knows if he's right, but based on the way I feel, it's probably close. I'm sorry, hon. I wish I had better news—surprise, your daddy's alive and he's okay!—but that's not how this story ends. The cancer was always real, and it was always going to get me in the end.

I love you. I want you to know it. What I said to you back at Erick's place, I meant every word. You're the best thing in my life and you always were. Thank you for being who you are, and don't mourn me again. You already got that over with.

But now, I'm sure you figured it out, but in case you haven't:

I faked my death.

Erick helped.

I made him swear he wouldn't tell you about it. I love you, hon, but you're a terrible liar. You got that from your mother. If you knew, Gallo and Frost never would've believed it, and they would've hunted me down during my final months. That I lasted this long is a minor miracle.

Here's the thing. Erick is still under the impression that my "partner" stole the money and disappeared. You all assumed my last heist was that truck robbery, but that's not it.

My last heist is this one. It's giving you the money I stole like I always planned.

On the back, you'll find instructions for how to access a Swiss bank account. You'll find it contains every dollar I took, minus a million bucks. Had to keep a little something for my final days. You understand.

All that money is yours. I suspect you don't need it now that you're with Erick, but if you ever do—it's there.

I stole it to leave you a legacy. Something to remember me by that isn't just heartbreak and hatred. That's why I never left Vegas. That's why I sent the stupid email. It was always meant for you, Heloise, and I had to track you down so I could give it to you. I'm sorry it was such a mess, and I could've done it better, but hey, it worked out in the end.

There's not much else to say. Don't feel sorry, and don't come looking.

I'm already gone.

I love you,

Dad.

It takes a while to process what it says. I sit in the studio, reading and re-reading, and eventually use my laptop to check the account.

He wasn't lying. There's a lot of money just waiting there in my name. I don't need money, but my father nearly killed himself getting all this cash for me.

I'm not sure what to feel. Dozens of emotions swirl, filling my head. Confusion, anger, hurt, sorrow, joy, everything. At some point, Erick comes in and kisses my hair, his customary greeting. "You okay?" he asks. "Marina said you've been off ever since getting a letter this afternoon."

I hold it up for him. "Dad sent it." He stares but doesn't seem surprised. "So it's all true then, huh? You helped him fake his death."

Erick pulls up a chair, places it facing me, and sits down. He leans forward, looking into my eyes. "I am so fucking sorry I didn't tell you right away."

"Dad says he convinced you not to."

"We cut a deal. I couldn't let him stick around here, and I couldn't let him go, either. He came up with the fake death thing, and he also made me swear not to say anything about it. I told him I wouldn't for one year. After a year, I was going to tell you and come clean. I'm really, really sorry."

"Why?" I ask, blinking back tears.

"Because it was the only way he could spend his last days in freedom. I thought you'd want that, even if you had to go through some hell to get to this point. I wanted to give you that."

I nod, wiping my eyes. "I feel like I lost him all over again."

"You didn't, Hellie. You didn't. He's been gone since the day he left, only he's been hanging around on borrowed time, spending his last days in comfort instead of dead in some ditch. I know lying to you was wrong, but it was either that or risk letting the whole thing fall apart, and I couldn't do it. I'm so, so sorry you had to go through all this. I really am. I'm so sorry."

I stare at him for a long moment then throw myself into his arms. He grabs me, the chair squealing back, and he hugs me to his chest. I'm on my knees in front of him, my face pressed into his shirt, sobbing like a total moron. Crying because of this incredible gift he gave me, crying because I lost my father for a second time, crying because they both did these painful things for me.

Erick's been carrying around this secret. He's known for months that he was going to tell me soon. Dad broke the news first, lucky him, but I can only guess at the stress of it eating at the back of Erick's mind. I feel sorry for him, though not too sorry, since he should've told me from the start. But if I'm honest with myself, if I really look closely at how it all went down, he was right to keep me in the dark.

"Who else knew?" I manage to ask once my tears slow.

"Ren. That's it. Nobody else. Just me, Ren, and your father."

"I'll have to thank Ren then."

"Don't worry about it, I already gave him a nice bonus for all his hard work."

I laugh and kiss him. It's an ugly, sloppy, tear-filled kiss, but he doesn't shy away.

"I love you," I say.

"I love you too. More than anything."

"Good. Because I think my father didn't tell you everything."

His eyebrows raise. "What did he do?"

"The partner you've been looking for doesn't exist. My dad had the money hidden in a secret Swiss account all this time, and he gave it all to me."

Erick says nothing. It's hard to read his face. Half amusement, half frustration, but eventually he only grins and shakes his head. "That motherfucker."

"I know."

"It's all there?"

"All but a million he kept for himself."

"I'm sure he blew through that already."

"I hope so." I touch Erick's face. "You're not mad?"

"Not at all. Keep it. That money's yours. It's the last great haul of an old-school con man, a dead and dying breed. Your dad was a piece of shit, but I've got to admit some admiration."

"Thank you." I kiss him and press my forehead against his. "I guess that means I'm rich now."

"You've been rich since the day I stole you."

"Fair point."

"What do we do now?"

I kiss him again. And again. "I was thinking I'd paint for a while. Get some emotions out. Do you mind?"

"Not at all. Do you mind if I watch?"

"I'd like that."

"Good." He kisses me softly.

I get to my feet and shuffle over to my canvas. It's blank this time, prepared with white Gesso. He pulls his chair back and gets himself comfortable.

I pause only to look as he rolls up his sleeves.

My gorgeous man.

Saving my father's life—if only for a few months—is the greatest gift anyone could give to me. Erick went against his own interests to make it happen, and he did it because he loves me.

Now, I'll make him a thousand paintings, each painting for him, and maybe they'll live up to how I feel for him too.

Chapter 46

Hellie

One Year Later

Marina shoves a bowl of cereal at me. "Eat."

"I'm not hungry."

She stands, hands on hips, and glares. "You turned down eggs. You turned down bacon. You ignored fruit. You will eat the cereal and thank me for stooping so low as to offer it to you. Now do not insult me further. Eat."

I pick up the spoon. "Yes, ma'am."

"Good." She stalks off, muttering to herself.

I manage a few bites. I'm nauseous and exhausted, my ankles swollen, my belly beginning to grow, but all things considered, I'm okay. Marina's been on my ass to keep shoveling food down my face, which isn't exactly the most pleasant thing in the world, but she's right. I need to keep my strength up now that I've got a baby growing in me.

Marina fusses around, brings me juice, crackers, tea, anything she can think of as I try to read the paper. It's early, but Erick left for work nearly an hour ago now. I'm antsy, already thinking about what I'll spend the afternoon painting. I've been doing this series focusing on moments from my father's life—the truck at the bottom of the canyon, the armored truck, money in a pocket, fake documents, his face always obscured. When I'm finally ready to get up and get working, Erick appears in the kitchen doorway, wearing his customary fitted suit and looking like a straight-up slice of heaven.

"Hello, my devil girl," he says and comes over to kiss me.

"Hey, what are you doing here? I thought you were on the Strip today."

"Something came up last minute and I decided to stay home."

"Sounds good to me." I get up and kiss him. He puts a hand on my belly, and even though I'm only two months along, he swears he can feel the baby moving around. "I'm headed up to the studio if you want to come."

"Actually, I was hoping you'd take a little detour with me first."

"Well, sure, what do you have in mind?"

"Come this way." He takes my hand and tugs me along.

I follow him, not sure where we're going. We move to the back door, out onto the patio, and that's where I stop in my tracks.

There are plants everywhere. Colorful plants, flowers, the sort of stuff that can't survive in this climate. It's like he transplanted an entire jungle into the back yard, so dense and thick it almost feels like the foliage is taking over the world. I breathe hard, head spinning, staring around, completely overwhelmed.

"What did you do?" I ask, my hands covering my mouth.

"You said the one thing you dislike about the desert is the lack of color. I know it won't last, but at least for today, I brought the color to you."

"Holy shit." I laugh and move out the door, heading down into the chaos. There are manicured lanes between the various outcroppings. Reds, yellows, blues and purples, plants I don't know and can't name, all beautiful. "This is what you've been up to?"

"I had some help." He walks with his hands behind his back. "Do you like it?"

"I love it." I turn to face him. "But why now?"

"I have one more surprise." He takes my elbow and steers me along the central walkway. Ahead, there's a small archway made of wood and vines, and underneath is an easel holding a painting, but it's covered by a cloth.

"Erick. What did you do?"

He plants me in front of the painting and slowly removes the cover. I stare in total shock, unable to comprehend what I'm looking at.

The girl at the piano. Her father's back to the viewer. Her mother's face glowing with light.

"I started looking for it the day after your father retired. I knew you'd be hurting from his fake death, and I wanted something to make you feel better after I told you the truth."

"Erick."

"It took a lot longer than expected, but I found a lead two days after you told me you were pregnant. It was meant to be, Hellie."

"Erick. Stop. Wait."

"It was being kept in a warehouse in Moscow. Cost a small fortune to pry it away from the owners, but money does work wonders sometimes. I suspect this painting has been in storage since the day it was stolen all those years ago."

"It's real, isn't it?" I step forward, heart racing. I can see the differences now, between my version and this one. It's so obvious to me with hindsight. How could anyone mistake my monstrosity for this piece of divine inspiration?

"It's real," he confirms. "The real version. Your copy is floating out there somewhere still, and nobody will ever know about this one. But it's yours."

I stand inches from the canvas, staring, my mouth open. It's incredible, beyond incredible, a small miracle. I turn around to hug him—

But he's down on one knee.

"Erick," I say again, feeling dizzy.

"Heloise. Hellie. My devil girl. I love you so much, and I want you to be mine forever, in the same way I'm already yours. Will you marry me?"

I croak. It's undignified but no other sound comes out. I have to nod, over and over, as he slides the ring onto my finger—a beautiful cluster of shimmering diamonds scattering the desert light.

I pull him up, hug him, and kiss him hard. "I'll marry you," I finally say, which makes him laugh, and we kiss until my mouth feels numb, and I'm crying a little bit, surrounded by green that shouldn't be here, a life growing in my belly, an impossible painting on display for nobody but me and him to enjoy.

"Your father would've been proud of you, you know," Erick says, kissing my neck.

"I agree," I say, laughing and hugging him. "But you never know, he still might be. Now, let's get this painting inside before it melts."

"Sounds good to me."

***Want more? Read a bonus scene right now! It's a few years earlier, and Erick spots Hellie for the first time...* Go here to start reading:** www.BookHip.com/DDGJCBW

Read the first Crowley family novel! Finn and Dara's story is steamy and banter-filled. Check it out here: www.amazon.com/dp/B0C87QQDND

Join my Facebook group, BB's Book Addiction. Head on over: www.facebook.com/groups/bbhamel

Keep reading for a preview of *Marriage of Sin!*

Preview: Marriage of Sin

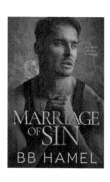

Chapter One: Dara

There is no way in the world I can face my bank account sober.

But I also need to make sure I can afford to drink before I go into this bar and drown all my problems in overpriced wine.

I take a deep breath as I thumb through my phone. Around me, traffic buzzes along Boylston Street in downtown Boston, kicking up fumes. Young couples sit outside of bars talking in the early evening shade cast by enormous office and apartment buildings, dads push strollers, old people walk dogs, and here I am a few blocks away from where I work sitting on a bench beside a scraggly tree about to find out just how bad my life's gotten.

Is this rock bottom? Let's find out.

I unlock my banking app, close my eyes, take a deep breath, and open them again.

Zero dollars stare back. Zero in checking, zero in savings.

My heart sinks into my feet. Zero, zero, zero. Nothing across the board. I knew it would be bad—but this is so much worse than I ever could've imagined.

"Lucas, you motherfucker," I whisper, horror and anger warring against sorrow.

I really wish I bought that drink first.

But at least I didn't sit through the indignity of my card getting declined.

This wasn't how I thought today would end. I figured it wouldn't be great—getting woken up at six in the morning by my roommate and the man I thought I was going to marry, only to find out that they've been sleeping together behind my back, and oh, yeah, they're in love, that's not easy.

That was a pretty spectacularly horrendous way to start the day.

But it somehow took a nosedive at five-thirty when I was leaving the office, only to get a text.

Lucas: I'm so sorry about this morning.

Lucas: And I'm so sorry about the money and your things.

Lucas: It's just, I'm in love with Christine, but we're both broke. You'll be OK, right? You have that amazing job. You'll be fine.

I stared at my phone for the five-block walk to a local bar called Trevi's before I finally worked up the nerve to find out what he meant by *the money.*

Which is why I'm staring at a bunch of big, fat zeroes.

I open the messages app and start texting furiously.

Dara: You emptied my bank account???

Dara: And what do you mean my things????

Dara: Lucas, you piece of shit, what did you do???????

I'm in full-on panic mode. I knew Lucas was a monster, but I never imagined he would sink this low. When we met in school, he was a lovable dork, a guy that loved cheap beer, football, and bad horror movies. I fell for him when he rubbed my feet during a marathon of Halloween movies.

I thought he was the one. Lucas isn't anything exciting, but he's been dependable, always there for me, always asking how my day went, always offering those lovely foot rubs of his.

So what if there weren't fireworks? There weren't nuclear bombs? It was steady. Comfortable.

Now it's like my skin's been peeled off, leaving me raw.

I'm about to call my ex when I hear my name called out. I flinch, look up, and find my manager, Johnnie, standing a few feet away flanked by a couple of Patagonia Bros in matching vests I don't recognize.

"What are you doing all alone out here?" Johnnie asks, flashing me his patented Country Club Smile. He runs a hand through his wavy hair. "Come to think of it, I don't think I've ever seen you outside of work, Dar."

I grimace at the nickname. Nobody calls me Dar except for Lucas, even though I've asked him not to half a dozen times. "I was about to get a drink actually," I say quickly, glancing down at my phone. The screen remains dead and quiet. No reply from the piece of crap that ruined my life. I'm thinking about calling the police, about getting the FBI involved, but mostly about tracking him down myself and killing him with my bare hands.

But I know it won't help.

Because whether I catch Lucas and strangle the life from him or not, my heart's still broken.

And my bank account's still empty.

"You should come with me, Patagonia Bro 1, and Patagonia Bro 2 over to McNally's. Come on, Dar, you seem fun. Let's have a good time, yeah?"

He doesn't actually say *Patagonia Bro*, but I blank out their names on purpose. I don't have time for this, but Johnnie's my manager at a heavily male dominated accounting firm, which means I have to smile, bat my eyelashes, and play nice. Otherwise, they call me a bitch behind my back, and I don't get promotions or raises.

"Sorry, I'm meeting a friend," I lie, shifting uncomfortably. "Otherwise, I'd totally come."

"A guy friend?" Johnnie sits next to me while his Patagonia Cronies leer at me, both of them grinning, like this is totally normal behavior. Johnnie's breath reeks like liquor. Did he cut out early and start drinking or something? "What's his name? Actually, don't worry, it's fine. I just figured, you know, since there's a vibe here, it might be fun to explore it outside of a professional setting."

His eyes are glassy as he glances down at my tits. Yep, definitely shitfaced.

"I'm sorry," I say, blinking rapidly. "A vibe? What are you talking about?"

"Ah, damn, don't get all feminist on me, okay, Dar? It's just, I notice the way you look at me when you come into my office. I notice the blouses with the top two buttons undone? You're pretty hot, you know? A solid six, but you could be an eight if you worked out more. You wear some borderline inappropriate attire, but nobody cares because you have absolutely *fantastic* tits."

I feel like my head's about to explode.

Johnnie's always been a prick. He's one of those Nantucket Assholes with a trust fund the size of Georgia and a yacht to match. He only has this job because his uncle's a founding partner. Johnnie's got fewer brain cells than my bank account has dollars, which is still zero, by the way.

"There's absolutely no vibe," I say quickly, standing up. "And you have to be absolutely fucking batshit *insane* to talk about my clothes and my fucking tits right now."

Under normal circumstances, I'd never talk to a vindictive little prick like Johnnie like that, but I'm way past my last nerve, basically working on reserve nerves at this point, and I'm lashing out.

Johnnie's face falls. His Patagonia Cronies stare at him like they're about to laugh—which makes his face turn a disturbing shade of pink.

"You fucking bitch," he says, standing up to stare down at me. "You do realize I'm your manager, right?"

There it is. I was waiting for that. The threat in his tone is clear.

"I'm not in the mood for this," I say, shaking my head. "Just leave me alone, okay? I'll pretend you didn't just say the most asinine, sexist thing in the world, and you can swallow your pride for once in your life."

"Fuck that," he says quietly. "You can't talk to me that way."

In all my time at Bankman Associates, I've held my tongue. I've kept my head down, smiled politely, nodded at inane comments, laughed at inappropriate jokes. I've done all the things women have to do in a toxic workplace environment. I've done it, because the job pays exceedingly well, and I was raised to value money more than anything else.

More than my own self-esteem, apparently.

But this is too far.

Ten hours ago, I had a boyfriend.

A nice boyfriend. Nothing spectacular, but still. A guy I thought was going to propose soon. We had plans, long-term plans. We were merging financial assets. I had a lot of hard-earned money saved in the bank, ready to be spent on a wedding, or a down payment for a house, or maybe on baby clothes and a crib.

Now, I'm twenty-four years old, and I have none of that.

Instead, a white-hot rage (admittedly pointless and impotent) burns in my belly.

I jab a finger at Johnnie. "Listen to me, you walking stock option. I need you to apologize right now. I need you to accept the consequences of your actions, because other people have feelings. You realize that, right? You can't go around saying whatever you want, fucking whatever moves, stealing whatever you need, throwing away whatever you don't care about, cheating on me with my fucking roommate, all because you're a selfish piece of fucking *trash*."

I'm projecting here.

A little bit, anyway.

Johnnie's gaze darkens. "You just crossed a line, Dar," he says through his teeth. "I don't know what's gotten into you, but you're *not* going to get away with embarrassing me in front of my bros."

He grabs my arm. I stare as his fingers dig into my flesh, biting down hard. I yelp, more from shock than from pain, but he doesn't let me go.

I start to freak out.

Johnnie's a big guy, easily over six feet. His Patagonia Cronies are also tall, both of them looking like they're from Abercrombie catalogues, like they're one step away from the polo club, and neither seem to mind that their friend is publicly manhandling a girl.

This is getting out of control very quickly.

At least until a shadow appears at Johnnie's side.

"You should let her go." The voice is low and resonant with malice.

A man's standing there. Stubble on his chin. Big hands balled into fists. A pristine suit, slim fitting.

I stare at the stranger, at the tall, broad, athletically built man, as a terrified pulse shivers down my spine.

He's handsome. Sinful, absurdly handsome. Like, beyond inappropriately handsome. Dark, wavy hair pushed back in a lazy sweep. High cheekbones, tanned skin, blue eyes like early morning frost. A reddish beard clings to his cheeks, trimmed, but somehow still unruly. He's in a suit, black and tailored to his muscular frame.

Holy hell, this guy is *hot*.

Stupidly hot. Like he's a very unnecessary distraction.

Johnnie's eyes bulge. For a second, I don't think he's going to release me. I imagine he'll use me as a human shield.

Instead, his grip slackens, then disappears. "Who the fuck are you?" Johnnie snaps.

The stranger looks at me for a beat before saying, "I'm her boyfriend."

Oh my god.

What the *hell* is this guy doing?

Go here to keep reading: www.amazon.com/dp/B0C87QQDND

Also by B. B. Hamel

B. B. Hamel is a Top 100 Bestselling author of steamy contemporary romance!

All my books are standalones, extremely steamy, and have a guaranteed Happily-Ever-After!

LOOKING FOR MY READING ORDER? Head on over to my Facebook group! It's pinned at the top.

www.facebook.com/groups/bbhamel

Series include Dark Mafia, Daddies, SEAL Team Hotties, Hate to Love, Second Chances, Baby Daddy, Miracle Babies, and more.

www.amazon.com/author/bbhamel

Thanks so much for reading! As an indie author, your support means absolutely everything to me.

XO, BB

Printed in Great Britain
by Amazon